KING ME

A FOREVER WILDE NOVEL

LUCY LENNOX

Cover Art by: AngstyG at www.AngstyG.com

Cover Photo: Wander Aguiar www.wanderaguiar.com

Editing by: Sandra at www.OneLoveEditing.com

Beta Reading by: Leslie Copeland at www.LesCourtAuthorServices.com

KEEP IN TOUCH WITH LUCY!

Join Lucy's Lair
Get Lucy's New Release Alerts
Like Lucy on Facebook
Follow Lucy on BookBub
Follow Lucy on Amazon
Follow Lucy on Instagram
Follow Lucy on Pinterest

Other books by Lucy:
Made Marian Series
Forever Wilde Series
Aster Valley Series
Virgin Flyer
Say You'll Be Nine
Hostile Takeover
Twist of Fate Series with Sloane Kennedy
After Oscar Series with Molly Maddox
Licking Thicket Series with May Archer
Licking Thicket: Horn of Glory series with May Archer
Honeybridge series with May Archer

Visit Lucy's website at www.LucyLennox.com for a comprehensive
list of titles, audio samples, freebies, suggested reading order, and
more!

ACKNOWLEDGEMENTS

Many, many thanks:

To my sister for her help with line-edits, concept discussion, trouble-shooting, and blurb help. This book would be a scrap heap without her help.

To my daughter for her help troubleshooting the beginning. Our late-night convo in the kitchen is something I'll never forget.

To May Archer for help with the plot and inspiration regarding Falcon Crest which is where I got the name Falcon.

To Leslie Copeland for support and excellent beta reading at the drop of a hat.

To my editor Sandra for her visit on a beautiful sunny day in Vancouver. Oh, and for the edits I guess.

To Wander Aguiar for taking gorgeous photographs.

To AngstyG for nailing the cover and giving me the inspiration to set part of the story in Budapest. Without you, I wouldn't have learned about the crown.

Finally, please note the art mentioned in the book is real, but hasn't necessarily been stolen. This is fiction. Go with it.

WILDE FAMILY LIST

Grandpa (Weston) and **Doc** (William "Liam") Wilde (book #6)
Their children:
Bill, Gina, Brenda, and Jacqueline

Bill married Shelby. Their children are:
Hudson (book #4)
West (book #1)
MJ
Saint (book #5)
Otto (book #3)
King (book #7)
Hallie
Winnie
Cal (book #8)
Sassy

Gina married Carmen. Their children are:
Quinn
Max
Jason

Brenda married Hollis. Their children are:

Kathryn-Anne (Katie)
William-Weston (Web)
Jackson-Wyatt (Jack)

Jacqueline's child:
Felix (book #2)

PROLOGUE
KING - TWO YEARS AGO

Never pick a fight with your boyfriend when you're in the middle of stealing a Van Gogh. Because he might just decide you're not worth a hundred million dollars and it'd be better for him to ditch your ass at the scene of the crime.

Hypothetically speaking, of course.

"Elek, what the fuck?" I hissed, finding it difficult to hide my exasperation. "We're in the middle of a job. Now's not the time to start talking about what comes next."

I bent back over the hundred-million-dollar painting lying on the floor in front of me, carefully running my gloved hand along the ragged edges of the canvas to smooth it before gently starting to tuck it into a roll. It felt almost sacrilegious rolling a painting as valuable as this into a tube, but it was the only way to practically transfer it.

"You won't even consider it," Elek continued, as if I hadn't spoken. "It's an easy job. Security is minimal. We'd barely break a sweat." He paced through the room as he talked, the beam of his flashlight sweeping in arcs across the floor.

My shoulders tightened, a rebuke on the tip of my tongue, but instead I closed my eyes and blew out a breath, trying to keep calm and focused. I hated distractions while I worked. Which Elek knew, but it never seemed to stop him.

I tried to tell him distractions made people sloppy. They got you caught. I should know—as an art history student, I'd taken an interest in art theft and forgeries which included quite a few stories of art thieves getting caught. I'd thought that perhaps it might lead me toward the FBI or working for an auction house or insurance company sniffing out fakes.

But then I'd met a charming older man and ended up on the other side of the equation.

Distractions.

"This should be obvious, yes," he said.

He wasn't going to let it drop, which meant the only way to end the conversation was to respond, "I just don't see the point."

He stopped his pacing and turned toward me. "It's on the list," he said evenly. "That's the point."

I resisted the urge to roll my eyes. Elek and his damned list. Over the years he'd compiled a wish list of items he wanted for his own personal collection. In the past he'd only stolen items on the list if the opportunity arose—like if he was on a job at the same location as one of the items on the list, he might make a detour to nick it. But recently he'd been planning jobs around the list itself, which seemed like a lot of risk to take just to steal something we couldn't turn a profit on.

I shrugged. "It's not a job I'm interested in."

"Since when does your interest in a job matter?"

I rocked back on my heels and looked up at him. "Since I started thinking for myself." I knew as soon as I said it that I shouldn't have. His eyes narrowed and his nostrils flared as he drew in a sharp breath.

I held up a hand, hoping to placate him. "Look, let's just get this finished, and then we can discuss it when we get home."

Elek met my eyes for a long moment. Then he nodded. "Sure thing, *macska*."

I turned back to the painting, starting to gently slide it into the tube. The next thing I knew, the light from Elek's flashlight swung in a sharp arc, and then there was a loud crack followed by a bright explosion of pain radiating across the base of my skull.

My first thought was confusion.

My second was shock.

My third was that head wounds tended to bleed and I didn't want to get blood on the canvas. I fell back away from the painting, landing on my hip. My entire head rang with pain, and I squeezed my eyes shut, fighting against it.

"Elek?" I asked.

I felt his hand, warm and reassuring, take mine. "Sorry, *macska*," he said softly.

I was about to ask *sorry for what* when I felt something sharp and plastic tighten around my wrists.

My eyes flew open. "What the fuck?"

I was so disoriented by the pain that it took me a moment too long to understand what was going on. By then Elek had bound my hands and was dragging me toward the wall.

Instinct took over and I struggled against him, but that earned me a knee to the stomach. While I was doubled over, trying to catch my breath, he finished zip-tying me to the radiator.

"What are you doing?" I gasped.

"This is the end of the road for us, kitten." He didn't even bother looking at me when he spoke. Instead he knelt over the painting, and I winced as he shoved it into the protective tube as if it were a boy band poster being sold on Black Friday at the mall.

My mind spun, not just from the pain but also the confusion. "I don't understand. What happened?"

He stood, surveying the study with a critical eye, making sure no evidence of the break-in remained. Except for me of course.

Fuck. If I got caught in here… I fought against the zip ties, not caring that the sharp edges bit into my skin.

Elek's gaze landed on me, and it was creepily devoid of emotion. "It seems our interests don't align as well as they once did."

I blinked at him. Was he fucking kidding me? "Is this about the job? I'll do the damned job," I shouted.

He shrugged, tucking the tube with the Van Gogh under his arm. "Too late. I don't know when I let you get so much control. I don't need this. I made you into the tool I needed, and I can do it again with someone less trouble. Maybe make them even better."

Anger boiled inside me. I strained forward against the restraints. "Good luck," I spat. "There is no one better than me."

He lifted an eyebrow and grinned. "Any art thief not currently tied to a radiator at a crime scene would seem better, eh, *macska?*"

I growled low in my throat. I was going to throttle him the moment I got out of here.

If I got out of here.

Fuck.

My heart, which had already begun hammering harder than normal in my predicament, stuttered for half a beat before thundering so loudly, my ears whooshed with it. It was like a scene out of a movie—the one where the bad guy double-crosses his partner in crime. Only we weren't just partners in crime, we were also partners in life.

Or so I'd thought.

"Elek," I said, trying to keep my voice conciliatory. "Let's talk about this."

"Sorry, *macska,*" he said again, sounding about as sincere as a child apologizing for taking candy he shouldn't have.

With that he turned and left. There was utter silence for a few moments, broken only by my strained breathing. I waited for him to turn back. To come cut me free.

Instead I heard the sound of breaking glass and a shrill alarm cut through the night. Emergency lights along the wall began to flash.

The motherfucker tripped the alarm. On purpose.

Which meant the police would be here in minutes.

I was seriously screwed.

I redoubled my efforts against the restraints. The plastic was slick now, probably from my blood, but I didn't care. It was a small price to pay if it meant evading capture. They still weren't budging. I was going to have to think of something else.

My head pounded, my nerves lit like live wires from adrenaline. The flashing lights and screaming alarm only made it worse. Panic threatened, but I held it at bay. It wasn't my first rodeo—okay, heist—and, thanks to Elek, I'd spent the past three years earning a reputation as one of the most successful art thieves in modern times.

I could figure this out. I was not only quick on my feet, but well versed in high-level security systems. I was familiar with the layout of the interior minister's house, I just hadn't anticipated needing an exit plan that included getting out of plastic handcuffs.

I looked around, assessing my options. The empty study was still in the wee morning hours, and the wood paneling of the large room glowed honey brown in the flashing security lights. The thick picture frame in front of me housed a blank space as if the Van Gogh had never been there.

If I'd been wearing my normal gear, I'd have had pockets full of tools I could have used to free myself. But tonight I was dressed in the same slim black trousers, white button-down shirt, bow tie, and hipster framed eyeglasses I'd worn as a server earlier that evening at the cocktail reception held in the interior minister's house before I'd hidden in a storage closet for hours until it was time to let Elek into the building for the heist.

Even a damn corkscrew could have come in handy right now. But my pockets were empty. Elek had promised I didn't need anything since he'd bring it in when he came. In hindsight, believing his bullshit was a critical mistake. And without something to cut through the plastic, I wasn't getting out of here.

My skin flushed hot, my mouth going dry. This couldn't be happening. Elek couldn't have done this to me. We were partners. We loved each other. We'd made plans for the future together.

It couldn't have all been a lie on his end. No one can be that convincing.

"Elek," I shouted to be heard over the alarm. "Please don't do this." I swallowed back the sour taste in my mouth at having to beg. "Please come back."

His voice crackled through my earpiece, indicating the distance he was putting between us with his escape. "Sorry, kitten. You'll be okay. Play dumb."

I tried not to think of how familiar his voice was, how just the night before he'd murmured his Hungarian endearments into the back of my neck as he pressed me into the sheets of the bed, holding my hands high above my head and resting his weight on me.

My stomach churned, anxiety reaching a fevered pitch. "Elek, dammit," I ground out. If begging didn't work, maybe threats would. "If I get caught, I'm sending them after you. I'll make a deal, immunity for the real art thief."

He had the fucking audacity to laugh. "No you won't. Because you forget about the forgeries."

Fuck. He was right.

My brain spun in a million different directions. Part of me wanted to replay every moment of the previous three years with Elek, dissecting whether or not he'd been lying to me this whole time. If any of it had been real. Could I have really been *that* naive and stupid?

Another part of me was desperately struggling to figure a way to get out of here. Some argument I could make, some object I could trade. Anything to make Elek come back for me.

And then there was a third part that was always curled up in the corner of my brain worrying about what my family would think and what I would ever say to them if word got out their beloved son, grandson, brother was the infamous art thief nicknamed Le Chaton—the man currently being hunted by Interpol, the FBI, and French National Police.

I couldn't let any of that happen. I needed to get out of here. "Elek—" But I didn't know what to say.

Was any of it real? Did you ever love me?

That's what I wanted to ask. But the answer was pretty obvious given my current situation. However he may or may not have felt about me in the past, I meant nothing to him now. My eyelids slid shut, a burning at the back of my throat. His betrayal cut so sharply it was like a knife had been driven through my chest.

"You didn't have to do this, Elek." My voice cracked. "Whatever you wanted, I would have given it to you."

There was a pause, and I strained to hear his reply under the cacophony of sirens and alarms. "I know, *macska*." He let out a laugh. "Now you sound like my wife."

"Wh-what?"

Nothing.

My mind exploded with questions. "What do you mean wife? What are you talking about?"

He couldn't have a wife, I told myself. There was no way he could keep a secret that big from me. But then again, he'd just tied me to a radiator and left me to get busted by the cops, so it wasn't like he was the most trustworthy man in the world.

But a wife? We lived together for fuck's sake. How would that even be possible? Except then I remembered how much he traveled delivering the pieces we stole. And how adamant he was that he do it alone. I'd always assumed he wanted to keep his art underworld contacts to himself and I was happy to let him. Now I wondered if he could have been using those trips as a cover to sneak home to a second family.

"Dammit, Elek! Why are you doing this?" I cried through the comms unit again.

I waited for him to explain but was greeted with only static. He was either out of range or had decided he no longer had any interest in talking to me. I'd been dismissed.

That's when it really sank in. He'd actually left me behind. He wasn't coming back.

I was on my own.

The sound of approaching sirens was like a shot of adrenaline to my heart. The police would be here any minute. My pulse kicked into overdrive, sweat beading along my forehead.

"Think, King, think," I hissed at myself, pushing Elek's taunt of having a wife from my mind. It was clear there was no escaping the zip ties which meant the police were definitely going to find me at the scene of the crime. From their point of view, there were only two possibilities to explain my presence: I was the criminal, or I was an innocent bystander.

My choice was pretty obvious. I did a quick mental check for any evidence they might find on me. The only actual incriminating items on my person were the earpiece and latex gloves I wore. Since the gloves were the same ones we'd used to load canapés onto the trays for the reception, I stripped them off and shoved them in a pants pocket, hoping I could explain them away easily enough. Thankfully, Elek had bound me to the radiator face-first which meant I could use my hands if I contorted myself against the restraints enough. The unforgiving plastic hurt like hell and cut into my skin as I fought to reach my pocket, but it was worth it to get rid of evidence.

The earwig also needed to be destroyed and hidden. I struggled to remove the little thing and crushed it with the heel of my shoe into as many tiny pieces as I could before scattering and crushing them deep into the pile of the Persian tribal rug nearby with the heel of my shoe.

I bent as best I could, trying to probe the base of my skull where Elek had struck me with his flashlight. I let out a hiss when my fingers found the knot, but there wasn't as much blood as I expected. Damn.

Blood would be more convincing.

From the front of the house I heard banging and knocking. The police arriving. I was running out of time. My pulse spiked, my heart going into overdrive. This was my life on the line. If I couldn't sell that I was innocent, I was screwed.

Holding my breath, I gritted my teeth and slammed my head forward as hard as I could against the solid metal of the radiator. Pain exploded in my cheekbone, radiating through my skull so intensely it sucked the breath out of my lungs and brought tears to my eyes. Within seconds, I felt the warm sticky trickle of blood and leaned my face down to my hands to feel the cut. Sure enough, faces bled like crazy. I ran bloody fingers through my hair and then pulled my knees up close to my chest and tucked my head against them, making myself appear as small as possible.

I was used to trying to calm myself, to pushing away panic and anxiety and fear. Now I had to embrace it. I closed my eyes, letting the full force of my emotions rise to the surface. Letting them overwhelm me to the point that it became difficult to breathe.

I was on the edge of a full-bore panic attack by the time I heard the first set of footsteps approaching.

"Don't shoot!" I cried out in both English and French. "Il est parti par là!" With my hands tightly strapped to the radiator, I couldn't point toward the exit Elek had used, but I could hitch my shoulder in that direction.

The Parisian gendarmes came in shouting instructions for me to put my hands where they could see them. When I didn't do what they commanded, they shouted louder, more frantically.

"I can't!" I yelled, yanking my wrists against the plastic ties.

Their voices blended with the blaring siren, creating a cacophony of chaos. I grew terrified they might think I was resisting arrest and become violent.

At that point it was easy for me to let go and allow my fear to take over.

I burst into tears.

"I'm innocent! I didn't do this," I repeated over and over in English and French like a desperate chant. "I swear. Please help me!"

Law enforcement officers buzzed around, making sure I wasn't carrying any weapons but not really asking me any questions. They seemed more interested in clearing the building and staring at the gaping blank space where the Van Gogh used to be. By the time someone approached me who actually looked to be in charge, I was hoarse, bleeding, covered in snot, and worn-out.

Perfect.

Right as he reached me, the security system alarm cut off. The silence was deafening. For a moment everyone hesitated, the change so sudden and severe. Then the man spoke, and in the sudden quiet, every nuance and cadence of his gruff voice stood out.

"My name is Special Agent Falcon. I'm an FBI agent working with the global art crimes task force here in Paris."

Oh shit.

I blinked up at him as the American accent hit me and the name sank in. I recognized it immediately. I'd read it in dozens of articles and heard it mentioned in the news and on the radio whenever a famous piece of art went missing. For the past few years he'd been hunting Le Chaton. Now he'd found him.

Now he'd found *me*.

I looked him over, sizing up my adversary. He sported a two-day beard made up of mostly pepper with a few sprinkles of salt. Despite the scruff, I recognized the square jaw and chin dimple from his many appearances in press conferences. He was taller than I expected, and wider through the shoulders, the rest of him trim and lean. His shirtsleeves were rolled up his muscular forearms, and his striking gray-green eyes focused on me between furrowed brows. His hair was cut short like I'd expect of an FBI man.

In person, Agent Falcon was goddamned flipping gorgeous. I blinked and almost slipped out of my chosen role of panicked innocent victim to peruse the thickly muscled body looming over me.

He took in my appearance with a frown. "What happened here?"

I hiccuped. "I... I... Oh, you're American, thank god. Y-you see... th-there were some men here and they... oh god, I think I'm going to be sick. I feel dizzy."

My eyes fluttered closed, and a strong, warm hand landed in the middle of my back to hold me steady. "Get me some snips," Agent Falcon barked at someone across the room.

He knelt on the floor next to me and pulled out an honest-to-god cotton handkerchief. I wanted to ask if he was a thousand years old, but the man was maybe in his late thirties, early forties tops. He put a finger under my chin and pressed the handkerchief to the cut on my cheekbone.

"Did you see who did this?" he murmured while working the cloth gently over the blood on my face.

I sniffled and blinked some more tears out, trying to appeal to his do-gooder protective side. The "doer of right and righter of wrongs" side. "They were wearing masks. Black ones and... they had on camo like... lots of pockets pants? What are those called?"

He glanced at me. "Cargo pants?"

"That's it. Sorry, I'm just..." I flapped a hand and winced when the zip tie bit at my battered skin. "So fucking scared," I admitted in a whisper. It wasn't a lie.

I'd given up everything for the man who'd been able to walk away as easy as going out for groceries. I wondered what he would say when I got back to our apartment. *If* I got home.

Not only had he been the one to manipulate me into this life of crime, he'd also been the reason I'd pulled away from my family. The Wildes of Hobie, Texas, weren't the kind of people who became global criminals. They didn't take from people. They gave.

And now my long string of bad decisions was going to land me in prison.

Someone raced over with a multi-tool and handed it to Falcon. He nipped off the tie while telling the person to send in medical help. "We'll get you fixed up, okay? And then I'll need to ask you some questions."

I sniffed again, rubbing my wrists. "Like what? I didn't do anything." I looked up at him in shock, trying like hell to project all my real-life terror into the innocent-victim act. "You don't think I did this, do you? Oh god. My parents are going to kill me. They don't even know I took this job."

"What job?" Falcon asked, looking between me and the doorway in anticipation of an EMT maybe. He wasn't fully listening.

"Building's clear, sir," someone said to him after announcing it in French to the rest of the first responders.

"Thanks," Falcon murmured. His eyes returned to mine. "You were saying?"

I wiped at my eyes with the heel of a hand, deliberately mashing my injury and yelping in pain. "Oh god. Ow. Um... the catering. I worked with the... appetizers. You know... serving them on trays for the party? Someone at the art school said it was easy money and would get you around some really cool pieces you couldn't see otherwise. But... if I'd known it was going to be... dangerous." I looked down at my hands and sniffed again lightly, rubbing at my raw wrists. "My parents made me swear not to take a job outside of my work-study program," I said under my breath. "When they find out..."

Falcon's hand squeezed my shoulder. "Just take a deep breath, and we'll get this sorted out. Here comes someone to take a look at your injuries. Hang tight."

A medical first responder came bustling in with a kit and checked the knot on my head before cleaning the laceration on my cheek. Throughout her ministrations she asked me questions in French about what had happened. Knowing Agent Falcon was listening, I told her about the man who'd knocked me on the head, leaving me dazed and half-conscious and unable to resist when he'd forced me into the storage closet behind the kitchen toward the end of the party. I described him speaking a foreign language I didn't understand and told her it sounded like maybe Russian. I explained how several hours had passed before he pulled me out of the room toward the study where I'd tried to get away. "That's when he smacked me and I fell against the radiator. He tied me in place and just left me here." *It all happened so fast, I didn't really see what was happening...*

The woman tutted over me while she cleaned me up and used some kind of skin glue to close the wound on my face. When she was done with the bandages, she went to work on my wrists, cleaning and applying ointment to them before bandaging them too.

When she was done, I pulled my knees up again and buried my face in them to wait. *I'm just a passive little wallflower victim here... so very scared, Officer Handsome.*

"You need to come with me," the now-familiar voice said. I lifted my head up to meet Falcon's gaze, trying to make mine look as tired, scared, and innocent as possible. The agent's eyes flared wide for a split second before his face returned to its formidable neutral position. "Let's go."

His gruff words didn't fool me. I'd seen the momentary empathy in his stormy eyes. And all I needed was a spark of empathy to manipulate the guy. I was as good as freed already.

And already I'd started thinking ahead, to what came next.

Elek.

Just the thought of the name caused a tide of rage to rise inside me. Elek would rue the day he left me at the mercy of the FBI, Interpol, and the French police. He would regret walking away from me without a care in the fucking world. As if I'd meant nothing to him. As if I *was* nothing at all.

As soon as Falcon let me go, I was going to teach Elek Kemény a lesson.

By leaving me to be captured, he'd tried to take everything from me. I would return the favor in spades. Except I would find success where he had failed.

He'd underestimated Kingston Wilde. He'd taken advantage of me, used me, and cast me aside.

And he would pay.

CHAPTER ONE

FALCON - CURRENT DAY (TWO YEARS LATER)

"Is he... is he fucking kidding? What's he doing?"

I watched the video again, grumbling under my breath about the audacity of Le Chaton. Sure enough, that was Kingston Wilde walking straight out the front door of Pergamonmuseum in Berlin twelve hours earlier when the Greek coins and ingots had been stolen.

"Your jaw is literally hanging open," Linney said in her soft Irish lilt. "Why are you so surprised? We knew he was behind it. Who cares?"

"Yes, but... he doesn't get caught," I said. "This is... this is ridiculous. He's just..." I flapped my hand at the monitor. "Ridiculous," I repeated for lack of a better word.

"Maybe his arrogance will be his downfall one day," she said, typing something into her laptop. Three empty coffee cups sat stacked around her messy desk, and a ceramic mug of tea steamed closest to her hand. It was after five in the morning and we'd been up dealing with this through the night.

I pressed Pause on the video just at the moment Kingston turned so that his face was fully visible to the camera. It was so brazen, so obvious. Le Chaton was as arrogant as Linney had said, but he wasn't stupid. "This can't be right. Have we verified the recording with the techs?" I asked her just as Zivon, our best tech, entered the room rubbing his eyes.

Linney nodded, her blonde hair just as neatly tied back as it had been Sunday afternoon when we'd gotten the call to come in for another case. As soon as we were done interrogating a witness to a forgery—a truly bad one—we'd turned the man over to be booked into custody.

That's when we'd gotten the news about the Berlin job and the missing Greek coins.

"They say it hasn't been altered," Linney said. "Three different cameras got the same man, the same images. It's him. Berlin agrees. That's why they called us."

Why would he have walked right out the front door? Something wasn't right. Le Chaton didn't show his face. He wore a mask and gloves. The only reason we knew his real identity was because Ziv had written an algorithm to compare nearby CCTV feeds from all of the art crimes in order to match faces. Not too long after the van Gogh job, Ziv's algorithm had found the same familiar man in nearby areas after three of the thefts. One had been in Barcelona, one in Geneva, and one in Johannesburg. Facial recognition had finally matched with an American passport photo for Kingston Wilde of Hobie, Texas, a man who'd studied art history at the Sorbonne in Paris and still lived there.

The moment I'd seen the passport photo, I'd had a shock of recognition. I'd seen him before, but it had taken me a moment to remember from where. It had been the man zip tied to the radiator at the Van Gogh job the year before. The man I'd stupidly let walk away from the scene of the largest art heist in decades.

The mistake that had cost me my promotion to special agent in charge of the Global Crimes Task Force, a fact I was still bitter about and planned to rectify by putting Kingston Wilde behind bars.

Unfortunately, being in the same metro area during three similar art robberies didn't count as sufficient evidence to do much more than ask him a few questions, and I wasn't about to approach him again until I had solid evidence to put him away with. I'd tried it a few times before with no success. The man was incredibly talented at talking his way out of things and explaining them away as mere coincidences. I knew this from experience now. For a brilliant strategist, the man played adorable and bewildered very well. Every time I'd questioned King about his whereabouts, he'd turned into a scared, timid little babbling creature who left me even more confused than before I'd begun.

It was like he put me into some kind of trance, one I couldn't admit to my team may have come from how beautiful and vulnerable he looked whenever I was around him. It was humiliating as hell, and I hated him for it.

"So… what?" I asked my teammates, shaking off the memory of the beguiling cat burglar. "The idea is that he's heading straight to Athens to give them these ancient coins? Or is this another case with a note?"

Ziv spoke up. "No note at the scene."

For some reason, the thief we referred to as Le Chaton had begun leaving judgy little notes at the scenes of some of his thefts. And, well, they weren't actually thefts either. The notes in these particular cases were always the same:

I was here despite your "security measures." You need to step up your game. Here's how I got in.
  —The Cat

And then it would be followed by a list of security weaknesses and how he'd bypassed them all. Like he was doing them a service by telling them exactly how to beef up their security systems to protect against thieves like him.

There was no rhyme or reason for which jobs had the note and which ones had a missing piece of art instead. We'd spent hundreds of hours trying to figure it out despite my boss, Nadine, telling me to get a life and let it go. Since those cases were technically simple breaking and entering or trespass cases, they didn't matter much in the grand scheme of things. Not like when high-value art pieces were actually stolen.

But I couldn't let it go. Because with so many other details about Kingston Wilde, it didn't make sense, and I needed to figure it out.

Linney shrugged. "Athens is definitely where he'd think they belonged. Fits his MO. Why not beat him there and catch him in the act? It's either the National Historical Museum or the architectural one he'll return them to. We can put a response team at each."

Ever since the Van Gogh job, Le Chaton's focus had seemed to change. Originally, the pieces he'd stolen had ended up on the black market, usually sold to the highest bidder and never to be seen again. But now he tended to zero in on previously stolen items. The "heist," if you could call it that, was him sneaking into a place to return the piece to the person or museum he thought was the rightful owner. We'd kept that detail from the media so far because god only knew how the press would jump on our new "Robin Hood" figure.

And the asshole was still on the hook for a two-hundred-million-dollar missing Van Gogh among plenty of other things. Also, stealing from unlawful owners was still theft. Even if everyone and their brother thought they deserved it.

"Play it again," I said over my shoulder. Ziv hit Play and the video started from the beginning. The image was clear as day. King's longish dirty-blond hair flopped over to one side, and my fingers twitched down by my thigh like they wanted to rake the hair back from his face or grab hold of it to shake some sense into him.

Or shove the man to his knees.

I blinked and cleared my throat, trying to focus.

"That face," Linney murmured. "Hell, I'd give him the *Mona Lisa* if he asked nice."

"Amen," Ziv added under his breath.

They were right. Kingston Wilde was beautiful. There was no

denying the outside package was pristine and distracting. But we were after what was on the *inside*. Specifically, the knowledge of locations of the countless works of art this sophisticated thief had absconded with from wealthy residences around the globe, including a Cézanne from a pharmaceutical CFO in Boston, a Degas ballerina from a real estate mogul in Florence, and an Andy Warhol from a lesser royal in Saudi Arabia. And how the hell had he continued to get away with it when we'd had our best team on the case for almost five years?

The only lead we'd had at first was a strange, repeated recounting of a shadow climbing through the trees on some of the properties he'd hit early on in Paris when his escapades had just become problematic enough to justify creating the task force.

The first witness to recall the creature in the trees had called the thief "Le Chat Sauvage" which had driven me so crazy, I'd suggested changing it to Le Chaton just to take some of the power out of it. Besides, the man was no "wildcat" even though his identity had continued to elude us for years until we'd finally caught the break with the video feeds.

But now he was straight-up taunting us.

"Maybe you should pay him another visit," Ziv suggested.

"You know I can't do that," I snapped. "I look like an idiot every time I question him."

Linney turned to Ziv with a cheeky grin on her face. "Last time King even winked at him. You should have seen Falcon's face. I thought he was going to clench his jaw hard enough to break teeth."

My cheeks heated. "Shut up," I said, deliberately keeping my jaw relaxed when all I really wanted to do was grind my teeth at the memory. "This isn't productive. Find out where he went after he walked out of the museum. I want every piece of video you can find. Check airports, metro stations, bus—"

"Yeah, yeah," Ziv said in a dry tone. "We got it." The two of them turned back to their computers and got to work.

Our art and antiquities expert, who'd been sitting quietly at his desk in the corner, eyed me over his cup of tea. I recognized that look.

"Mouse, what've you got?"

His soft voice carried across the space. "Where are the coins?"

I furrowed my brows at him, but he continued before I had a chance to ask what he meant.

"Falcon, you're talking about twenty or thirty pounds of metal. Where is he hiding them in these videos? He's not even walking funny."

"There are any number of ways for him to get the coins out of the building," I explained. "It's his presence on the same day in addition to all the other—"

Mouse held up his hand to stop me. "That's simply another coincidence, or so his defense attorney would claim, and you know it. If we want to pin this on him, we need to link him to the actual movement of those coins, either out of the Pergamon or into the museum in Athens."

"I understand that, but at the moment, I'm a bit short on video showing him actually reaching in and removing the—"

He held up his hand again, and Linney snorted out a laugh. It wasn't like our quietest teammate to cut me off like this.

"Yes, I understand," Mouse continued. "And we know the video feeds in the coin room were put on a loop during that time. But what about the loading doors or mailing room? What about the employee entrance? By walking out the front door, he got our attention so focused on him, we haven't taken the time to look at everything else."

Linney sighed. "He's right, Falcon. We fell for it."

"No we didn't." Ziv clicked at lightning speed on his keyboard. "I've already checked all those feeds and found nothing. I'm checking again."

An alert popped up on my screen at the same time my phone started ringing with a call from my supervisor.

"Agent Falcon," I clipped, standing up to find somewhere quieter to take the call. Before I could even step outside the large shared space of our team's office, Nadine stopped me in my tracks.

"The Holy Crown of Hungary has been stolen." Her clipped words sent a chill through my chest. If I wasn't mistaken, that was a piece kept under round-the-clock guard in the Hungarian Parliament Building. It was one of the highest-profile pieces of crown jewels in the world. The kind of item that was utterly unstealable the way the Titanic had been unsinkable.

"How?" I sputtered, wondering if King Wilde had gone completely off the deep end. He was the only one we knew with the skills to pull something like that off. "When? How?"

"Yesterday. And it doesn't matter how. Drop what you're doing and get to the embassy so you can call me back from a secure line. There are extenuating circumstances, and it's urgent."

I snapped my fingers to get everyone's attention. "Define urgent," I said, wondering if she was getting pressure from diplomatic angles.

"It's a matter of national security. Get there now. Also, Agent Falcon?"

"Yes, ma'am."

"Berlin just called. The coins were in a museum air vent with a note explaining how he bypassed their security."

After she ended the call, I stood there for a moment, my jaw clenched so tightly I could hear my teeth grinding. Fucking Kingston Wilde. What the hell was his game this time?

CHAPTER TWO

KING

Strutting out the front door of the museum in Berlin had been the ballsiest move I'd done yet. It had put me on record at the scene of one of my crimes in a way that hadn't happened since the Van Gogh job in Paris. What the hell had I been thinking?

It was without a doubt the stupidest move I'd ever made on a job. Well, besides having trusted Elek Kemény. But that could be explained away by my youth and naiveté at the time. What exactly explained my ridiculous desire to taunt Agent Falcon into arresting me?

The Greek coins in Berlin had been the last job, and I guessed I just wanted to go out with a bang. The only thing left on Elek's wishlist after the coins and ingots was the Holy Crown of Hungary which was virtually impossible to steal. Since the Berlin job had been the last item on the list I could protect, I'd taken the chance of getting caught on video.

It was stupid, but I wanted proof *I'd* been the one to fuck with his precious wish list.

My revenge plan had been twofold. First, prevent Elek from getting his hands on any more items on his wish list. Second, find and replace every forgery I'd ever used on a job with the original work, even if that meant stealing the original from whomever he'd sold it to, essentially erasing any evidence that could be used to tie me to past jobs. That way when I decided to walk away, I could get away clean.

I'd tackled the forgeries first, leaving only one still unaccounted for.

Since Elek had the one remaining forgery, I hadn't dared try to recover it. It was one thing to steal from a museum, and quite another to steal from an art thief. The former used predictable, reasonable methods of security. The latter was wily as fuck.

It was better just to leave it be and get out of the game while I was ahead. Or so I kept telling myself, even though I had the original already tucked away and ready to take my forgery's place if I ever had the chance. It was a Delacroix self-portrait that had been nearly impossible to sneak out of the Louvre's archives. Of all places to have to infiltrate. I'd hated doing it, but if by some chance I ever got the chance to replace my forgery with it, I didn't want Elek to ever know I'd been there and done it. The last thing I needed was an angry Hungarian ex gunning for me.

The end of my revenge spree couldn't have come at a better time. I needed a break. Hopefully a visit home would help ground me a little and I could reset my priorities. It was time to put this upsetting chapter of my life in the past once and for all. Get out of the heist business while I still could.

I'd done almost all I could to keep Elek from what he wanted. I'd broken into every museum and residence containing items on his wish list and informed them how to beef up their security so even I wouldn't be able to break through it. And if I couldn't find a way past a building's security system, there was no way Elek ever could. He just wasn't good enough.

If I decided to tackle the final item... well, it was complicated. The Holy Crown of Hungary was surrounded by live guards around the clock. So I kept trying to tell myself to let it go.

The question now was... what came next? What would my life be about if I wasn't planning and executing an art theft? At this point, I had obscene amounts of money stashed away, mostly rewarded to me with gratitude for returning priceless pieces to their rightful owners but also from fencing lesser works that had value but little meaning to anyone. I wasn't proud of it, but I also didn't lose sleep at night from robbing assholes who thought they could proudly display a stolen Van Gogh or Holocaust diamonds and no one would ever know or care.

Hell, one of the jobs I'd done the year before had included a book of Picasso sketches that had been displayed in the dogs' bedroom at the home of a lesser royal in Bahrain. Returning the sketchbook to the Picasso Museum in Paris had been extremely satisfying, and I hadn't minded grabbing a diamond-studded collar and leash set at the scene of the crime as a tip for my good deed.

But I couldn't expect to stay undetected forever, so I needed to quit while I was ahead. Otherwise Agent Falcon with the FBI would be thrilled to string me up by my balls one day and pin me for everything I'd ever stolen. Maybe that was why I'd let myself be seen on camera walking out of the Berlin museum. Now I would be squarely on Falcon's radar. There'd be no way to travel undetected which would make future jobs more difficult. It was like crossing a bridge toward my new life and burning it down behind me so I wouldn't be tempted to go back.

The flights from Berlin to Dallas took all day, but when I landed and saw my sister MJ waiting for me in the arrivals area, I almost wept with relief.

"You look like shit," she said in her usual hold-nothing-back manner.

"I feel worse," I admitted, hugging her for a longer time than normal.

She squeezed me for a long beat before saying the words I'd been thinking the entire flight.

"Nothing a little Wilde lovin' can't fix. Let's get you home."

Home. God I needed that.

Once we got in the car, MJ turned to me. "Spill it."

She always knew when I was keeping something from her. I let out a breath and ran my hand through my hair, employing my usual tactic of distracting the conversation away from me. "Tell me about Neckie. How's she doing since the baby?"

Even though MJ's face softened at the mention of her girlfriend, she didn't take the bait. "You can see for yourself at the bonfire tonight. Tell me what's going on. I've never seen you quite this bad."

After opening my mouth to change the subject again, I closed it. I was just so fucking tired of lying to my family. They thought I was a personal art curator who traveled around the world helping obscenely wealthy people add to their collections. Over the years, I'd implied things like confidentiality agreements and nondisclosures kept me from being able to talk about it much.

I sighed. "I need to make a job change."

She muttered, "About damned time," before pulling out of the parking space. "What precipitated this decision?"

I looked out the window, trying to figure out just how much I could tell her. "My current job is very stressful. It's not a good long-term situation."

MJ was quiet for a time while we made our way to the interstate. Once we were speeding along out of the city, she spared me a glance. "Do you have any idea how frustrating it is to be an attorney and not be able to help your brother out of legal trouble?"

I gawped at her. "What? Who's in legal trouble?"

"Don't play stupid, King. I'm the one who reviews all of your legal papers. Leases, taxes, etc. And you live way beyond your means. Whatever you're into is going to come back to bite you in the ass. Why won't you confide in me and let me help you?"

I huffed out a breath and sank deeper into my seat. "It's embarrassing."

MJ laughed. "Do you think you're the only Wilde who's done something embarrassing? Wow. You obviously haven't been paying attention lately. Did anyone tell you about Hudson accidentally proposing to Darci? Or about Felix falling in love with someone without realizing the man was a royal? Or West almost letting Nico walk out of his life for good because of his stubborn pride? We are all fuckups, Kingston. All of us."

"What about you, smarty-pants?" I asked her.

"I wasted ten years I could have spent with the love of my life because I was too chickenshit to ask her out in high school. Now stop trying to move the conversation off of you."

I drummed my fingers on my knee for a moment before coming to a decision. "If I ever got arrested by the FBI for a crime committed in a different country, would you be able to help me or find someone who could?"

Her eyebrows shot up. "The FBI?"

I sighed. "Just answer the question."

She thought about it for a moment. "It depends on what kind of crime it's for."

I'd wanted to ask her these questions for years, and now here we were. It felt strange to finally tell someone the truth.

More or less.

"Hypothetically speaking of course," I began, "what if it was art theft?" I braced myself for her to respond with outrage or condescension.

Surprisingly, MJ smiled wide. "I knew it! You're part of a cabal... wait! You're mixed up with Italian mafia... or... No! It's the Russian mob."

Not the reaction I'd been expecting. "I'm being serious."

Her brows furrowed as she glanced over at me. "For real?"

I swallowed. "Not for real, obviously. I said hypothetically."

She nodded slowly. "And hypothetically, how the hell would you have gotten involved in an art theft?"

My back teeth ground together as memories of Elek came unbidden into my mind. I hated that after two years he could still elicit such a rise out of me. I'd hoped taking my revenge would rid him from my life and mind for good, but still the thought of him sent a storm of emotions through me. "Hypothetically, I was young and stupid. I trusted the wrong person who told me they loved me."

She glanced over at me again and reached out to squeeze my hand. "Oh, babe. I'm sorry."

I felt a burning in my throat. "Don't. I don't… just… don't. Okay? I need legal help, not… whatever that is."

MJ's eyes narrowed. "Yeah, well, if you ask me, you need love help too. It's plain as day on your face. When was the last time you had a boyfriend?"

I held up a hand. "No. We're not doing this. Art theft, remember? Art. Theft."

"Okay. Art theft. What kind of evidence would they have on you?"

Before I could answer her, she added, "And stop saying hypothetically, I'm your attorney. It's already privileged."

I let my head fall back against the seat and began recounting all of the jobs I'd done that the authorities were aware of. I didn't bother mentioning the ones that had never been reported. I'd stolen from many people who'd rather suffer the loss in silence than call in law enforcement. In fact, those were the best kind. But they were also the most dangerous. On jobs where the artwork was legal and insured, people tended to let you take it without risking getting hurt. Not so much with drug lords, corrupt oligarchs, and owners of stolen goods.

As I enumerated the jobs, MJ's jaw began to drop.

At one point she cut me off with a slash of her hand. "That's enough. Jesus, King." There was a strained look around her eyes. "What the hell? And why? Why in the world would you get into something so risky? I don't understand."

"I don't want to talk about that part." I sounded like a bitchy teenager.

She pressed her lips together, clearly trying to decide whether to push the issue or not. I was relieved when she chose to move on. "So this guy Falcon has been trying to pin you for a string of art thefts for years with no success?"

I nodded. "Yeah, and—"

"Wow, you must be really good at it," she said, cutting me off again. MJ definitely qualified as one of my bossier sisters.

I couldn't help but puff up a little. "The best," I said, flashing her a smile.

She rolled her eyes. "I'm not sure that's something you should be bragging about. But... good job? I guess?"

Typical sister response. "Anyway," I continued. "I'm done with it. So now I need to decide what I want to be when I grow up."

MJ pressed the button to crack open her window letting in a flood of crisp fall air. Despite it being October, the sun was shining directly into the car, heating it up. "Before we talk about that, let's sort out the legal dilemma. You said they had evidence against you?"

"No. They don't. Not that I know of. I mean, I guess there could be something I've messed up and overlooked, but I really don't think so. If they did, I'd probably already be in jail by now. So the biggest threat at this point would be them finding someone I've worked with on a heist and convincing them to testify against me."

"Pfft," MJ said, flapping her hand away from the steering wheel. "White, good-looking American boy like you? Unless you murdered someone, chances are you'd beat any testimony from a fellow criminal."

"This agent really wants to put me away," I admitted. "He's been after me for years."

She thought that over a moment. "Do you have any leverage?" she asked. "Like information they'd want?"

I grinned. "Tons. I have the location of every named work of art I've been involved with including a long list of locations where authorities can find famous stolen works that are still in the wrong hands. Pieces that have been missing for decades."

Silence for a beat before MJ turned to me with wide eyes. "You know where famous stolen artwork is?"

Finally something I said seemed to impress her. "Yeah. A lot of it. I've either come across knowledge of it or seen it while on a job.

And I have it all listed in a notebook. I guess I've always thought of it as a bargaining chip."

It was something I'd started creating after I realized Elek had such a hold over me. If he ever decided to turn me into the authorities, I needed a way out. So I'd started the little book of art crime intel as a kind of insurance policy.

My sister's forehead was creased in thought. "That's good, King. Really smart. If anything happens to you, don't give it to them right away. You know that, right? Wait for me or an attorney I arrange for you. We'll be able to determine the best way to use it for your benefit. And for the love of god, if you're arrested, don't—"

"Say anything," I finished. "I know. Believe me, I know that."

Silence descended again. For a while I thought she was contemplating my eventual arrest and trial. Part of me wanted to reassure her that it would never happen, but another part of me wanted to let her figure out a plan just in case.

After all, the best thieves always had a back-up plan in the event of the worst-case scenario.

When she finally spoke again, it surprised me. "Have you thought about moving home?"

I blinked over at her. "To Hobie? Me?"

She rolled her eyes. "Don't be such a snot. Yes, you. We miss you, jackass. You could teach art at Hobie High or, hell, open up a gallery on the square. There's plenty of tourist business now that lake season is basically year-round. You could make a good living. Doc and Grandpa could help you with seed money. You know they'd love to do anything to keep you nearby."

Before I could stop myself, I snorted at the thought of needing their money.

"Oh my god," MJ screeched. "You're rich as fuck, aren't you?"

I felt my face heat. "Let's just say, I brought your girlfriend a diamond nose stud as a thank-you gift for giving birth to my niece."

MJ's face softened for a split second before she glared at me. "Was it stolen?"

"No," I said with a laugh. "It's a legit purchase from a jeweler in London. I swear. I can even give you the receipt."

"Mmpfh. I'll allow it. Mostly because she'll be sexy as fuck with that thing in. She has a lovely nose."

"You're whipped."

MJ's grin was wide and free. "So very happily whipped. You should try it."

It was my turn to scoff. "Not sure about that. My life is complicated enough as it is without a partner."

Agent Dirk Falcon's square jaw and dimpled chin rose unbidden in my mind and set my heart rate on edge for some reason. Maybe it was a subconscious reminder that I already had a man in my life who made things complicated enough without adding a love interest to the mix.

After arriving in time for a big bonfire with half the town and almost all my family members followed by a long sleep in the ranch bunkhouse, I made my way to Doc and Grandpa's kitchen for breakfast. Several of my siblings were already lounging around in their pajamas with hands wrapped around cups of coffee. Grandpa's familiar, wide shoulders took up space in front of whatever he was making on the griddle, and the smell of bacon made my mouth water.

"There he is," Doc said with a wide grin and open arms. I gave him a hug and kiss on the cheek.

"Everything looks and smells amazing. I should have come home months ago," I admitted.

"Years ago," someone coughed into their hand.

"No shit," someone else said.

I ignored it and headed for the coffee. My family meant well, and they showed their love with teasing, but I still felt hollowed out with guilt.

West looked up from his phone. "Where you been lately? Last I heard, you were in Bahrain. Was it another art consultation?" He lifted his eyebrow and emphasized the words art consultation like they were code for something.

"Can't we all just put it out there that he's CIA," Hallie said without looking up from her own phone. "We've been whispering about it for years now."

"I'm not," I said for the millionth time. "I promise you my degrees in art history are real, and they're not something the CIA has a huge need of." At least that part was true. "Besides, you know how much I hate guns. Pretty sure CIA agents have to be well trained in firearms."

"Cover story," someone coughed again. I identified my brother Otto as the cough-er. He grinned and winked at me.

"Whatever," I said, taking my first sip of coffee and avoiding eye contact with MJ. "Subject change please."

Hallie held up her phone. "Could you hack into this if you had to?"

I paused.

"A-ha!" she said triumphantly. "Case closed."

West grabbed Nico's coffee mug to get him a refill. "Have you ever participated in a dead drop?"

I paused again. Lying to my family was one of the lines I tried never to cross. Which they made extremely difficult at times.

"Duuuuude," Saint said. "And I thought being a SEAL was impressive."

"It is," his boyfriend, Augie, agreed, rubbing Saint's upper arm and sneaking in a squeeze of Saint's enormous biceps. "It so is."

"I don't work for the CIA," I insisted.

"Okay, fine. Some other covert agency," Hallie said, waving a hand. "Whatever. Point is, our bro is a spy. Totes cool."

Winnie grunted her disapproval of her twin's trendy speak. "Does it matter? The important question is... are you happy?" Then she shot laser eyeballs at me.

Fuck.

"So... how 'bout them Cowboys? Think they're gonna go all the way this year?" I asked.

The room full of non-sports fans gawped at me.

Doc tilted his head and grinned at me. "Oh, you're into American football? Interesting. Define a safety."

I drew a blank. "Shut up," I muttered, sipping the coffee again. "Tell me about your great-grandchildren. Someone said you've been playing favorites."

The bait worked. Doc sputtered and began extolling the virtues of all of their great-granddaughters. West winked at me and walked over to exchange the refilled coffee mug for the baby in Nico's arms. Seeing West as a dad was so natural and right. He'd always been responsible and caring. I was thrilled he'd found a loving and interesting partner to share his life with.

As I looked around the room at the rest of my siblings and cousins, I noticed just how many of them had found love since I'd seen them last. So many of them seemed happy and fulfilled. Was I?

It wasn't even a question. The answer was a resounding no. I was tired and bitter, alone and so fucking stressed all the time. My life had been wearing me down one job at a time.

Aunt Gina had been watching me from across the room since I'd walked in. I'd noticed her studying me at the bonfire the night before as well, so when she approached me and stood next to me at the kitchen island, I wasn't surprised.

"If your life isn't working out the way you planned it, King, then change it." She reached for my hand and held it. "You are smart, well educated, and driven, not to mention only twenty-eight years old. It is never too late for a fresh start."

"I'm fine," I said more out of habit than anything else.

Her soft fingers brushed across my forehead before she leaned in to press a kiss there. "A man your age shouldn't look like he's been used as a pommel horse, Kingston. Maybe it's the travel that's wearing you down. Either way, you deserve to be happy and free."

Free.

The word resonated through me, making me yearn. The only

way to be free—to *stay* free—was to be done with that life, to convince myself to let the Berlin job be the last one. I needed to let go of this obsession with getting back at Elek. He wasn't worth the complicated and risky attempt to sneak into the Hungarian Parliament Building for the Holy Crown. It needed to end here. I had to put this life behind me once and for all.

So I tried. And over the next couple of weeks with my family, I began to relax and finally feel like I truly could make a fresh start. By the time we traveled to Napa to celebrate Doc and Grandpa's vow renewal, I almost felt free in the way Gina had described. I began to think of art theft in the past tense. I would miss my little cat-and-mouse game with Agent Falcon, but it was finally over.

And it truly was. Until that fucker dragged me back in again.

We were all sitting around the lobby lounge in the vineyard lodge having drinks and shooting the shit the night before Doc and Grandpa's wedding when I spotted a man enter through the main doors. At first I thought my brain was playing tricks on me or maybe I'd had more to drink than I'd thought, but as he came closer I realized Agent Dirk Falcon was actually there in California, in the same fucking room as my entire extended family.

My heart thundered in my chest. This was it. There was only one reason he'd be here. He was coming for me. Which meant he had something. I'd overlooked a detail. Or maybe my little stunt in Berlin had finally been the last straw, giving him enough cause to finally put me away.

I froze for a beat before standing up and glaring at him. "This is a private party."

"I'm sorry. It can't wait." His voice was clipped, professional. It gave nothing away.

I couldn't believe that fucker dared to do this in front of my entire family. How the hell had he even tracked me here? "Are you here to arrest me, because if so—"

"No, no. Not that. I…" Falcon looked around at my family and seemed to realize we had a rapt audience. "I need your help. I have a plane waiting on a private airstrip nearby. We need to be in..." He looked around again. "We need to leave right now."

I blinked. The fuck? Was the man actually asking me to go with him? Voluntarily? It didn't even cross my mind he might be serious about needing my help. It was just a ruse—a trap to get me into custody without a struggle. "I don't work for you," I sputtered.

Falcon's eyes narrowed. Dammit, the man's intensity only made him more attractive to me. "You do now. Let's go."

A million thoughts raced through my head, not the least of which was the notebook of stolen-artwork information in my room. If I left it with my stuff, it could get lost or even shipped back to my apartment building in Paris where any number of things could happen to it including it being found easily in a search of my things. I glanced over at MJ who—thank god—gave me a discreet nod. My sister had my back. I just needed to make sure she had easy access to the notebook so she could take charge of it and get it back to Hobie safe and sound.

And if by some chance the agent let me go to my room alone... I could try to get out of there and take off.

I let out a breath. "Let me gather my things."

My brother Saint stood up. "What the hell is going on? Who are you?" He demanded of Falcon before turning to me. "King, who is this guy?"

I tried to reassure him. I didn't want my family anywhere near this situation. I'd successfully kept my past from them up until now and didn't intend for them to find out the truth like this. "It's fine. Really." Then I turned to Doc and Grandpa. "I'm very sorry to miss the wedding."

Grandpa's eyes were as warm and loving as always. "We know you love us no matter where you are tomorrow. We just want you to be happy."

I huffed out a laugh that sounded bitter even to my own ears. "Yeah. Happy." I glanced at Falcon, wondering if this would be the last time I saw my grandfathers. Would he extradite me? To where? For which job?

Falcon turned to my family. "I'm really sorry to do this. He's needed on a... very important project."

At least the man had the decency to lie to them. I wasn't sure what was causing him to protect me that way, but I'd take it. Now all I had to do was get him to stay there and wait for me.

"My room is the closest one right there," I said, pointing to the hallway. I ran a hand through my hair, letting my shoulders sag and trying to look as defeated and resigned as possible. "I'll be right back."

Falcon's eyes began to narrow suspiciously at me, but thankfully someone distracted him long enough for me to cross the lobby to my room. As soon as I was through the door, I raced into action, opening the in-room safe and reprogramming the code to MJ's birthday before tossing all of my contraband in there along with the journal and grabbing my legal Kingston Wilde passport and my still-packed duffle bag.

Then I quickly eased open the sliding glass doors on the other side of the bed and snuck into the night.

CHAPTER THREE

FALCON

I had to be the world's stupidest law enforcement officer. Something about King's eyes seemed to put me into a trance. When I was around him, I wanted to protect him instead of arrest him, which is why I'd done the unthinkable and let him go to his hotel room unescorted.

When it became clear he'd bolted, I'd wanted to smack myself for being so naive, so gullible and easily manipulated. All he'd had to do was look at me with that expression of defeat, and I'd assumed that's how he actually felt. The man was a master manipulator. When was I going to learn he was a liar and a faker?

I'd honestly contemplated calling in my resignation right then. I didn't deserve my position on one of the world's top art heist task forces. After I'd let him go at the scene of the Van Gogh heist two years ago, I'd learned my lesson. Or so I'd thought. Never in a million years had I thought he'd make a scene in front of his entire extended family.

But he hadn't made a scene, had he? He'd simply wandered to his room and disappeared into the night. *Like any seasoned criminal would have done.*

I sighed and banged my head on the steering wheel of the rental car. How the hell was I going to explain this to my team? To my *boss*? We'd have to start back at square one to find him again, and I'd be lucky if Nadine even allowed me to stay in charge of this op.

Think, you idiot. He can't have gotten that far.

But that wasn't true. If he had access to a vehicle, he could have gone in any direction, north toward Oregon, east toward Nevada, or even back to San Francisco where he could get lost in a sea of strangers. The best thing I could do was get back on the plane and check in with my team in Paris. See if they could track him down electronically somehow.

I pulled the car into the lot and made my way to the small jet. The tiny airport was half-asleep this time of night, and the cool November air felt good on my hot cheeks. Humiliation was an even harder pill to swallow the second time around.

After trudging up the folding stairs, I ducked into the plane and made eye contact with the flight attendant. She gave me a flirty smile followed by an odd wink.

"Let us know when you're ready. Take all the time you need." She glanced toward the seating area and smiled in that direction too.

I spun around to find King Wilde kicked back in one of the large leather seats with his ankles crossed on the low coffee table in front of him.

He was clicking around on his phone like he'd been killing time waiting for me to arrive.

An intense feeling of relief rolled through me, followed by ire. "What the fuck?" I sputtered. "Are you... what... why are you here? Are you insane?"

He looked up at me with those same deep-set eyes I could get lost in. His dirty-blond hair flopped over his forehead in a way that itched to be pushed back. I clenched my fingers into a fist as he spoke calmly. "It's the crown, isn't it? You think I took it."

I stared at him. How the fuck did he know this was about the crown? No one knew it had been taken. The Hungarian govern-ment had wanted the theft kept under wraps to avoid a public back-lash, so they'd closed off the rotunda where it was displayed. The

Holy Crown of Hungary was a national treasure, symbolic of Hungary's special state as recognized by God. Admitting it was missing would be a major embarrassment and create a media firestorm.

It was so important to the Hungarian government that the crown was kept under constant surveillance with armed guards standing watch over it at all times. It should have been impossible to steal. And there was only one thief in the world with the skills to pull off such an impossible job.

Le Chaton.

Except we had evidence that Kingston Wilde was in Berlin at the same time.

I clenched my jaw. "What crown are you talking about?" I'd been played by him enough and didn't intend to let him trick me into giving him information he didn't have.

King lifted an eyebrow. "Seriously? Is that how you want to play this?" When I said nothing, he let out an exasperated sigh. "The Holy Crown of Hungary, also known as the Crown of Saint Stephen, was stolen from the Hungarian Parliament Building in Budapest."

"How the fuck did you know about that?" I asked, my voice rising in frustration despite my best efforts to keep it calm and measured.

He lifted a shoulder. "I have my sources."

"Or you were involved," I countered.

"Nope, sorry."

"And I'm supposed to believe you?" I asked with a laugh.

King shrugged. "Doesn't matter. There's not one single molecule of evidence I was even in Budapest. Ever. So try again."

He was so damned arrogant. "Maybe you had a partner on the ground you were directing from afar."

King furrowed his brow and tilted his head, sending the floppy hair into his eye. My fingers twitched as he brushed his own through the messy locks and nodded. "I don't have a partner."

A shadow fell over his expressive eyes, but I assumed it was more of his acting bullshit. I pushed aside the desire to know what had caused it.

He was the enemy, I reminded myself. Just because I needed his help didn't change the fact we stood on opposite sides of the law on this. "Look, the reality is that it doesn't matter if you took it or not. We need it back."

His eyes changed instantly to curiosity and... *intrigue.* "Why?"

"How about because I said so?" I snapped, tired of his attempts to swing the power from me to him.

"Then I guess I'm out of here. Good luck," King said with a shrug, standing up and making his way toward the still-open door of the plane.

Dammit. I moved in front of him, blocking his exit. He pulled up short, but the area at the front of the plane was cramped, forcing us into close proximity. I caught a whiff of something clean and sharp, and I had to keep from leaning in to smell more of it.

"King, wait." God, I hated to do this, but if by some chance he wasn't the one who took it, he was sure as hell the only one who might know more than we did about it. And the stakes were way too high to let him walk away.

We needed him.

He glanced toward the open door and then back at me blocking his path. "What?" he asked wearily.

I needed leverage, something to force him to stay and make a deal. "We found your DNA on one of the Greek coins."

He stared at me in shock. "No you didn't."

I nodded with complete confidence despite the fact I was lying my ass off. "The lab techs said it was from sweat. I guess it was overly warm in the ducts."

Bluff. Total bluff.

I could tell he was trying hard not to believe it, but there was no way for him to know for sure. I just needed that hint of uncertainty and he would be mine.

"We're prepared to offer you full immunity if you'll help us."

He lifted an eyebrow. "Immunity for what?" He leaned against the galley wall, crossing his arms and projecting a calm confidence. "I read in the papers the coins you're referring to weren't actually taken but had simply been misplaced."

I really wanted to wipe the smug, arrogant grin off his face. "The coins, maybe, but half the ingots in the collection were never returned."

His mask slipped for a split second. I could tell he wanted to argue with me, to tell me he'd left the entire collection intact. But that would be an admission of guilt.

King's nostrils flared. "Bullshit."

"The museum estimated the worth of the stolen pieces to total around forty thousand euro. And since your DNA is on the remaining coins..."

His eyes narrowed at me. I could tell he wanted to call my bluff badly, but he couldn't be sure some museum employee didn't take the chance to pilfer from the collection when it was found in the ductwork.

King pushed away from the galley and paced deeper into the plane. He stood, staring out one of the windows for a long moment. Then he turned to face me. "I want immunity for everything through this crown operation."

I barked out a laugh. "Keep dreaming."

"I'll take my chances, then." He started toward the door again, and pushed his way past me.

Nadine's voice replayed in my head from the night before. *"Give him whatever he wants. We need that crown more than we need to put away a do-gooder cat burglar."*

We'd already spent over a week trying to run down leads the usual way but had found nothing. Nadine was getting pressure from above, and the stakes were high enough to do whatever it took to get our hands on the crown.

At the risk of everything I'd worked on in four years of trying to put Le Chaton away.

"Stop," I barked.

He stopped at the door but didn't turn around.

I clenched my hand into a fist several times before finally forcing myself to say the words. "We will give you immunity for everything up through now with the exception of the theft of the crown," I offered.

He turned around and considered me for several beats, long enough that I started to feel a trickle of nerves that he might not take the deal. Which would have been idiotic of him, but there was a lot about Le Chaton I'd never understood.

"I didn't take the crown," he finally said.

"Then you don't need immunity for it," I countered.

He thought about it a moment, then nodded. "Okay." He came back, squeezing past me again and re-taking his seat.

I blinked at him in surprise. I'd honestly expected more of a fight. I'd been prepared to offer him immunity for the crown as well if push came to shove, but he hadn't pressed for it. Either he truly didn't take the crown, or he was that confident he hadn't left any evidence behind. To be fair, it made sense he hadn't taken the crown in Budapest since he'd been on record in Berlin at the time. But that didn't mean he hadn't been involved. But if he had been, why help us find his accomplice?

I stepped toward the cockpit to speak to the pilots. "Get us in the air to Paris please."

When I turned back to King, his eyes were focused and he seemed to have dropped his don't-give-a-shit act. "Why Paris?" he asked.

"The rest of the team," I told him succinctly, slipping back into the seat across from him.

He nodded. "After we pick them up we need to fly to Greece. Mykonos."

My back bristled at his nerve in making such a demand, but it was tempered by my curiosity. "What's in Greece?"

He hesitated a moment before responding. "The crown."

My eyes bulged. I waited for him to laugh as though he were joking but he remained dead serious. "Wait, you know where it is?"

He shifted in his seat, looking less like the self-assured Le Chaton and more like a nervous kitten. "I have an idea where it is."

I took that information in, turning it over in my mind. "Because you were involved?"

"I told you I had nothing to do with it."

I shrugged. He could say a lot of things but that didn't mean I planned to believe him. "Then how else would you know?"

The plane began moving, and he looked out the window, watching the ground slip by faster and faster until it fell away beneath us. It wasn't until the plane had been swallowed by clouds that he said, "There's only one person I know who wants the crown badly enough and might possibly have the skills to acquire it."

He fell silent again, and I wanted to reach across the narrow space between us and take him by the shoulders and shake him. Did every conversation with him have to be this difficult? It felt like pulling teeth. "Who?"

His fingers drummed against the armrest, tapping out a rhythm only he seemed to know. His eyes shifted to meet mine, and I was struck again by how striking they were. "My former partner."

I tried to hide my surprise. "I thought you didn't *have* a partner," I accused.

A muscle twitched along his jaw. "*Former* partner."

Interesting. Apparently I'd hit on a sore spot. "How long since you two worked together?"

"Not since Van Gogh."

He couldn't hide the hint of anger in his voice. It seemed there was little love lost between King and his former partner.

And suddenly a piece of the Kingston Wilde puzzle slipped into place. I'd always wondered how he'd ended up trapped in that room without the Van Gogh. The easiest explanation was a partner who'd fucked him over, but we'd never had any evidence to support the claim. Given the way King's body tensed at the mention of his former partner, I'd wager our hypothesis was correct.

"Tell me about Van Gogh."

King let out a soft laugh, a dimple appearing next to his lips for only a tiny fraction of a second before disappearing again. "Nope."

God, he could be infuriating. "We had a deal, King," I reminded him.

"The deal is I help you find the crown, nothing more. Who I am —my past—none of that is on the table."

"It is if your partner is the one who took it," I told him.

"*Former*," he ground out through clenched teeth. His eyes caught mine and held them in challenge.

One I refused to lose. I nodded. "Right. Former," I said as though humoring him.

His jaw twitched. As I expected, my response got under his skin, and he glared at me before shifting his attention to the window.

Silence fell between us as the plane broke through the clouds into a sky lit by a full moon.

After a moment, King let out a long sigh. "I didn't take the ingots." His voice was low and carried the sound of utter defeat and exhaustion in it, expressions I'd been fooled by before.

"Right," I scoffed as if I believed my own lie. Because of course no one had actually taken the ingots, but I liked holding it over his head anyway. Leverage seemed to be the only language a man like King knew how to speak.

We were blazing into the sky when he finally looked up at me. "I don't give a shit whether you believe me or not, *Dirk*."

He closed his eyes again and reclined his chair as far back as it would go. I shifted in my own seat, trying hard not to let the sound of my name spoken in his sultry voice wake my lonely dick up.

While he dozed, I studied him without remorse. Finally, after all these years, Le Chaton was there within arm's reach. My fingers itched for a set of handcuffs. How many times had I imagined slipping them around his wrists? Tightening them down? Seeing the moment in Kingston Wilde's eyes when he realized I'd won? That he was mine?

But now instead of being in handcuffs, he was practically a member of my team. And I knew next to nothing about him. He was a complete mystery. I knew plenty of things about him, but nothing about why in the world this small-town kid from Texas would have started stealing high-priced art.

King's family had plenty of money. His father was a top-level international money man, and his grandfathers owned half of their little corner of Texas. Most of his siblings had impressive resumes and made plenty of money. King himself had a master's degree in Art History from one of the top specialty schools in the world. He could have a high-paying job anywhere he wanted to.

I shifted in my seat, reclining the back and then straightening it again, unable to get comfortable. I wanted to ignore King the way he was ignoring me, but it was impossible. Finally, I gave up trying. "How did you get into this business?" I asked.

He opened one eye to peer at me. "Same old story since time began," he muttered before closing the eye again.

He clearly wasn't interested in chatting, but I didn't care. "A woman?" I pressed. "You wanted to impress a chick?"

He lifted a shoulder. "Something like that."

"Tell me. Nothing you can say can be used against you, remember? Immunity means no matter what we find, you can't be charged with any of those previous thefts."

He opened his eyes again and narrowed them at me. "And once my attorney, MJ Wilde, gets paperwork to that effect, you let me know. M'kay? Until then, I'm catching some sleep."

Fuck.

I stood up and moved to the back of the plane to get a little distance from him before making the phone call to Nadine to give her an update. It took several attempts, but thankfully King's sister was still awake in California.

"Let me talk to him," she snapped into the phone. "And you're on my shit list for taking him away from here before our grandfather's wedding ceremony, you asshat."

I did feel bad for that. "Sorry, but it's important."

"More important than celebrating two men who... you know what? Never mind. Give me my brother."

King was actually snoring when I walked back up to his seat.

"He's sleeping," I said before holding the phone so she could hear the snores.

"He's faking. Give him the phone."

I blinked at the man in front of me. The corner of his wide lips was damp with drool. "King?" I asked softly before placing my hand on his shoulder. I could feel heat and firm muscle through his thin sweater. He continued snoring.

MJ's voice blared out of the phone, scaring the piss out of me. "It's me, you jerk-off, and you're keeping me from getting in bed with a beautiful woman!"

King's eyes opened with a roll, and he took the phone from me, wiping the drool away with the back of his hand. "Cool your jets. I'm up."

I couldn't hear her side of the conversation, but I hoped like hell she was happy with the paperwork she'd received from my office.

When the call finished, he handed me the phone, saying, "We're all good on the immunity." Then he closed his eyes and went back to sleep.

I blinked at him. "What the fuck? No. Now tell me how you got into this line of work," I sputtered. "I want some information."

He didn't lift his head from where it was angled on the back of his seat, but it was dark enough outside that I could see his eyes open in the reflection of the airplane window.

"It wasn't a chick," he said. "It was a dude. And I was the idiot who believed every damned word out of his lying, cheating mouth. And now I'm going to take great pleasure in taking the one thing he cares about most away from him."

I stared at him in shock. Not just at the intensity of emotion in his voice, but that he'd shared so much about himself so freely. And while I should have been thinking about how this affected the mission ahead, my brain was too busy ticking frantically through everything I'd ever known about him. In five years of following his heists and two years of knowing his actual identity, never had I learned of his sexuality.

Knowing he was gay or bi shouldn't have changed a single thing. We had a job to do. He was an asset, a tool. His purpose was to retrieve an item of utmost importance to American politics and Hungarian heritage. Whether or not he was attracted to men was completely irrelevant.

I sank into the seat across from him again and sighed.

Yeah, right.

CHAPTER FOUR

KING

When we landed in Paris, I insisted on going to my apartment to pick up some tools of my trade. If I was going to get a crack at Elek's house, I needed to be prepared.

"We can get whatever you need," Falcon grumbled. "No need to go to your place."

"Really? Do you have a Flexy Navigator drone attachment for an XLF-360? Hm? Or an infrared motion-detector sweep that fits a broad-spectrum infiltrating cam like the YuliPro? What about a—"

He cut me off with a flap of his hand. "Fine, whatever. But I'm cuffing myself to you this time."

Falcon clearly didn't have any idea what I was talking about. Of course, neither did I since I'd made all of those things up. But I needed several key items from my apartment regardless, and it was worth the embarrassment of being cuffed to him like a criminal.

Thankfully, the man got an important phone call while we were at my place, so he let me rifle through my supply closet untethered. I gathered everything into a duffle and slung it over my shoulder before holding out my wrist to be re-cuffed.

"Why do you need that tube?" he asked, eyeballing the painting tube I'd laid on top of the duffle.

"It has a delicate tripod in it," I said. "To mount the infrared motion-detector sweep—"

"Fine, whatever," he said again, yanking me into the hallway. I let out a breath and followed him back to the Uber where the driver didn't even bat an eye at the handcuffs.

Paris was like that sometimes. It was one of the reasons I liked it so much. That and the art, of course.

By the time Falcon's little team of busybodies joined us on the plane, my stomach was tumbling with nerves. Why had I agreed to this? Of course, I knew the answer. I'd agreed because the minute I'd left the vineyard, I'd called one of my contacts in Florence to ask what was going on in the art world that I didn't already know about.

That's when I'd learned that Elek's own personal holy grail, the Holy Crown of Hungary, had been stolen right out from under the noses of the Hungarian parliament guards. It simply wasn't possible for that to happen without him at least having knowledge of it, and it was way more likely that he'd actually managed the job himself with the help of some kind of crazy-ass risk takers.

Either way, I wanted in. There was no way in hell I could stand by and let Elek simply walk away with the Holy Crown of Hungary, a coronation relic from the year 1000. It had adorned the head of over fifty Hungarian monarchs through the years since being presented by the Byzantine emperor. It's very image was incorporated into the Hungarian coat of arms. It had been hidden, lost, recovered, and taken abroad several times over its thousand-year history, including being entrusted to the United States after the Second World War to keep it safe from the Soviet Union. President Carter himself had decreed its return to the people of Hungary in 1978 only after assessing the stability of the Hungarian government.

It belonged to the people, not Elek Kemény.

Oh, who was I kidding? I didn't care nearly as much about the Hungarian people as I did keeping Elek from having anything he wanted that badly.

So I'd swallowed my pride and skulked to the closest airstrip to the vineyard and waited for Falcon in the FBI's private jet. The very presence of Falcon and the jet indicated the importance of whatever this mission was, and it had taken all of my self-control not to start off by rattling off a thousand questions to him like an eager child.

I'd done my best to play it cool instead, like I could walk away at any minute if this began to bore me.

As if.

When we returned to the plane, Falcon's team joined us. I stood and stretched before reaching out my hand to shake.

Falcon was all business. "Kingston Wilde, this is Aislinn Brennan, the Interpol liaison on the team."

I gave her my flirtiest smile and was pleased to see her fair skin flush in response. "Nice to meet you."

"Call me Linney," she said in a lovely Irish lilt. She returned my smile and shook my hand before finding a seat on the other side of the aisle from where I'd been sitting.

Up next was a short guy who looked too young to be employed by any law enforcement agency. He had brown hair, brown eyes, and a button nose. The kid was kind of cute, if a bit nondescript.

"This is—" Falcon was cut off by the smaller guy.

"Doesn't matter. They all call me Mouse." His voice was so soft, I had to lean in to hear him. The skin of his hand was just as soft, and his smile was sweet. "Nice to meet you. I'm a fan of your work."

"Jesus, Mouse," the other man said from behind him. "I don't think you're supposed to tell him that considering he's a *criminal*."

Mouse shrugged, still holding my hand. I noticed Falcon's eyes on where our hands joined, so I held Mouse's grip even longer just to piss the senior agent off a little.

"Pleasure to meet you, cutie," I said, causing Mouse's face to go up in flames.

"Jesus Christ," Falcon muttered.

Mouse skittered past me to sit next to Linney, which left the final member of the crew.

Falcon clapped the stranger's shoulder. "Ziv Batkin. One of the best hackers in the world."

I eyed the man, wondering what crime he'd committed to land

him a job in law enforcement. Because if he was truly a world-class hacker, he certainly hadn't gone to work with them voluntarily.

"Nice to meet you," I said, shaking his hand and offering him a smile too. Everyone knew it was easier to catch bees with honey, and I'd never shied away from using my charm to win people over.

Ziv narrowed his eyes at me. "Mpfh. We'll see," he said before joining Linney and Mouse in the grouping of four captain's chairs across the aisle from me.

I lifted my eyebrows at Falcon. "Seems like a motley crew you have there."

"They're the best," he snapped.

"Easy, killer. Clearly they're the best if they caught the elusive Le Chaton in…" I sat back in my chair and looked at my nonexistent wristwatch. "Five years, was it?"

Falcon grunted and dropped back into the seat he'd been in on the long flight from California. The one directly across from mine.

I stood up again as soon as he settled in. "Mind if I disembark to stretch my legs a bit? It's a long flight to Athens."

"Yes, I mind. We're leaving any minute, and I'm not taking any chances of you bolting again. Sit your ass down."

My eyes flew to Falcon's face. My, my. I kind of liked bossy, angry special agent man. I wondered what he'd do if I teased him a little.

"What're you going to do if I run off again, *Dirk?*" I asked, emphasizing his first name in a low purr only he could hear over the sound of the plane's systems ramping up. "Spank me?" I leaned down and whispered that last part in his ear, assuming the buttoned-up FBI agent would have a healthy dash of homophobia.

"Not like you don't deserve it," he countered just as quietly. "Someone needs to put you in your place."

My stomach tightened at the implication. Holy fuck. If Agent Falcon was into men, I was into a heapload of trouble. I had a history of letting my dick steer me way wrong in this business, and the senior agent was exactly my type—older and bossy with a nice healthy dash of gruff and sexy mixed in.

I played a mental game with myself to keep my skin from flushing with heat. After trying to get the other agents wrong-footed with my own charm, it wouldn't do to be thrown off by Falcon's innuendo. I was better than this. I could control myself.

After turning around to face away from him, I leaned over and reached into my backpack, looking for absolutely nothing but giving him a nice, healthy peek at my assets just to regain the upper hand.

He made a breathy grunting sound deep in his throat, and I let out a silent sigh of relief. Upper hand reestablished. I didn't spend an hour every night on squats, crunches, and pushups for no good reason. If by some oddball twist of fate I'd lucked into working with a *gay* FBI agent, and he thought I was attractive, it meant I'd have a way of manipulating him.

And it was looking more and more like I'd need that sooner rather than later if I was going to use this opportunity to get revenge on Elek. I was going to steal that fucking crown right out from under his nose and make sure he could never get his hands on it again. And if, in the process, these guys were able to catch him with stolen goods and put him in jail, well, then, that would be the cherry on top.

After we were airborne, Falcon got everyone's attention to discuss the plan.

"King is going to tell us where he thinks the crown is being held, and we're going to go in there and steal it."

I stared at him, replaying his words in my head to make sure I'd heard him correctly.

"Do what now?" It was one thing for me to plan on swiping the crown during the op, and yet another for Falcon's FBI team to commit an actual art heist. "Why not just arrest the guy? You're the cops. If you know he has the stolen crown, can't you just go in with a warrant? And why is this a matter for the international task force?

Why not Hungarian law enforcement or Greek law enforcement for that matter?"

I had seriously thought they would let me lead them to Elek and then arrest him. My hope was to snatch the crown away from him before then just to prove I could. I'd return it to the Hungarian people, of course, but I wanted the satisfaction of stealing it from him. Now Falcon was suggesting the FBI itself was going to steal it. So why was I even there?

Falcon pressed his lips together for a beat before explaining. They were really nice lips. "The Hungarian government asked for discretion."

Something about this was setting off warning bells. "That doesn't make any sense."

"We didn't ask your opinion," he said tersely. "Moving on..."

He gave the floor to Linney, who explained that she'd uncovered some information once I'd eventually given Falcon the address of the target residence on our flight from California to Paris.

"We pulled up schematics of the house," Linney said.

"Wait, how did you get information like that so fast?" I asked.

Linney glanced at Falcon before speaking. "We have someone who can hack into any system. Unfortunately, the information Ziv has access to only goes so far. So we have you as backup."

I lifted an eyebrow at her. "It's always nice being the second choice."

Ziv snorted. Falcon sighed and looked over at me. "You couldn't possibly have thought you would be my first choice."

"Point taken," I admitted. "So you need a plan to get in there and take it. Do you have any idea of how you want to do it? Or am I expected to come up with that too?" I shot her a wink and a smile.

Linney shrugged, blushing a little. "A little bit of both to be honest. We have specs for the security system, we can get an eye on the comings and goings of all of the staff, and we can probably track the target's movements. But we don't know where in the house he'd keep something like this. And we don't know what we don't know about pulling off a successful heist. Obviously you have tricks up your sleeve we're unaware of. We're hoping you can help us figure out some of those aspects of a successful job."

I sat forward and rested my elbows on my knees, meeting Falcon's eyes. "The bureau is capable of planning a heist like this without my help. There's obviously something else going on here. I want to know what it is."

Linney answered for him. "Doing it with your help lessens the risk factors. And speed and discretion are of utmost importance here."

"Why?" I asked, still looking at Falcon.

"That's not really any of your business," the senior agent said. I rolled my eyes. His attitude was annoying no matter how peeved he was at me for eluding him all this time.

Mouse spoke up in his small voice, surprising more than just me. "Does it matter?"

Was he kidding? "Yes it matters. Of course it matters."

Mouse smiled at me knowingly. "No it doesn't. You're going to do this anyway. Not just because you have immunity at stake but also because you can't stand the idea of the crown being in the wrong hands. Admit it."

I hated a know-it-all, and it seemed this airplane was full of them. Falcon snorted and Linney grinned. "He's right." Falcon added. "You'd do this without us. Just for the sake of it."

I leaned back in my chair and crossed my arms. "You'll never know, will you? Since I've already agreed to work with you on it. What happens to the crown after we take it? Is it going back to the Hungarian Parliament Building?"

Linney glanced at Falcon, waiting for him to answer the question.

"Yes, of course," he said, clearly leaving something important out.

I narrowed my eyes at him. There was no way I trusted the man. That's why I'd had MJ sign off on the immunity deal before I got too involved. I was going into this mission with the assumption that at some point Agent Falcon would try to screw me. I just didn't know how quite yet.

But if I was the one stealing the crown, the joke was on Falcon. He who had the crown had the power, and I didn't plan on handing it over until I knew for sure I was in the clear and the crown was being returned to its rightful owner.

Linney opened up her laptop on the coffee table in front of her and angled it so I could see the screen. "Can we get back to the plan? Here are the schematics for the house. I want to know how you would enter it so we can start working on a timeline for the retrieval."

I scanned the monitor trying to hide my wince at seeing the confirmation in plain sight of what I already knew. That Elek had built our dream house. All ten excessive bedrooms of it perched on the edge of the sparkling Aegean.

I exhaled, trying my best to relax and not think too much about it. "Okay, let's get started. First of all, these aren't the right schematics."

Linney looked up at me, her expression a cross between outrage and horror. "How do you know?"

Falcon's eyes bored into me. He knew I knew more than I was saying. After rubbing my hands over my face, I glanced at him. He was going to find out anyway as soon as I started planning the op. "Because I designed this house. And I know it like the back of my hand."

Everyone stared at me in shock. Ziv whistled low in his throat. Mouse sucked in a soft breath. Linney's eyes went straight to Falcon's.

And Falcon's nostrils flared in anger. "Get on with it."

CHAPTER FIVE

FALCON

It was hard enough dealing with King when he was acting surly, but when he turned on the arrogance, it was impossible. Still, I couldn't seem to drag my attention away from him. And since he obviously had critical information for our mission, that was just fine with me.

He ran his hand through his hair. "Let's just concentrate on the schematics for now. There is actually a tunnel from the wine cellar to a spot way out in the rocks by the ocean wall. At least, that was the plan. We'll have to do some on-site surveillance to determine if it was actually created. The rocky terrain could have affected how it was ultimately built, if it was built at all."

Linney began typing on the laptop, muttering, "Let me see if we can catch anything like that from the satellite images."

As we moved further into the strategy session, King's hair got messier and messier from running his fingers through it. I eventually figured out that it was a gesture he made while thinking things through, and by the time we were halfway to our destination, his hair was sticking up so much, he looked like he'd just been fucked.

The exact moment my brain threw that image up onto my mental movie screen, King looked over at me. "What?" he asked, tilting his head at me in confusion. It only made a piece of his hair flop over again.

"Huh? Nothing," I grumbled, standing up and turning away from him before he could catch sight of my tightening pants. I made my way forward to the galley for a coffee refill.

"Is he always this grumpy?" I heard him ask the others.

"Only when he's chasing something that's eluding him," Ziv responded pointedly.

I smiled as I reached the galley, but the flight attendant mistook it. She jumped up. "Sorry, sir. What can I get for you?"

"Oh, just coffee. I can pour it myself. Sit back down. I didn't mean to disturb you."

The attendant had spent a good portion of the original flight to California keeping me company with funny tales of trips she'd taken when she'd been a flight attendant for one of the major commercial airlines.

"It's my job, Agent Falcon," she said with a smile, nudging my hip with hers to move me out of the way. "If passengers start pouring their own coffee, I'll be out of a job."

"You must be exhausted by now. Isn't there a mandatory cap on your shift?"

I leaned a hip against the counter and watched as she remembered how I took my coffee and fixed it perfectly.

She chuckled. "I guess you didn't notice me sleeping most of the flight from California to Paris. I was kicked back in one of those lay-flat seats."

I glanced back to see what seats she was referring to and noticed King's eyes on me. I quickly turned to face the flight attendant again. "I guess I was distracted with work."

"I guess so," she said, handing me the hot drink. Her other hand landed on my chest and pressed a path to my shoulder. The intimate touch jarred me, and I blinked at her. "You had something on your shirt," she said softly.

"Are you coming back or what?" King's voice made me jump out of reach of the delicate hand on my shoulder. I cleared my throat and turned to glare at the thief who'd somehow snuck up behind me.

"You don't have to be rude," I said, pointedly.

"You don't have to be flirting with this poor woman who's just trying to do her job." King flashed the woman his blinding smile. "Might you happen to have a bottle of water handy?"

The woman was suddenly flustered, and I wanted to growl my impatience at the asshole standing next to me. I had no interest in the woman, but King didn't know that. And what the hell was up with him flirting with absolutely every human being he encountered? It was aggravating as hell.

"*I'm* flirting?" I asked in astonishment. "That's like Renoir calling Monet an Impressionist."

King's eyes flared wide. "Oh my. The man has read *Famous Art Styles for Dummies*. I'm impressed. Or should I say impres*sionist*?" He took the offered bottle of water before the flight attendant moved past us to offer the others refreshments.

I was focused so much on King, I barely noticed her walk away. "I know a little more than that. I'm a senior agent in charge of an international art crime team. And I wasn't flirting with the flight attendant," I said in a lower voice. "Don't be an ass." I decided not to mention that I was gay. It was bad enough I was attracted to him. If the man found out about it, his ego would grow big enough to force the rest of us to jump out of the plane.

King cracked open the bottle of water and glugged down a few sips. I forced myself not to watch his Adam's apple move. When he put the cap back on, he lowered his voice again so only I could hear him.

"The man who has the crown is Elek Kemény."

I stared at him, surprised he was finally giving me some useable information. Unfortunately, it was false information.

"According to property records, it's actually Elek Károlyi," I corrected. "A Hungarian national who—"

"*Actually*," King interrupted, "it's Elek Kemény. He uses the name

Károlyi because he has grandiose delusions of being a descendant of the royal family of Hungary."

That stopped me in my tracks.

King nodded and pushed himself off the counter he'd been leaning against. "Yeah. And you think *my* ego is big. I'm surprised your 'best hacker in the world' didn't catch that oversight." His use of finger quotes was obnoxious. But he had a point.

"That's why he wanted the crown," I said, more to myself than anything.

"Bingo. Give the man a cookie. He thinks the royal bling belongs to him."

I reached out and stopped him before he could go back to his seat. "But he's not actually descended from royalty, is he?"

King's slender biceps flexed instinctively under my fingers which caused me to realize I'd grabbed him by the arm. I dropped my hand like King's body was toxic. His eyes moved from where I'd held on to him to my eyes. This time, I couldn't look away from the bobbing of his Adam's apple as he swallowed. When he spoke, his voice was still low, but it had taken on a rough quality that went straight to my balls. It was the sound he might make late at night after someone had fucked his throat. And the fact I was even thinking that meant it had been a hell of a long time since I'd fucked anyone's throat or any other body part for that matter.

"Well?" he asked.

I blinked at him. "Well, what?"

"Dude, I just asked you if you knew the history of the Hungarian royal family."

I shook my head. "Not really. I mean I know Károlyi was a previous president of Hungary, but I don't remember that being a royal surname. And since the monarchy was abolished in the early part of the last century, it doesn't really matter. Does it?"

"It matters to him. And I'm sure it matters to other children or descendants of the royal family. Ultimately, though, it comes down to a legal matter. And *legally* the government of Hungary owns the crown. A random citizen can't just decide it's theirs and take it."

I lifted an eyebrow at him. "Can I quote you on that, *Le Chaton?*"

King surprised me with a laugh, a robust deep sound that made me smile. Seeing him let go like that made me realize how tense he'd been despite his flirty nature. I wondered if it had been his fear of finally being caught or simply the way he was when he was preparing for a heist.

We moved back to our seats and joined the rest of the team again. Mouse asked King a question about what kind of security he thought would be on the display case the crown lived in, and King began describing pressure plates, sensitive electronic connections, and even some advanced kind of lockable brackets we had never heard of before. Hearing him describe how to get around the most advanced art security in the world was fascinating. As much as it bothered me to know that he could overcome some of the best security museums had to offer, it sure was a relief to have someone like him on our team. I thought about how many other cases and other thieves we would be able to catch if someone like King was with us permanently.

I also remembered the notes he'd left at all of the museums and high-profile residences explaining how he'd breached their security systems. Could I convince him to explain that to us at some point?

Mouse looked up at King expectantly. "How do you get past those brackets? Are they just something you can unscrew once you turn them off?"

King smirked at him. "Hell no. You have to deactivate them on the computer first," he said, glancing over at Ziv. "The source code is on a constant rotation which makes hacking it a bit like trying to shoot a moving target."

Ziv nodded. "I've seen that before. It's nothing I can't handle."

King seemed to stifle a sigh. "Well, I can help if you need it. I've done it before. But we can cross that bridge when we come to it. I'll need—"

"I said I could handle it," Ziv said through clenched teeth. "You stick with your part of this job and let me handle mine."

"And what exactly is my part?" King asked.

"Oh, I don't know. The sneaky criminal shit?"

I moved my hand in a slashing motion. "Cut it out. First we get the plan in place, then we can worry about who is doing what. Our biggest challenge is going to be getting both sets of fingerprints for the biometric scanner on the door to the room."

King looked over at me in surprise. "Two sets? Elek and who else?"

"We were hoping you would know that."

King's fingers went straight back into his hair. "Fuck."

CHAPTER SIX

KING

The first place my mind went was to the last time I heard Elek's voice, and he'd mentioned a wife. But I'd researched the hell out of him and not found any evidence of a spouse.

I sat back and thought it through, ignoring Falcon's attempts to get my attention.

Why exactly was I doing this? The task force assumed I was doing it because of a desire for immunity, but they were wrong. I didn't need immunity. They had nothing on me and wouldn't have anything on me moving forward. I'd been too careful. Hadn't I?

So, why say yes?

Okay, fine. Immunity. I honestly didn't know for sure whether Agent Falcon had something on me. It had definitely been hot in the air duct, so I couldn't rule out the fact I may have dripped sweat on something. I didn't think so, but I couldn't be sure. And if one of the employees had nicked some of the collection... well, spending any amount of time in a German prison didn't sound like something worth risking.

Especially if working with them could get me both immunity *and* the crown.

Ever since hearing that the crown had been taken, my fingers had itched to get it out of Elek's hands. And the only way I could do that on short notice was to have additional resources. The kind of resources Falcon and his team could provide.

Was I still that hell-bent on revenge?

Hell yes.

The man had betrayed me. He'd left me at the mercy of law enforcement. You didn't do that to your partner, and you sure as hell didn't do it to your lover. That was the part of this I could never forgive.

Plus, he'd shorted me out of my share of a two-hundred-million-dollar payday. That was a pretty big fucking deal. But it wasn't like I didn't have plenty of money now. I'd had several years to amass my own wealth so I didn't ever decide to rely on a sugar daddy again.

Third of all, I couldn't stand the idea he had something he wanted so badly.

"Could it be a boyfriend's," Ziv asked when I didn't make a suggestion.

"He has a boyfriend?" I asked, feeling my stomach turn inside out.

Falcon's brows furrowed. "Wouldn't you know?"

I shrugged. "Not only have I not seen him in two years, even if I had, I wouldn't necessarily know about his sex life. It turns out the thief is also a liar."

Ziv hid his words in a fake cough. "Takes one to know one."

Mouse looked at me with pity. "Don't listen to him."

Ziv rolled his eyes. "According to social media, Elek has taken up with the son of a friend. Even if he's an old family friend, I still don't think he'd give a new boy toy that kind of access. Maybe it's one of his security guards."

I thought for a minute. "No. He'd keep the crown in his bedroom and he doesn't let his guards have access to the bedroom." I met Falcon's eyes. "The lover's prints are probably the ones you want."

He could tell I knew what I was talking about. "How do you know?" he asked anyway.

I thought about all the nights Elek had instructed me on how to prepare myself and be ready and waiting on his bed when he came home from a trip.

"I just know," I said.

Falcon assessed me for a moment in which I silently begged him not to push me on this.

"Okay. Then we need to find out where they're going to be in public so we can try and get their fingerprints."

Ziv clicked around on his laptop for a while before finding something. "Here are posts about a gala coming up. Hold on... let me see..." He clicked some more with Mouse reading over his shoulder.

"There!" Mouse said, pointing to a post. "They'll be at the gala this week in Mykonos. It's a charity thing the guy's family puts on."

Falcon turned to speak to Linney. "Figure out how to get us an invitation. Mouse, you and Ziv need to figure out how we're going to capture the fingerprints with some kind of tech we can get past gala security. Linney, you'll need a dress, and I'll need a tux."

"What gala? Is Elek going to be there? And what about me?" I asked, selfishly wanting a chance to look Elek in the face again.

"We can't risk him seeing you. The only semi-public event we know he's planning on attending is the Lazarus gala in two days. According to Ziv's intel, Elek's old friend Kristo Lazarus is the one throwing it, so the son, Elek's rumored new fling, should be there too."

The name Lazarus didn't ring a bell, but then again, I knew enough now to know there'd been plenty Elek hadn't shared with me about the rest of his life. I pictured Elek, *my* Elek, with a new man on his arm. How did I feel about it? Jealous? Mm, not really. The very minute he left me at the scene of the crime in Paris, he'd ceased being the man of my dreams, and in the years since, I'd grown up enough to realize what I'd had for him was puppy love, not real love. While I hadn't been home to Hobie much in the past few years, I'd seen the special kind of connection between my siblings and their partners. It was enough to open my eyes to what true love really was. And then there was the love between my grandfathers which I'd always assumed was a one-in-a-million kind of love.

Sitting at the vineyard among the Marians and Wildes was all I'd needed to see how wrong I'd been.

So, did I wish Elek was still mine? Hell no. But thinking of another man spending time in that house and enjoying the money I'd help make was galling.

"I'm going to that gala," I said defiantly.

Falcon ignored me and continued to talk to Linney about logistics. I met Ziv's eyes and could tell he was the kind of man who might enjoy lighting a spark on a mission if it wouldn't bring the whole thing toppling down on us.

I needed to concentrate on wooing the one member of the team who seemed to understand me the best but liked me the least. But how? I was no "world-renowned" hacker, but I knew enough to prove to him he wasn't the only techie on the team. So maybe I needed to use my own computer skills to send Ziv a message.

I leaned back and closed my eyes, thinking through what I knew about the Mykonos house and the elements I'd specifically designed for it in order to foil would-be burglars. The question was whether or not he'd had the presence of mind to add any additional ones after we'd broken up.

Elek wasn't really a forward thinker in that way, so I doubted it. However, one rule of any heist was to expect shit to go wrong and be prepared to handle it on the fly. So we would have to assume he'd added security protocols we didn't know about.

"How important is this operation to the art crimes task force?" I asked, wondering just what kind of risks we could take. It was one thing if failure was an option and quite another if someone's life was on the line.

Ziv snorted again. His disdain was duly noted.

Linney was actually the one who answered. "It's not the task force. This is specifically a matter of interest to the FBI and US government."

"I don't know what that means," I said. "Why just the US and not the art crimes task force? What interest does the US have with a Hungarian artifact?"

Falcon was conspicuously silent.

"Listen," I explained. "Risk assessment is an actual thing in planning something like this. If timing isn't critical, it means a failed attempt can be repeated again a short time or long time later. And if that's the case, we don't have to be quite as thorough in covering all of the contingencies. In other words, we can try it one way, and if it fails, we can come back and try it another after regrouping."

"It can't fail," Falcon said.

I threw up my hands in frustration. "Because you're a perfectionist son of a bitch or because—"

Falcon's eyes narrowed. "It can't fail," he repeated through gritted teeth. "All I can tell you is that neglecting to get our hands on this crown could mean the breakdown in geopolitical relations as we know them. There is more to this than a stolen piece of history, King. While lives are not directly at stake, peace certainly is. This crown falling into the wrong people's hands could be disastrous for multiple governments. Is that enough to press upon you the importance of succeeding on this op, or did you need me to make it more clear?"

It was on the tip of my tongue to ask him to make it more clear, only because I wondered if his teeth would actually break. But from the seriousness of the faces around me, I could tell it wasn't time for jokes. This was truly a big deal to the US government beyond the mere issue of stolen antiquities.

In addition to their serious expressions, the fact the government was sparing no expense to send an entire team of agents overseas in a private jet to pursue this mission was impressive. I wasn't so far gone as to eschew the concept of patriotism and service to my country. But I also wasn't altruistic enough to discount how this opportunity could also benefit *me*. If retrieving the crown was truly that important to the US powers that be, maybe I could finally get the final piece of evidence Elek had on me while I was there.

I took a breath and nodded. "It's crystal clear the op needs to succeed. So here's what I'm going to need…"

CHAPTER SEVEN

FALCON

The rental van was waiting for us when we finally landed on the sleepy Greek island of Mykonos. Ziv took charge of driving us to the rental villa that would serve as our operations headquarters for the duration of our stay in Greece.

King took one look at the sprawling whitewashed villa perched on top of a hill and the panoramic views of the Aegean sea beyond and started laughing. "Don't you know the bulk of serious heists are planned in abandoned warehouses? Haven't you seen any movies at all?"

"Shut up," I muttered. "You try finding an appropriate place in a tiny Greek island on short notice. It was more important to be discreet than cliché. This is the standard luxury-villa style around here. It's part of blending in."

Linney spun around, taking in the warm sunlight dappling through olive trees off to the side of the gravel driveway. "It's absolutely stunning. Do you have any idea how long I've fantasized about going on holiday to the Greek isles? If only we weren't here in December, I would've brought my bikini." On the other side of the house was an informal garden with wooden benches and a small stone fountain that had most likely been turned off for the winter.

Beyond the garden in the distance was the barest sliver of the blue waters of the Aegean. We were probably about a quarter mile away from it, and the only thing between us and the seaside cliffs was the wild grass and tumble of half-buried stone that made up some kind of nature preserve.

As soon as I unlocked the door, Mouse raced past me, presumably to claim first dibs on the best bedroom. The last overnight operation we'd done had been short on bedrooms, so he'd been forced to sleep in a glorified closet. Linney sauntered past mumbling about setting up the "command center," and Ziv called out to remind her to make sure the room had an ethernet feed or Wi-Fi since he wasn't about to let her use his special satellite connectivity.

"When geeks go wild," King said with a chuckle as he moved past. "Reminds me of..." He stopped before sharing something that was obviously personal. "Never mind. Where do you want me to put my stuff?"

"There should be a bedroom with two doubles in it. You'll be in there." I didn't add the ever-important detail that he'd be sharing the room with me. I was too tired from the long traveling days to get into it with him again so soon. Instead, I set my bags down by the front door and wandered into the large farmhouse-style kitchen to make sure the groceries we'd arranged for had been delivered. If not, we'd need to run back into the nearby village before it buttoned up and went to sleep.

Thankfully the place had been fully stocked to our specifications, and I even found a premade casserole that only needed to be heated up in the oven. Just as I was trying to figure out how to work the unfamiliar controls, Mouse wandered in and took over.

"You're a terrible cook," he admonished. "It's better for all of us if you let me do this. Why don't you scrounge us up some plates and silverware? And they probably left us some sparkling water and wine to go with it."

I let the younger agent boss me around until it was time to eat. When I went poking around to find King, I discovered him facedown on one of the double beds with still-damp hair and nothing but a towel wrapped around his waist. He'd clearly taken a shower and then passed out without even getting under the covers.

Instead of waking him, I nudged the door almost all the way closed and moved farther into the room to get a better look at him.

I wasn't usually a dirty old man, but this... this situation was different.

Or so I told myself.

Kingston Wilde was made up of slender muscle and youthful perfection. His skin was smooth and flawless, and it wrapped around fit musculature in a way that reminded me of his feline moniker.

The man had an ass on him that attracted my attention like a nice pair of breasts probably would have if I'd ever been straight. The bubbled roundness of his butt sloped up from his lower back where twin indentations sank into his winter-pale skin. I wanted to lick into them one at a time and then peel that fucking towel off his ass to see what lay underneath.

The arm closest to me was lifted above his head and curled around a pillow. I could see a glimpse of brown armpit hair which had always been a particular weakness of mine on a man. The stretch of his arm exposed the side of his ribs, making him look vulnerable. His hair had been drying into a crazy mess, which made my fingers itch once again to tunnel their way in and straighten the floppy locks.

I sat on the bed next to his and opened my mouth to say something. Before I could get the words out, he blinked awake and gazed at me. Our eyes met and held for a beat way longer than any normal interaction. My heart raced and stomach clenched. This attraction I had to him was dangerous.

"Dinner's ready," I said in a gruffer voice than I'd intended. I cleared my throat. "I didn't know if you'd want to get up or sleep through."

He turned on his side, not taking his eyes off me. The towel opened just enough to show me the furred expanse of his inner thigh. I wondered if I fainted from lack of oxygen whether or not I could pass it off as travel-related sickness.

My eyes blinked back to his. Again, he held them longer than expected before speaking.

"I'm definitely up."

The tone in his voice seemed odd, and I couldn't help but glance back down at where the towel was open. I'd only intended to get another peek of his creamy skin, but this time I noticed the tent in his towel. In addition to realizing he was hard, I also noticed how it had opened the towel even more, giving me a much more intimate view.

"Shit. Yeah. Uh. Sorry." What the fuck was wrong with me? I didn't stutter like a child or apologize for... looking straight ahead. "Anyway. Dinner. Or whatever. Up to you."

I stood and turned fast enough that I could pretend he wouldn't have been able to catch the fact I was hard too. The last thing I needed was his ego growing any larger.

Waking up hard from a nap was one thing. Getting hard while creepily staring at your sleeping... business colleague was a different thing altogether. One was normal. One was actually creepy.

Messing with an asset was against the rules. Which didn't matter since I was not going to be attracted to the conniving criminal whose sole purpose seemed to be tempting me into forgetting myself.

Jackass.

Clearly he was trying to get under my skin. And for some reason I was having a hard time remembering that. The man was a manipulator. He played people like chess pieces. He was so used to using his looks and charm to get people to do what he wanted, it was like second nature. I'd already watched him do it with everyone he'd come in contact with since leaving Napa.

I shook my head and pushed from the bed, starting for the door. I hesitated with my hand on the knob, waiting to see if King would say something. Apologize, maybe. Or call me back. But he said nothing. I left the room, using every bit of strength I had not to look back at him.

I returned to the kitchen to find the rest of the crew already settled into their spots around a large heavy farmhouse table with plates and silverware laid out and the casserole on a trivet in the center.

"Help yourself," I grumbled, taking my place at the end of the table.

"What's got you in a twist?" Linney asked.

"Nothing," I said, reaching for the serving spoon. "I'm just anxious to get this show on the road. How's it coming on securing the gala invitation?"

Ziv shoved the rest of a roll in his mouth before answering. "No luck yet. I'm trying something different though."

King came sauntering in, dressed in a form-fitting dark T-shirt and designer jeans. He'd brushed his hair, the still damp locks swept back over his eyes and tamed, for the moment. Without even looking my way, he took his place at the other end of the table and reached for the pitcher of water. "Why don't we just take one from a known attendee's house?"

The rest of us stared at him until he noticed the silence and looked up from where he'd been pouring a glass of water for himself.

"What?"

Mouse dove right in. "Well, let's see. First, it's illegal. Ahem. Then it's immoral—"

"Which wouldn't bother a notorious cat burglar at all," Ziv noted.

Mouse ignored him. "And third, how the heck would we know where the person had the invitation stashed?"

King took his turn with the casserole dish and shrugged before grabbing the spoon. "Oh c'mon. How many places in a house would someone stash a party invite? Three or four max. Fridge door, kitchen junk drawer, home office, or tucked in a day planner in a purse or briefcase."

He was right, and I had to admit it was tempting.

Linney seemed to be considering the idea. "What happens when that person shows up without their invitation?"

King took a huge bite of the dish before swallowing and responding. I forced myself to eat instead of watching his damned throat again.

"Who cares? If they show up without their invitation, they claim they misplaced it because, really, no one will believe it was stolen from their home, and then they find someone who can verify their identity. Easy enough."

Ziv glared at him. "And if they realize that particular invitation has already been used for admittance?"

King shrugged again. "You said there were going to be several hundred people at this thing. Are they really going to make a big fuss and ring the alarms over one illegal attendee?"

"The French ambassador is going to be in attendance, so they might very well ring the alarms," I added.

King's eyes swiveled to mine, and his lips quirked up in a grin. "Gauthier is going to be there? For real?"

Mouse referred to his tablet. "Mm-hm. Gauthier Roux is confirmed. Why, do you know him?"

King nodded. "Hell yes, I know him. That's our in. He'll get me on the list. The invitation will be under the name David Kennedy which means I'll need my David Kennedy identification credentials." His voice drifted off for a second while he thought. "Which are in Paris."

Mouse looked excited to finally have something to do. "No problem. I'll just make you new ones. You'll have to provide me with the information of course."

"Great. I'll give him a call right now," King said pushing back from the table.

"Hold up," I said, raising a hand. "You're not going to the gala, remember? So you won't be needing any credentials"

King's jaw tightened. "If you want me to use *my* source to get you in, then I'm certainly going with you."

"I already said no," I snapped, perhaps more forcefully than I intended, given the way Linney's eyes widened in surprise as she traded a glance with Mouse.

King's gaze held mine for a long beat. "Then I guess I won't be calling Gauthier after all." He lowered himself to his seat and dug his fork into the casserole as though he didn't have a care in the world.

It was like he was deliberately trying to get under my skin.

It was working.

Ziv, Linney, and Mouse all sat quietly, watching the two of us. Eventually, Linney cleared her throat pointedly and made a head gesture at King. She didn't have to say the words out loud—we needed him to get us that invite. Which meant I was going to have to be the one to back down first. Dammit.

"Fine," I said through clenched teeth.

King looked up at me, his expression a mask of innocence. "Fine, what?" he asked.

I wanted to throttle him. "Fine, you can go," I ground out.

His mouth broke into a wide smile that did funny things to my chest. I hated that he could irritate me so much one second and still somehow make me want him the next.

"Excellent," he said, standing again. "I'll go ahead and take care of that right now."

"It's eleven o'clock at night," I said in surprise. "Don't you think that's a little late?"

King's smile turned into a smirk. "Trust me. He's not asleep yet. The man can't drift off without finishing the *New York Times* crossword in bed first."

He winked at me before pulling his phone out of his pocket and sauntering off.

I didn't want to picture how he'd gotten that intel about what the attractive ambassador did late at night in his own bed. Because I didn't want to see King in that picture with him, sheets tangled around his hips as he slept next to him. Instead, I dug back into my dinner and forced myself to go over what we'd need to accomplish the following day.

"Easy, boss man," Linney said softly, reaching out for my wrist. "You're going to bend the fork if you keep stabbing the plate like that."

I looked down, noticing for the first time that my hand was fisted so tightly around the fork that my knuckles turned white. I tossed it onto the plate and stood up. "I'm going for a run."

Three pairs of eyes stared at me before glancing at one another. As I took my plate to the sink, I heard Ziv say something about the long days of travel stiffening me up.

Linney's chuckle was all knowing, and Mouse's lighter voice was playful. "You might be right about something stiffening up."

Ziv groaned, and Linney laughed even louder. I bit my tongue to keep from snapping out something rude over my shoulder as I strode out of the room in search of my running gear.

CHAPTER EIGHT

KING

I wasn't really friends with Gauthier. I mean, I'd met him a couple of times through mutual friends, and the man had definitely hit on me at the time, but it wasn't like we were besties. I'd made up the thing about the crossword puzzle. Falcon didn't need to know any of that though. And I knew I could get an invitation simply by calling Gauthier's personal assistant.

But it was fun to watch to Falcon squirm. Squaring off against the testy agent was like partaking in a complex yet enjoyable dance. And it had been a long time since I'd had a worthy dance partner. Getting under the grumpy agent's skin was the most fun I'd had in a long time.

After sending an email to Gauthier's assistant, I went back into the kitchen to help clean the dishes. Ziv, Mouse, and Linney were reminiscing about an operation that had gone wrong at the High Museum in Atlanta. The minute I walked into the room, their laughter stopped.

"Don't stop on my account. That's one of the museums I've never been to before. I'd love to hear what you guys got up to there." I gestured to the sink to take over from Ziv. He lifted an eyebrow and handed me the wet sponge.

"By all means, help yourself," Ziv said with a smirk. "I'm beat. See you guys in the morning."

Linney and Mouse bade him good night before returning to their cleanup duties. Mouse dried the dishes that I washed, and Linney wiped down the big kitchen table. After a few moments of silence, Mouse looked up at me shyly.

"Did you really steal the Cellini salt cellar?"

I barked out a laugh. "Yeah, but that was kind of a joke. I mean, the last guy who did it was an idiot. I guess I wanted to prove that you could take the damn thing without ending up on surveillance video. I returned it, you know. It wasn't like I wanted to keep it. It's safely back at the museum where it belongs."

Mouse's eyes were bright with inquisitiveness. "See? That's what I want to ask you about. Why go through the risk of getting caught stealing hundreds of thousands of euros' worth of precious artwork if you're just going to return it?"

Linney had stopped wiping down the table and stood watching me. I was feeling relaxed, and part of me enjoyed the casual friendship the team seemed to have. Maybe in some way, I wanted to feel a part of it.

I shrugged. "Some pieces belong in certain places. Like Holocaust spoils. It's heartbreaking to learn about items that were stolen or hidden during World War II and are now owned by the wrong people. I can't tell you how many Holocaust pieces I've returned to their rightful owners." I turned the water off and rested my hip against the counter, drying my hands on a nearby kitchen towel. "That's what really started it for me. Well, I mean, not what *started*, started it, but why I continued after the Van Gogh job."

Linney crossed her arms in front of her chest. "What was different about the Van Gogh job? What went wrong? It's been driving Falcon crazy all this time."

It was my own fault we'd come around to this. I should have anticipated the question. My usual inclination to keep my cards so close to the vest caused me to clamp my lips closed at first.

"Nothing you say here can be used against you, you know,"

Mouse reminded me. "You can tell us without worrying about it getting you in any trouble."

He was right. The immunity offer had been ironclad. According to my sister, I could speak freely. That still didn't make it any easier to let go of deeply held habits of keeping quiet.

Linney tilted her head. "No honor among thieves?"

"Something like that. I was double-crossed. Might as well be in a heist movie. I trusted the wrong person, and it came back to bite me in the ass." I couldn't help but add a little dig. "Luckily the responding agent was a softie."

Linney's nostrils flared in annoyance. Mouse on the other hand snorted a soft laugh.

"Never again," Linney warned. "Falcon will never give you another inch. You mark my words. The man has learned his lesson."

I strongly disagreed but was smart enough to keep my mouth shut about it. Plus, there were certain inches I wouldn't mind the sexy senior agent giving me.

Mouse shot her a look. "You want to put money down on that?"

"Shit," Linney muttered. "I'm out. See you in the morning."

For some reason I felt like I needed to share the truth. Maybe I didn't want Mouse thinking the worst of me. "I was young and stupid, Mouse. I let someone talk me into doing something I shouldn't. And when I finally realized what I'd become, it was too late. Or so I thought. So I did the only thing I could think of to try and make some of it right." I didn't tell him the ironic part, that when I finally decided to put it all behind me, the one organization that had wanted me to quit all this time was the one forcing me back in.

Mouse thought for a minute. "I read about the Aleutian totems. Was that you?"

I nodded.

The corner of Mouse's mouth curved up. "I know I shouldn't be telling you this, but that was amazing. What you did for those people. Their cultural heritage had been looted right out from under them and used as tourist bait by those... I mean... well, anyway... have a good night. And don't worry, Falcon doesn't snore."

I watched him leave the kitchen. Why did it matter to me whether or not Falcon snored? After I finished straightening the last bits in the kitchen, I turned out the lights and made my way to the front door to make sure it was locked before heading to bed.

Once I'd changed into sleep pants, I slid between the cool sheets and let out a breath. Even though I'd taken a cat nap before we ate, I was still wiped out from the travel and ten-hour time difference.

So I fell asleep right away. Sometime later, I awoke to the sound of tapping on my window. Who the hell would be out in the middle of nowhere on this Greek island? I rose and peered out.

Falcon's face glared angrily from the other side. "Let me in," he mouthed. I scrambled to open the window and grinned out at him.

"What are you doing?" I asked. "Why are you outside in the middle of the night?"

"Can you open the front door instead of the window please?" he asked in annoyance. "I'm not exactly petite. And not all of us sneak into houses through windows."

He had a point. I made my way to the front door, chuckling. After unlocking it, I noticed he was wearing jogging clothes that were plastered to his body with sweat. They outlined every muscle, and it was impossible to keep my eyes from tracing over them.

"Did you go for a run?" I asked stupidly. Of course he had gone for a run. It was just that his physique had scrambled my brain a little bit.

He raised an eyebrow at me. "I'm going to chalk that one up to you still being half-asleep. Who the hell locked the door?"

I blinked at him. "Um, Ziv, I think." Served the asshole right. I turned toward the kitchen, expecting Falcon to head off to bed.

Instead, he followed me in to grab a bottle of water from the fridge. I moved to the coffee maker and hunted supplies to make half a pot.

"You're making coffee at two in the morning?" He took a swallow from the water bottle.

"Well, I've already had two sleep sessions now. The chances of me being able to fall asleep a third time are pretty slim. I might as well get up and spend some time with those schematics." I finished prepping the coffee maker and hit the button to start it. After finding a loaf of bread in a cabinet, I tossed a couple of slices in the toaster on the counter.

I glanced over at Falcon. "Want some?"

He shook his head and leaned back with his hip against the counter. "Tell me more about Elek."

Nosy motherfucker. "No thanks."

He ignored me. "I mean, having a relationship history with him could mess with our operation. That's why I'm asking. So who was he to you? Or maybe who is he to you *now* is the better question."

Falcon wasn't wrong to ask. I knew that. If I were in his shoes I would demand to know also. But that didn't mean I wanted him to see such a vulnerable part of me. My history with Elek was embarrassing, plain and simple. Admitting how naive I had been when I first came under Elek's spell and how quickly and easily I'd trusted him was humiliating. And telling it to someone strong and powerful, someone who seemed to have his own shit together, someone like Falcon, wasn't easy.

"We fucked. There, you happy?" I took the toast out of the machine and slapped butter onto it. After retrieving the cream from the fridge, I doctored my coffee and took everything to the kitchen table.

Falcon took the seat next to mine. "I'm not trying to get into your business. You and I both know that your personal history with him, whatever it is, could be a real problem in this operation. I simply want to be prepared. Anything you know about him could help."

I nodded and took a bite of my toast. After swallowing, I ticked off some points on my hand. "First, he's not the smartest guy in the world. Which is good for us. Second, at one point, I used to have the ability to get him to do what I wanted. I don't know if that's still the case, but it might be. In which case that could benefit us. Third, the fact I have a personal history with him means I know him better than any undercover operatives ever could. I know his habits, his schedules, the kind of people he keeps around him, and unless things have changed, I even know the man he would have hired to put in the security around the crown."

Falcon seemed to relax. "Okay, you're right. Those are good things. I just don't want any surprises, as I'm sure you can understand." He stood up and pushed the chair back under the table. "Good night, King."

I enjoyed the sight of him walking away and tried not to think of how good he looked in his workout clothes. Instead, I got to work.

Two hours later, I realized the late hour had caught up to me, and I decided to get some more sleep if I could. When I walked into the room, I was shocked to see Falcon's sleeping form in the bed next to mine. How could he not have realized this room was already taken?

I stepped back out into the hallway and looked for an extra bedroom. I'd already noticed the rooms Ziv, Mouse, and Linney had selected. And now I realized there were no additional bedrooms. No wonder Mouse had reassured me that Falcon didn't snore.

After returning to the room, I slipped into my bed and tried like hell not to stare at the man across from me.

I failed.

CHAPTER NINE

FALCON

The following day dawned bright and warm, warmer at least than the day before. The first place my eyes landed was on the bare shoulder of the man in the other bed. King Wilde.

Why had I thought sharing a room with him would be a good idea? It wasn't. It was a stupid, idiotic, ridiculous idea. Because now, I was having thoughts.

I shook my head and stood up. No time for thoughts. No thoughts. None at all. I grabbed my things and headed for the bathroom. A shower would do nicely, even if it did need to be on the cold setting.

By the time I got dressed, everyone had already gathered in the kitchen, and someone had made a platter full of eggs and some sausage. A bowl of cut-up fruit was in the center of the table, and I could smell the coffee the minute I walked in the room. Today was going to be a good day. The run the night before must've helped clear my head because I felt more ready for the day than I had since before finding out about the crown.

As I poured my coffee, Ziv turned around beaming. "Your boy came through for us. The invitation arrived this morning. David Kennedy plus one. Now we just have to decide who his plus one is."

I nodded. "And we also need to decide who David Kennedy is. Because it sure as hell is not going to be King."

A familiar snort came from behind me. "Falcon, the man knows me on sight."

"So does Elek," I pointed out.

He ignored me. "You don't understand. Gauthier knows me very well. There's no way someone will be able to take my place. They announce people at galas like this. Plus, I might even be able to get him to acquire the fingerprint we need."

My jaw literally dropped. "Are you fucking crazy? We are not going to get the French ambassador to Greece to participate in our illegal operation on foreign soil. Have I mentioned yet that what we are doing here is not exactly sanctioned?"

Now it was King's turn to stare. "No, actually, you didn't mention that. But that's fine, I'm used to unsanctioned operations."

The man loved to tease, even if it gave other people heart palpitations.

"The answer is no. No foreign-dignitary involvement in the op. I can't believe I just said that out loud," I muttered. "Maybe it's the lack of coffee."

While I poured a cup, I tried not to think about just how close King would have to be to the ambassador to ask him to do such a thing. That wasn't the kind of thing you asked an acquaintance to do, and it wasn't the kind of thing you even asked a friend to do. It was the kind of nefarious activity you might ask your spouse to do, or your boyfriend. And I didn't want to think about him dating the damned French ambassador to Greece.

I could see Linney thinking from here. So when she spoke, it wasn't a surprise. "He's right though. He has to be the one to go in with the invitation. Otherwise, the ambassador's security personnel could cause us problems."

I knew she was right. But I didn't have to like it. "Fine. I'm going in too."

King looked like the cat who'd stolen the cream, and suddenly I felt like I'd been played. Was I destined to always feel this way with him?

As he took his seat at the table, I glared at him. "That doesn't mean you're going to be the one to procure the fingerprints. There's no way I'm going to let you get close enough to Elek's new boy toy to do it. So stop looking at me like that."

"Like what?" King asked, batting his eyelashes.

Mouse chuckled. Ziv rolled his eyes. I let out a sigh. "Like you just put my king in check. I wish you'd stop looking at this like a game."

King's eyes hardened, and his expression turned serious. "And I wish you'd stop treating me like a child. Maybe if you told me what the stakes truly were, I would take this more seriously. But until you trust me to be a true member of this team, I'm going to try and keep as much control of the situation as I can. And you and I both know that you would do the same in my position."

"I'm not authorized to give you more information," I told him for the millionth time.

Linney snapped her fingers to get our attention. "Can we stop with the dick-measuring contest and get to work please?"

I nodded and reached over to pull my laptop out of my bag. After setting it up on the table and booting it up, I pulled up the spreadsheet that had the master list of things we needed to do on it. I checked off the entry about acquiring an invitation to the gala.

"So now we need to get tuxedos for both of us," I said, looking at Mouse. "Do you think you can work on that?"

Mouse was already making notes on his own laptop. I looked over at Linney. "Any luck on the fingerprint-capture technology yet?"

King interrupted. "Before we get to all of that, I want to talk about something else. I think we should make an attempt to enter the house before the gala."

Ziv scoffed. "Why would we do that? We don't have the finger-prints we need."

King looked over at him. "What's your problem with me? You

should know by now that I want this crown returned to the Hungarian people as much, if not more, than the rest of you. Granted, I'm looking forward to screwing over Elek Kemény in the process, but I also care about returning a precious historically significant relic to its rightful owner. Which is the Hungarian people. And I'm assuming there's a reason we can't do that until we get the crown off Elek."

Ziv snapped back, "Forgive me if I'm suspicious of the art thief wanting to do something that might tip off our target before the primary op."

King's nostrils flared. I could tell he was getting annoyed as hell with Ziv's constant jabs. "You guys wanted me to tell you how I'd do this job. This is how I'd do the job. And you know I have a history of returning things to their rightful owners."

Ziv sat back in his chair, his eyes still on King. "This, coming from the man who took a two-hundred-million-dollar Van Gogh from its rightful owner."

King sat forward again. "Are you kidding? The interior minister we stole it from had bought the Van Gogh off the black market in the late 1990s. He paid peanuts for it, and he didn't dare show it in public until after he spent ten years falsifying provenance data for it."

We all looked at him in surprise. Could that possibly be true? I remembered going over that documentation with a fine-toothed comb. And I also remembered the fuss the owner had made over his insurance claim.

"Did the interior minister hire you to steal it for the insurance money?" I asked.

There was true surprise on King's face. "Fuck," he muttered. "I... I don't think so? I mean... I can't say for sure. But, honestly, the thought never occurred to me until now. I don't see how Elek could have afforded to build the estate without that full payday. But then again, there are a lot of things I didn't know about Elek at the time. I thought I knew him. Clearly I was mistaken."

Seeing this side of him, this unsure, less cocky side, was startling. It was hard to imagine Kingston Wilde as anything other than self-confident and fully cognizant of every job he participated in. But then again, I had to remind myself the King Wilde who started stealing art had been a young college student far from home, a small-town boy with stars in his eyes. Was it that hard to believe he had come under the spell of an older, wiser manipulator?

The thought of someone taking advantage of King in those early days bothered me more than I cared to admit.

"Why do you want to break in before the gala?" I asked.

King tapped his fingers on the table. "Number one, I want to get the lay of the land. I know the house as it was designed, but I don't know how it was actually built. Number two," he said, tapping his middle finger on the table next to his index finger, "there is a phenomenon in which a failed attempt can give the homeowner a false sense of security. It's the idea of 'what are the chances it would happen again?' Which means at a time when security should be higher, it's actually a little more lax." He tapped his third finger on the table. "Third, I need to get into the house, or at least close, to mount a signal jammer."

This time when Ziv reacted to King, he did so with less annoyance. I wondered why. "Why can't you just bring a jammer with you on the night of the main operation?"

Linney answered before King could, her eyes widening in realization. "I didn't realize this before, but in the satellite images it shows too much distance in the clearing between the road and the house. By the time any of us approached, the security team will have had a chance to ring the alarms."

King nodded. "And if, say, Mouse were to roll up in a delivery van, they can go ahead and signal for security to come, but it won't matter, because he's just there to deliver some flowers, let's say."

It was Mouse's turn to speak. "And we put the jammer in the flowers? I don't think that's going to work."

King shook his head. "No. While Mouse is delivering the flowers, I'll be in the tunnel delivering the jammer. They're already going to alert security, so if they think the tunnel has been breached, by the time they check it out, I'll be gone."

I could tell Ziv was thinking it through, and I was surprised when he smiled. "I see what you're saying, man. That might work."

King glanced at me in surprise. "It's a miracle. Maybe the man is turned on by breaking and entering."

I couldn't help but laugh. "Careful, he's one sneaky op from changing sides."

Ziv agreed, and Mouse nudged him in the shoulder. "I'm not sure Ziv wasn't a bad guy before he came to work with us," Mouse admitted with a grin. "He's certainly moody enough to be a criminal."

King faked a frown. "Oh, we're supposed to be moody? Good to know. Okay, let's plan the fake delivery for this afternoon. We'll need—"

Linney interrupted. "That soon? Do we even have the tech we need? And where the hell are we going to get a flower arrangement by then?" Her fingers started flying over the keys of her computer.

"Mouse," I said to the youngest operative on our team, "confirm we have a jammer in that shipment in the outbuilding. Linney, go ahead and source a florist. If there isn't one on the island—"

"There is," she confirmed. "I'm on it."

"Okay," I said, turning to King. "What else?"

He seemed surprised I'd gone along with his plan, and he seemed even more surprised I'd allowed him to schedule it so soon. I wanted to tease him about calling his bluff, but now was the time to work, not tease.

"I need a Narcol motion sensor button to attach to the tunnel door. It's a little device—"

"I know what it is," Ziv interrupted without looking up. "We don't have that kind. We have better. Much smaller. It should be in one of the boxes. Mouse, you're looking for a little blue box with a giant purple logo on it."

"Gotcha," Mouse said.

King's eyes jumped around from one teammate to the next,

clearly surprised at their capabilities. It made me wonder if he always worked alone, or if he had a crew who helped him on a regular basis. He certainly didn't act like he was used to having help.

King rubbed the stubble on his unshaven cheek. "Let's see... I don't think I'll need scuba equipment, but I'll double-check on the satellite imagery. I assume you have a mask and gloves. Hmm... A GoPro that can record video would be good, if you have it. Then we can create a record of the inside of the tunnel for planning our escape the night of the main op."

"We have that, no problem." I took a sip of my coffee and thought about King alone in the tunnel. I still didn't trust him, especially knowing he had history with Elek. "Ziv will go with you in the tunnel."

I could tell King was getting ready to argue with me. So I immediately changed the subject before he could open his mouth. "I jogged past the outer edge of the property last night and noticed an SUV driving the perimeter on a regular patrol. We need to take that into consideration and be ready in case we need someone to distract them."

Mouse frowned. "Why in the world does he have that kind of security on his house?"

King glanced at him. "It's his way of making himself feel important. He has friends with estates here who have that kind of security. It's most likely simple showing off."

"Compensating for something," I muttered.

"What about you?" King asked.

"I don't need to compensate," I said.

He blinked at me, his cheeks turning a little pink. "Good to know, Big Boy. I meant, what are you going to do about the patrol?"

"I can be ready to distract them if need be, but I have to be careful. I'm the only one who could get any of you out of the Greek jail cell."

Linney started teasing Ziv. "This time, remember not to take your wallet. Oh, and maybe don't start trying to explain yourself to local law enforcement. Do you want me to look up the Greek word for lawyer?"

Ziv kicked her under the table while Mouse got a fit of the giggles. I met King's eyes.

"See? These bozos speak for themselves."

Some of the tension seemed to leak out of King's stiff posture. "You guys have been together for a long time, it seems."

Linney stopped typing long enough to look up. "Four and a half years. Interpol put together the task force to investigate a particularly pervasive string of art thefts. Our sole focus has been identifying, tracking, and pursuing the infamous art thief named Le Chaton."

Surprisingly, even more tension seeped out of King. "Should it worry me that you're not very good at your job?"

Did he just...?

I made a move toward him, but Ziv grabbed my shoulder. "Boss, he's deliberately baiting you. Do not fall for it."

I knew he was right of course. But that didn't mean I didn't want to punch him in the face. If he only knew how many hours of sleep I'd lost knowing I was this close to catching him... If he only knew how many job opportunities I had passed up in order to stay on the team trying to catch him... If he only knew just how unbelievably difficult it had been for me to hand him blanket immunity in exchange for his help on this one job... I couldn't even think of it. My annoyance toward him had been banked by our current op, but those words had peeled back my civility, leaving my anger burning like wildfire out of control.

But I was the king of control. And I would not let him get under my skin.

"The reason we never brought Le Chaton to justice was because we are extremely good at our job. We are honest, fair, and thorough. We don't jump the gun. Which means we will not cut corners to make it work. So let's stop dicking around and get back to it."

After twenty minutes of shoveling breakfast down while tapping away at our computers and checking equipment, King looked up.

"I don't see any reference to his yacht." He scratched the scruff on the side of his face. "Wonder if he still has it. If so, we need to get eyes on it. It used to be the place he kept all his favorite pieces. He said it was easier to get them into international waters when the heat was on. Paranoid bastard." He muttered the last part under his breath.

King went back to studying whatever was on his computer screen while the rest of us stared at him.

Linney said it best.

"Well, shit."

CHAPTER TEN

KING

It felt good to slip into my black cargo pants in preparation for the mission. The dark clothing I wore was like a uniform of sorts. It automatically put me into the mindset of a job. When I buttoned them up, I was ready to work.

And when I pulled on the mask, I was even more ready to focus. That was when the stakes were highest and shit could go wrong. So when Ziv and I finally entered the dark and damp tunnel late that afternoon and pulled down our masks, my usual joking came to an abrupt halt.

"Lazy Daze is entering the bay," Ziv said over his earpiece. "Request clearance to dock."

I swallowed a laugh. After my yacht comment, Linney had decided to use maritime references as our code language for the op.

While we waited for Linney's smooth lilt to give us permission to continue, Ziv flashed me a suspicious look. "How the hell did you know where this place was? I would have never thought to look in a damned sewage drain under a bunch of bushes."

"I knew the general area where it needed to come out to provide the best chance at escape by road or water. And then it was just a matter of jogging around until I found it. Took fucking forever since I was trying not to look suspicious. If anyone was watching me, they had to think I have a tricky bladder," I explained.

"You were gone so long, Falcon checked the GPS to make sure you hadn't made your way off the island," he said.

That shouldn't have surprised me, but it did. "You're kidding? I didn't have to agree to this, you know. I'm here because I want to get this fucking crown out of Elek's hands. When will you assholes start believing me?"

Ziv held up both of his hands in surrender. "Relax. Jesus, I wasn't the one checking up on you. Blame the boss man. Besides, he has a lot riding on this. Last time he let an art thief slip through his hands, he got demoted." He gave me an accusatory glance before pulling his mask down.

I cringed. This was news to me. It was one thing to steal shit from people who didn't deserve it, but it was another to do something that negatively impacted an honest man's career.

And I knew Dirk Falcon was an honest man. It was something I'd already teased him about a few times. The guy was a rule follower and a complete square. I couldn't fault him for that. He was the kind of guy you took home to mama. Or... Doc and Grandpa in my case.

Not that I was taking him, or anyone else for that matter, home with me.

Ever.

But, god. I could stand to at least fuck the man. He was gorgeous and all grumbly sexy. I wanted to know what it would be like if he channeled all his frustration with me into a good session of hate sex. And after a mission? God, there was nothing better than the feeling of being shoved facedown in a mattress and fucked hard.

"Clearance granted, Lazy Daze."

I sucked in a breath, trying to pack away my little dirty fantasy about our fearless leader. Since the man was a rule follower, there wasn't going to be any hanky-panky happening on this op or between cops and robbers of any kind.

"Let's go," Ziv said, holding out his arm in a gesture for me to go first.

I preceded him into the dark space. We had to crouch since the walls weren't very high.

After a few feet down the rough and rocky path, Ziv whispered, "How did they even build this thing when so much of the terrain is rock?"

"Explosives," I answered. "It's probably why there isn't much height. They'd have had to go deeper to give people more head-space. Since this is only meant for a single-use getaway, it didn't need to be more than rudimentary and basic."

After a few more feet, he spoke again. "How can you be sure there aren't surveillance elements in here?"

I continued making my way forward at a fast clip. We'd determined we only had ten minutes to get all the way to the house and back before we risked being caught.

"There's no way to know. But there was absolutely no sign of electricity where we waited at the entrance, and I don't see any in here either. So anything would have to be on battery packs which would mean swapping them out regularly for recharging. And I just don't see his level of paranoia being that great. I think he'll assume no one knows about the tunnel, and if they did take the chance of entering a storm drain and stumble into the tunnel, they can't actually get into the house without setting off all the alarms."

"He knows you know about the tunnel," Ziv pointed out.

"Trust me, he wouldn't think I had the balls to steal from him," I admitted. "Besides, if I was running this op solo instead of working with you guys, I'd be coming at it from an entirely different direction." The end of the passage finally came into view.

"What kind of direction?" Ziv asked.

I turned and bounced my eyebrows at him. So much for not joking during an op. "The sexy seduction direction."

Ziv huffed out a laugh. "You'd fuck the crown out of him."

"Best way to get something out of a man's bedroom is to have a reason to be in the man's bedroom. Wouldn't you agree?"

I reached for the lamp attached to my safety helmet and turned it up to a brighter setting so I could record the details of the hatch with the GoPro camera strapped to my chest.

Ziv rattled off everything he saw so we'd have a verbal record in case the video didn't come out well. I wasn't surprised to see the type of alarm connectors Elek's security team had used on the hatch, but I was surprised to see them on *this* side of the doorway.

"Something's not right," I murmured, looking closer.

He must have known what I was thinking because he picked right up on it. "Maybe there's a set inside so he can alarm it for entry and exit."

"I would expect to see a camera here," I said softly.

"But we have the jammer turned on. So even if there was one, it wouldn't be able to record with us this close."

"There still should *be* one."

I felt around the edges of the hatch and the alarm connectors. The whole thing just looked so... basic. Like if Jimbo went to Walmart and asked them for a do-it-yourself secret-hatch security kit.

Ziv went to work mounting the jammer above the door. I was still shocked at how tiny it was. Working for the US government sure had its privileges, I guessed. The ones I could get my hands on were big enough to be spotted easily. This one was tiny in addition to Mouse doing an incredible job of making it look like what we'd imagined the inside of the tunnel looked like. It was covered in putty that made it look like dirty rock. While not perfect by any means, you'd definitely have to be looking for it to notice it.

As soon as we were done, I took one last quick look around before following Ziv back down the rock-strewn passageway to the end. Once we stripped off helmets and masks and stowed them away in the packs we'd left just inside the tunnel, we waited for the all-clear from Linney.

"Lazy Daze hold. Another craft is maneuvering out of a nearby slip."

The sound of the patrol car got louder before drifting off again.

"Lazy Daze, you are clear to dock. Reminder to proceed with zero wake."

I glanced at Ziv. "You going to be ready to run like the wind?"

The "zero wake" warning put us on notice to haul ass as soon as Mouse arrived in the van. It meant they had reason to believe someone might be watching or the patrol might come back around sooner than usual.

"Challenge accepted," Ziv shot back with a grin. "Why do you think Russians have more Olympic medals than Americans?"

The van pulled to a stop, and the side door nearest us flew open. Ziv shoved a palm to my chest and beat me there, turning to laugh in my face when I threw myself onto the metal floor of the van and slammed the sliding door closed behind myself.

"Because you cheat!" I panted at him with a grin. The adrenaline rush felt amazing after our long travel days and then the computer work earlier.

"*Tochno*," he said in a heavy Russian accent, leaning back against the wall of the van with a laugh and twinkling eyes. The hacker was enjoying the rush as much as I was. "*Exactly*. And don't you ever forget it."

I knew one appropriate Russian word, so I used it.

"*Mudak*," I said with a wink.

Asshole.

"Takes one to know one, my friend."

I considered the mission a success. Not only had we planted the jammer without getting caught or dead, but I'd also broken through Ziv's icy shell a little bit. There was something that happened to people when they did an op together. Even though our little semi-safe jaunt into the tunnel wasn't very risky, it was still a shared experience.

And I had to admit it felt nice to have someone at my side. It had been a long time since I'd trusted anyone to bring them into my work. I'd been so incredibly burned by Elek's betrayal, working heists solo had become a badge of honor.

Which was all well and good if you didn't want to divide your spoils, but it was shitty and lonely when you experienced this high and had absolutely no one to share it with.

When we returned to the house, Mouse jumped out of the van and raced over to a pair of scraggly bushes at the edge of the driveway before promptly evacuating his stomach.

"What the hell?" I asked, jogging over to see if he was okay.

He held up a hand. "I'm okay, just stay back."

I glanced over at Ziv in time to see him shrug.

"Go get a wet towel and some water," I called out. I approached slowly and gently reached out for Mouse's back. He wore a white button-down with an embroidered logo on the front indicating a local florist company. Falcon and Linney had gone out earlier to pick up the arrangement we'd preordered while Ziv had done some voodoo magic with an embroidery machine they'd packed in their gear.

When Ziv had hooked his computer up to the machine, I'd stared at him in shock.

"You'd be surprised how much we use this," he'd said.

"No I wouldn't. I have the upgraded version of the same thing," I'd admitted. "I just didn't picture a 'world-renowned hacker' using it," I'd teased with the usual finger quotes.

But now the embroidered shirt was a wrinkled sweaty mess. I rubbed my hand in circles on Mouse's back.

"Ziv's getting you some water," I said gently. "Take your time."

I could feel the trembling of his entire body through the shirt. Had he run into trouble and neglected to tell us? Or did he handle all op stress like this?

Instead of Ziv returning with a wet cloth, it was Falcon. He came storming out with so much anger on his face, I thought for a minute he was mad at *me* for some reason, but when he spoke, I realized he was mad at himself.

"I knew it was too soon. I tried to tell you that, Joshua." He elbowed me out of the way and put his hand on Mouse's back, reaching around to wipe the young man's face with the cool towel. "You can't be expected to—"

"I'm fine," Mouse said, standing up and grabbing the towel out of Falcon's hand. "I told you I'm fine, and I'm fine. I just wasn't expecting them to try and force me into the house."

"They did *what?*" I asked in surprise. "Why didn't you tell us when we got into the van?"

Mouse rolled his eyes and wiped at his mouth. "First of all, it was like Dumb and Dumber back there with all the bro talk. Secondly, I was concentrating on getting all of us out of there before the goons radioed the patrol vehicle to turn around."

He took the bottle of water Falcon handed him. I could tell the senior agent was still concerned for poor Mouse's nerves, and it made me wonder what the story was there. Clearly they'd had some kind of close call or difficult op in the recent past. Or Mouse had, anyway.

But it wasn't any of my business.

"I'm sorry," I said to Mouse before glancing up at Falcon over Mouse's head. "What can I do to help?"

"Go download your video footage onto the computer and make notes while your memory is still fresh. There's soup heating up on the stove, and if Mouse is still up for it, we'll have some fresh bread to go with it in a little bit."

Mouse had spent his lunch break putting together some dough and raving about the easy recipe he'd learned from his mom. Linney had told me later that baking was one of Mouse's coping techniques. I wasn't ever going to complain about that, and now I saw just how much the younger man had needed to do something repetitive and comforting.

"I'll go get ready so I can help if you need it," I told them before turning back to the house. "Great job on the op, Mouse," I called over my shoulder.

I heard the soft sounds of Falcon's murmured concerns as I made my way to the front door. It was a completely different side of the guy I'd been trying so hard not to notice up till now. It was much easier to think of him as the uptight asshole gunning for my capture and conviction than to see him tutting over a younger team member in need of reassurance. It reminded me of a night in middle school when I'd been caught sneaking out and my mother had raised the roof with her anger. She'd bitched me out for what felt like hours and then threw the book at me with all kinds of punishments and lost privileges.

But when I'd snuck out of my room an hour later to get a glass of water from the hall bathroom, I'd heard her crying behind the closed door of my parents' bedroom. It had taken me a long time to realize she'd been crying over me.

I'd thought her an absolute shrew at the time, someone who deserved whatever had caused her to cry. But when I'd finally realized how stupid I'd been, I'd felt terrible. She hadn't been yelling at me out of anger, she'd been yelling at me out of fear.

Out of *love*.

That experience had borne my brother West's favorite line. "She's not a bitch, she's a mom."

I made my way into the kitchen and took the seat next to Ziv, pulling out the GoPro to get to work. After cracking open my own water bottle, I smiled a hello at Linney. "Good job on comms."

She smiled back and nodded. "The person with the loudest voice gets the job."

"Mm." I thought about it. "I think it's the person with the loveliest voice."

Ziv shook his head. "Are you ever not flirting? I swear you could seduce a gravy boat."

"Have you ever seen the curves on one of those things?" I asked seductively. "And they live to serve. They'll give you what you want. All you have to do is bend them over."

Ziv and Linney hooted with laughter until the three of us settled down and got back to work.

"He okay?" Ziv asked softly after a minute.

"I think so. Falcon's with him." I turned to face him and Linney both. "What happened when he went to the house?"

Linney's eyes softened. "They said they didn't order flowers, which we expected. But when Mouse stammered his apology and asked if they knew where Santos Marinakis—the neighbor—lived, the men insisted he come in the house. He was standing on the doorstep already, and one of the security men grabbed his elbow and pulled. Mouse dropped the vase of flowers and it shattered at his feet. The man holding him shoved him against the side of the house and aggressively patted him down."

"Jesus," I said, surprised by the story. "Paranoid much. What the hell?"

Linney shrugged. "Thank god we'd been thorough and given him proper ID. All they found was his student ID and local driver's license along with a few euros. And it was to Mouse's benefit he was a stammering, shaking mess by that point. I would imagine that's what helped convince them he was the poor unsuspecting floral-delivery man."

"Poor Mouse," Ziv muttered. "After everything else the kid's been through."

I thought about why Elek would have such thugs at the front door. At our apartment in Paris, he'd had one man, and he'd referred to him as a butler. Not that I believed that's all he was. Tibor had been muscled and huge. The guy had never cracked a smile. At the time, I'd wondered why Elek needed someone like that, but then he'd explained that Tibor had been in desperate need of a job and Elek had been in desperate need of someone to keep his life and home organized.

Tibor had been in charge of Elek's security because even then Elek had owned plenty of precious artwork. He'd also been our driver. Since Elek had had Tibor since before we met, I hadn't ever really questioned it.

But now... now I did. Because Tibor hadn't ever confronted someone aggressively in my presence. And I'd lived under the same roof with the guy for two of the three years I'd been with Elek.

Ziv said, "I'm sure they've stepped up security since bringing in the crown."

Mouse and Falcon joined us at the table. Mouse looked much better, but I noticed Falcon took a seat close to him anyway. The leader of the group practically oozed protective alpha male, so it was no surprise he wanted to keep a close eye on the younger agent.

Linney made a few group announcements such as the tuxedo tailor coming the following morning and the success of the fingerprint capture test. I got the sense she was giving Mouse some time to recover before we started the debrief on the mini-op we'd done.

I continued to think through the things I'd learned both from the tunnel surveillance and the story about what had happened with the flower delivery attempt. Suddenly, I remembered something.

"Hey, were you able to plant a bug?" I blurted. I was dying to know what these security men were up to and whether or not the heightened security was because of the undercover agent or some other reason.

Linney stopped talking and glared at me. Falcon sighed and closed his eyes. But Mouse's face lit up with triumph.

"I almost forgot, but yeah. I actually planted all three of them. One when the guy pushed me, another when the second guy turned away to use his radio, and the third when I leaned down to gather the flowers up."

Falcon turned to Mouse with a burgeoning grin. "Special Agent Mickey for the win. Well done. I knew you could do it."

The baby agent beamed under everyone's praise. Which was great, but I wanted to get some intel.

"Any way we can turn on a receiver or something?" I asked. "So maybe we don't miss what they're saying…"

Falcon's proud grin dropped and his "King is a selfish bastard" glower returned. Which suited me just fine. I didn't have any room in my life for thinking this man was anything special. I was there to nail an art thief.

If only that scowl didn't make me want to nail all kinds of other things in the process.

CHAPTER ELEVEN

FALCON

We spent the rest of the evening going over what we'd learned. King was particularly bothered by the alarm connectors on the outside of the tunnel door as well as the heavy reaction by the security personnel at the door. I wasn't sure what Elek meant by alarming against escape from the house as well as entry, but I was fairly sure the extra muscle on site had something to do with the recent art acquisition.

If there was a more nefarious reason, then we were in trouble.

So far the bugs had picked up nothing but Hungarian, and while King knew more than I'd expected, he didn't know enough to translate everything we were picking up. Which meant we had to stream it back to our techs at home and have a translation team report back anything useful.

But it wasn't for lack of trying on King's part. He was downright obsessed with listening in on the off chance he could pick up something critical. Hours after everyone else had gone to bed, he was still sitting hunched over the large wooden table with the headset on and the laptop in front of him open to a translation search engine.

"Come to bed," I said before realizing how it sounded. I'd gotten out of the shower and dressed in sleep pants and an old T-shirt before wandering back to the kitchen for some water.

King looked up and rubbed his eyes with the heels of his hands. "I can't stop thinking there's more to this we don't know about." When he brought his hands back down to his lap, I noticed just how tired he looked. Inky blotches lined his eyes, and his hair was every which way, which I was learning was fairly usual for this late hour.

He looked edible.

"We can't figure it all out in one day. You need sleep. You were up late last night, remember?"

The corner of King's lip quirked up. "You'd make a good papa bear. Anyone ever told you that?"

I couldn't decide if that was a comment about my sexuality, my age, or my body hair.

"Relax," he said with a soft laugh. "I just meant you're protective. You look out for your team." He stood and stretched, revealing that tantalizing strip of skin above his waistband that had always been a weak spot of mine.

I tried not to look.

I failed.

King caught me staring. "Like what you see, Papa Bear?"

"Don't call me that, pup."

More deep laughter. It vibrated straight to my groin.

"You're not that old," he challenged. "Fifty-five... sixty tops."

I took a step toward him and glared down at him where he still sat at the table. "Insubordinate punk. I'll have you know I'm thirty-eight. Not that much older than your twenty-eight."

"You *sure* you don't have grandkids yet? Only someone sprinkled a fair amount of salt in your pepper." He reached up and ruffled my short hair.

I couldn't hold back my own laughter. "You're a brat."

"I prefer the term comedian."

"A troublemaker," I added.

"A moniker I can neither deny nor shake. Not sure I'd want to, if I'm being honest."

His hand was still in my hair, only it had slowed until his touch was more of a caress. My breathing did the opposite, speeding up until I expected him to call me on it.

"Come to bed," I repeated. This time my voice sounded strange to my ears. King's pupils widened, the shining darkness taking over the speckled green of his irises.

Fuck. *Fuck.* This was a bad idea. I could not... *we* could not go down this path.

"Make me."

His words were so soft, I would have missed them if I hadn't been staring at his plush mouth. My dick throbbed, tenting toward him in the soft fabric.

I teetered on the edge. All I would have to do is turn around and walk away, peeling my shirt over my head to send him the message I would give him what he wanted in the privacy of our bedroom. But there was still a niggling voice in my head chanting *master manipulator* over and over again. Did it matter? What was a quick bout of hot sex between consenting adults? A fuck wasn't the same thing as a relationship, or, hell, even a date.

It was just a fuck. A way to burn off stress on a mission.

Right?

King's fingers tightened on my scalp and began to pull my head closer. The small promise of aggression was like tossing fuel on a spark. I was going to let him do this. My eyes moved to his mouth in time to see his teeth scrape hard against his bottom lip.

I wanted to kiss them better. And then I wanted to scrape my own teeth across them so I could do it all over again.

"We found something!"

Mouse came racing into the room in his Avengers pajamas, bright-eyed and eager as if it wasn't two in the morning. King and I jumped apart, and I turned away for a minute to give my dick a chance to deflate. It didn't take long.

"*Fuck,*" King said. I might have imagined the slightly strangled sound in his voice.

"What'd you find?" I asked after clearing my throat.

"Well, actually it was Ziv." He looked around. "Where'd he go?"

Ziv came wandering in holding his laptop.

"The alarm equipment in the tunnel is a Russian surveillance brand. The company has a record of a shipment to the island the week before the crown was stolen. It's the same brand of the cameras the agent found at King's apartment in Paris."

Mouse and I stared at Ziv in shock as his words reverberated around the room.

King tilted his head. "*My* apartment in Paris?"

"No, mine," I blurted, stupidly.

His brows furrowed as he studied me. "You're lying. Right to my fucking face."

Ziv blushed deep crimson. "Boss, I am so sorry."

King's confusion began to cloud over with anger. "Did you have an agent on me in Paris? Why were there cameras at my apartment?"

This wasn't going to be pretty. But I had no other explanation than the truth.

"After Prince Rashid of Jordan discovered a certain someone had made off with his Jackson Pollock, he put pressure on the US to present its most notorious art thief for extradition." I watched his eyes for his reaction, but they weren't the indicator of his sudden fear. His face lost all color.

"And so," I continued, "we were given additional resources including a couple of undercover agents."

"Agents, plural," King mumbled before looking back up at me. "Two agents on just me?"

Ziv met my eyes and carefully shook his head. He was right. Until this op was over, we couldn't divulge that information.

"I'm not at liberty to give you any details," I said stiffly.

Anger flared in King's eyes and the set of his jaw. His fingers tightened into a fist on the thick wooden tabletop. "You're not... are you fucking kidding me?"

Gone was the tenuous unspoken truce we'd come to earlier in the day.

"I'm sorry," I said. And I meant it. I didn't want to be at odds with him. I'd been around him enough to know that he was either a sensitive man with trust issues or a damned good actor.

"No you're not," he spat. "All you care about is your op. Is anyone else under surveillance?" Suddenly, the realization dawned on him and his face fell. "Do you have someone undercover with my *family*?" He stared at me, his eyes begging me to reassure him.

I couldn't.

"Please..." King's voice cracked. "Please tell me you don't have an agent fucking around with my family."

I couldn't tell him that, so I kept my mouth closed.

"Dirk," he whispered, grabbing my heart and squeezing the shit out of it. "Please."

I swallowed around the thickness in my throat. "As soon as we get the crown back, we'll be out of your hair. You stay clean and we'll stay gone."

He studied my eyes for a second before shoving his chair back and heading for the door. "I'm going for a walk. Do *not* follow me."

I watched King walk away, wondering if I'd made the right decision. Sometimes my job had gray areas that were difficult to navigate. In this case, I had to balance the need to earn his trust for the success of the op with the need to cover our asses if the man disappeared before we got what we came here for.

"You were right," Ziv said. "I remember a year ago when you said his weakness was his family. I doubted you at first."

Mouse weighed in. "That's right. You said he was the only one of the ten kids who'd run off to live in another country, and it was probably because he wasn't as close to them."

"I was obviously wrong," Ziv admitted.

"He went to live in another country because that's where the Sorbonne is and he's an art scholar," I corrected.

"And that's where you think they met," Mouse said, remembering my original hypothesis.

I shrugged. "I'm not sure it matters now. But what does matter is getting him back on our side." I stood up. "I'm going to talk to him."

Ziv shook his head. "Bad idea, boss."

Mouse looked nervous. "I agree. Maybe give him some time unless you want your face caved in."

Time wasn't something I could give him. The gala was the following night.

After grabbing shoes and a couple of hoodies out of our room, I made my way outside and looked around, noticing the bright moonlight in the crisp air. I slipped into my shoes and yanked one of the sweatshirts over my head. Movement caught my eye from the direction of the sea, so I headed that way.

When I caught up to him, he was yanking a piney branch off a scraggly tree. The anger and frustration was clear in his body language as he fought the small tree for the limb.

I stood and watched.

"You going to use that to whip me?" I finally asked softly.

His eyes flashed to me. "Yeah, maybe. You'd certainly deserve it if I did."

The collection of soft needles finally pulled free from the trunk and he was left with something that would barely swat a fly away from a horse's ass.

He swished it through the air as he turned to continue his walk to the ocean cliff in the distance. I followed him quietly. King knew I was back there, but I didn't want to confront him before he'd gotten some of his adrenaline out.

"You don't fuck with a man's family, Falcon!" he snapped after a little while. "That's like... you just... you don't do that. It's a line you don't... you don't cross."

His voice was ragged, and I wondered if some of it was from guilt. Because it had been his own actions that had resulted in an undercover agent being placed with his family. He had to know that.

"What if it was your family, goddammit!" he continued without looking back at me. "What if I sent one of my own goons into your precious fucking family? Huh?"

"I don't have a family."

There was a hitch in his step before he continued walking. "I don't care."

He was lying, but I didn't call him on it.

When we finally got close enough to see the moon sparkling off the water, I realized it wasn't as steep a drop-off as I'd thought. The cliffs bordering Elek's estate were much steeper. Here, the ground gradually curved down until a shorter cliff. There were twin stone benches nearby made in the same style as the fountain back at our rental.

I took a seat while he paced and flapped his arms, spouting off all the reasons why I was the absolute worst human being on earth. While I hated seeing him so agitated and worried about the people he loved, I was secretly relieved to see such a genuine part of him.

This was the real King Wilde—vulnerable and untethered.

He turned and stalked closer until he was close enough to grab the front of my hoodie. He still hadn't let me give him the other one.

"I fucking hate you," he growled in my face.

I stood up slowly until I was looking down at him. His hand still clutched me close, and his chin was raised defiantly. Fire lit his eyes, and it tightened something in my chest. We stared at each other, his angry words hovering around us in the cold night air.

"You don't," I murmured softly. "You really, really don't."

His nostrils flared and his jaw tightened. "Fuck you."

I felt my body relax, and my mouth spread into a knowing grin. My hands reached for his hips.

"Gonna be the other way around, I'm afraid," I said, tightening my grip on him and pulling him against me.

That was all it took.

CHAPTER TWELVE

KING

I flew at him, ready to… I wasn't sure exactly. Take a bite of his face? Because the next thing I knew, I was crushing my mouth to his and gripping his head as tightly between my hands as I could. There was no way I was letting him go.

Falcon's arms came around my lower back and pulled me even tighter to him until I could feel his hardness pressing into my belly. My own dick humped into his leg without my permission as I devoured his face.

I hated him, but I wanted him desperately.

"Jesus," Falcon muttered between breaths before moving his mouth over to take my earlobe between his teeth. "So fucking hot. So pissed off. Makes me want to make you even angrier."

"Fuck you," I spat again. Apparently it was becoming a refrain. "You already make me angry enough—*mpfh!*"

His hand was around the front of my throat, squeezing but not hard enough to scare me, just hard enough to steal my breath from excitement.

"Less talking," he ground out.

"Fuck—*unnnghh.*" The hand tightened again, and he gave me a look that shot straight to my dick. Fuck, *fuck*. This man was the sexiest thing ever, and he was pushing all of my buttons in the very best way. I wanted to give over to him, let him take complete control over me.

"Please," I begged against my better judgment.

"That's better," Falcon said with a seductive smile, a look I'd never seen on his face before. A look that made my clothes beg to come off. "Much better."

Ugh, I did not want to give him the satisfaction of dominating me in any way.

But I wanted him to dominate me in every way.

"Please," I said again. Who the fuck was in charge of my mouth? That fucker needed a ball gag.

Falcon's thumb stroked up and down my throat until my eyes fluttered closed.

Do something to me, I thought. *Anything.*

His lips landed softly at the corner of my mouth. "You are a beautiful man," he murmured against my skin. My stomach tumbled with excitement at his words. "So responsive, so submissive... You have no idea how badly I want you. Your anger makes your cheeks pink." He continued to press kisses to my jaw, using the hand on my throat to tilt my head however he wanted. "Your passion makes your eyes shine." My dick needed more. I pressed harder against his leg. "And your desire makes you completely, utterly..." He pulled my shirt collar open to suckle on my collarbone. "Edible."

I whimpered. I wanted him to own me. It was my weakness, I knew. Giving myself over to dominant, older men. But fuck if it didn't feel amazing. And he'd had me tuned in to him for far longer than I cared to admit.

The cat-and-mouse game we'd played for years had been a kind of foreplay because this heat, this power between us was stronger than anything that could come from such a short time knowing someone.

I tried to remember why I was angry with him, tried to remember that I *was* angry with him.

But then the warm skin of his palm slid under the back of my shirt and onto my back, and I forgot it all.

"Falcon," I breathed into the top of his hair. It still smelled faintly of the soup we'd had for dinner and the fresh bread Mouse had made. "I want to come. I want... *oh god*, I want to come."

He shushed me, his hands wandering down the back of my sleep pants while his mouth stayed focused on the tender skin of my throat. When his palms squeezed my ass, my dick jumped and my balls tightened. I was going to embarrass myself.

"It's been a long time," I admitted.

"How long?"

Falcon's teeth nipped at the spot where my neck joined my shoulder. My T-shirt was beyond stretched out and probably damp from his mouth, but I didn't care at all. He was lighting me up so much I didn't feel the chill.

"Kingston," he said.

"Huh?"

A warm chuckle vibrated against my skin. "How long has it been since someone's had you? Since someone has been inside of you?"

His finger smoothed down between my ass cheeks and found the right spot, teasing it and pulling out a moan from deep in my belly.

"Too long." I gasped as he tugged at the sensitive skin around my hole.

Falcon moved his hand away from my ass until both of his hands were under my shirt, roaming up toward my shoulder blades. "Come to bed." His voice was hypnotic. "Come back to bed with me and let me have you, Kingston."

It was so tempting. I wanted him, but I knew that if we moved into the light of the house, near the rest of his crew, he would turn back into the rule-following hard-ass he was the rest of the time. Whereas here, now, he was something else. Something wilder and freer.

"I don't want to go back," I admitted, burying my face into his chest and clutching at his sweatshirt to keep him from pulling away from me. I wanted to lose myself in his warmth, his strength. Pretend we weren't who we really were.

"You're freezing. I can't let you stay out here any longer."

I laughed. The concern for my welfare made me feel light and happy, but it also sounded like papa bear.

After tilting my head back up to meet his eyes, I teased him. "*Let* me?"

Falcon's lips landed softly on the end of my nose. "Your nose is red," he murmured. "Put this on."

Instead of reaching for the hoodie he'd dropped on the bench, he peeled off his own and dropped it over my head before I realized what he was doing. Then he reached to put the cold one on himself.

The soft cotton felt warm and smelled like clean laundry mixed with the scent of his piney shaving cream. If I'd accidentally sniffed it earlier in the bathroom, it was because I'd mistaken it for my own, completely different-looking bottle.

I hugged the baggy top around me and enjoyed the immediate break from the cold night air. "Thank you."

Once he had on the other one, he stepped back into me and put his arms around me. "I want you, King. But I'm sure as hell not going to beg. And I'm not going to have sex with you on the cold rocky ground either. We're going back inside."

He pulled back and clasped my hand. Our fingers automatically threaded together like we'd held hands a million times before. It felt strange to hold hands with a sexual conquest. It was such a boyfriend or lover thing to do.

I knew he expected me to put up a fight, so I didn't. I went along willingly and even squeezed his hand partway back to the house.

"Thank you for coming after me," I said. "Um… that's… that's something no one has ever done for me except my family."

I clenched my teeth together. Why did I always sound like a nervous boy around him? I had my damned shit together, so why couldn't I sound like it?

Falcon looked over at me. "How do you mean?"

Why had I told him something personal like that? Something vulnerable?

"Never mind. That was stupid. I just wanted to thank you. Otherwise I'd still be cold." I swallowed. "The sweatshirt, I mean. That was nice of you. That's all I meant."

Falcon stopped midstride and pressed his lips together before opening his mouth to speak and then closing it again. I could tell he was arguing with himself over whatever it was he wanted to say. I assumed this was when he'd tell me we couldn't sleep together after all because of his work and his rules.

I waited patiently for what I knew was coming. When it came, it wasn't at all what I was expecting.

"King... the undercover agent with your family... isn't *with* your family."

My heart thumped. "What do you mean?"

He shook his head, clearly annoyed with himself for telling me. "The agent doesn't have any kind of personal relationship with anyone in your family. They're just embedded in Hobie to keep an eye out and ask around. It's not..." Clearly he was struggling with his ethics.

And failing.

"Dammit. It's not anyone trusted by your family. So you don't... you don't need to worry that..."

He raked his hand through his short hair before tugging on it and shaking his head with exasperation. "Fuck," he said. "*Fuck.*"

Then he strode ahead and let himself into the house.

I stood there, staring after him.

The blustery motherfucker cared enough about me to give me that reassurance against his better judgment.

But, why?

CHAPTER THIRTEEN

FALCON

I couldn't believe what I'd just allowed to happen. Who the hell was I? And how many times was I going to allow a pretty face—that *specific* pretty face—to get me to fold like a cheap house of cards?

Maybe I should request a reassignment.

The house was dark. I made my way to the bedroom and got under the covers of my bed before King could follow me in and gloat over my unprofessionalism. I'd known better than to give him even that little bit of information, but I hadn't been able to stand seeing him so upset. The amount of self-recrimination going on in my brain was overwhelming, so I began reviewing our plan for the following day to distract me from what had happened with King. *Concentrate on the future, not the past.*

Even if it was the very recent past.

And even then, the only regret was the unauthorized intel blabbing. I certainly didn't regret learning what King's mouth tasted like or how his entire body melted against mine the minute I took charge of him physically.

Great, so now I had a giant throbbing boner. And I was going to have to ignore it since I was sharing a room with the boner maker.

I heard him make his way into the room quietly, closing the door with a soft click. But instead of padding over to his bed on the other side of the room, he pulled back the covers on mine and slid in next to me.

There was no way in hell I was going to kick this sexy man out of my bed no matter how stupid I was in all other areas of my life.

I pulled him in closer and held him tight, noticing he'd removed the hoodie *and* his shirt. His bare back felt like heaven, and it led all the way down to his curvy, tempting ass.

We lay quietly, simply running hands over each other with metric tons of unspoken bullshit between us, until he spoke.

"He was friends with my art history professor."

King's voice was whisper soft in the small room, and his breath brushed against my shoulder. It took me a minute to realize he was talking about Elek.

"One day after class, my professor invited me to participate in a special challenge. He had an art collector who was supposedly obsessed with identifying forgeries." He shifted back a little so he could meet my eyes. We lay on our sides, facing each other, heads on separate pillows. The moonlight was barely there, but it was enough to show me the outline of his form in the darkness. "I assumed at the time it was because the collector was scared of acquiring a forgery one day by mistake."

I reached out and pushed his floppy hair out of his face, running my thumb down his cheek afterward to keep a connection with him. "What happened?"

"The man had brought five pieces for the professor to evaluate. I was so honored to have been chosen to help. The professor had blown all kinds of smoke at me about how clever I was, how special and high achieving. This was a rare treat that would be a boon to my resume."

King's fingers grazed softly through my chest hair as he continued. "I identified four of them as forgeries even though all five were actually fake. The art collector was stunned. He and the professor asked me to explain my findings. I told them the first one was a forgery since it used a fastener that was a hundred years newer than the purported age of the piece. The second was a forgery because I'd just seen the original at the Musée d'Orsay two days before. The third couldn't be genuine because some of the metal framing had zero scratches which was impossible for the combination of that kind of metal and age."

He rolled onto his back and ran his hand through his own hair. "The fourth was a joke. Turkeys weren't found in China in the fourteenth century for god's sake. And finally…"

King rolled back onto his side, reaching for my hand and threading our fingers together again almost without thinking. "Finally they showed me a lesser-known Miró sketch." King's hand tightened in mine. "It was a forgery I'd made." He said it softer than the rest, like he was terrified of admitting it.

Every molecule of the art crime investigator in me began processing this information at Mach speed until I realized this was his quid pro quo.

He was telling me this—giving me this—to pay me back for reassuring him about his family.

I squeezed his hand back. "Where'd they get it?"

"My apartment. Suddenly, I realized I hadn't been picked because I was teacher's pet. I'd been found out… or targeted. For some reason, I'd been specifically chosen because of my secret hobby."

"You were an art forger? For fun?"

Other than the Van Gogh job, I couldn't remember any Le Chaton cases where we'd discovered a forgery in place of a stolen original, but that didn't mean there weren't a million forgeries that had been put in place in heists we hadn't discovered yet.

"No. *No*, Falcon. I promise. I did it for me. I did it because… because I wanted to see if I could. To prove that I could. But I swear I never did anything with them back then. They were just for me."

I could hear the desperate sincerity in his voice. While I was relieved he hadn't been in the forgery business, I was more affected by his earnest desire not to disappoint me. He obviously cared about my opinion, and that was a gift of sorts. A concession.

"So how did they get a hold of the Miró forgery? I mean, how did they find out about it?"

"I found out later that someone I'd brought back to my place for sex had snooped around while I was sleeping. He ended up sleeping with Elek at some point and mentioned it. The guy was a fellow art student, so he'd recognized what it was and how good it was, I guess. The art world in Paris is smaller than you think."

He took a deep breath. "So Elek sent him back to sleep with me again to get more information. This time, the guy took photos of the work. Not only the Miró but also some of the other pieces I'd done."

"And Elek was intrigued enough to recruit you," I suggested.

King nodded. "And the way he went about it was public enough to ensure an implied threat to my position at the Sorbonne."

"Why did you say it was the real thing when it wasn't?"

"I wanted to see if either of them would correct me. It was strictly ego. Up till then, no one else had ever seen any of my forgery attempts. And here was a chance to have not only a renowned, esteemed professor of Eastern European antiquities at le Sorbonne, but also this wealthy art collector who seemed to know his way around an antiquity... it was hubris."

It was like watching a movie. The story was fantastical. "What happened after that? How did you come to... work with Elek?"

I hated picturing him with the older man. I'd now seen hours of video surveillance and reams of photos of the Hungarian bastard. The man was a fifty-five-year-old pompous jackass who equated flashy displays of wealth with self-worth. At least that's the way it had always seemed to me.

"When I said it was the original, the professor gasped and looked over at Elek, clearly impressed the man had brought an original Miró sketch to his office. I was surprised he didn't genuflect at Elek. Meanwhile, Elek's eyes twinkled at me with a knowing look. And when we were done, he invited me out for coffee. I should have said no, but I wanted my fucking sketch back. And I wanted to know what the hell was going on."

King rolled onto his back again. "That's when he offered me a fuckton of money for the sketch. At first… at first, I thought I was selling him pieces he could display in his home and impress his friends with. He requested these lesser-known pieces that weren't on prominent, public display. I got rich really quickly and thought… *this isn't so bad.* And in the meantime, the man was charming as hell. He'd immediately apologized for the way he'd discovered me and the way he'd manipulated me. He admitted that he was just so *enamored* with my *talent.*"

I could tell by the tone of his voice he was rolling his eyes.

"I was so gullible, Falcon. I look back on it now and cringe. But at the time… I was a twenty-four-year-old grad student with stars in his eyes. And here was this wealthy art collector who wanted to wine and dine me while praising me to the heavens."

"How did it turn from creating forgeries to participating in art heists?"

"After about six months, Elek took me to a fancy cocktail reception at the interior minister's house. We mingled with all of these high-level politicians and local celebrities. It was a far cry from little Hobie, Texas. I was finally in the kind of social sphere where there was true art on the walls. Except… except I realized that one of the pieces was mine."

"Shit."

"Yeah. At first, I assumed he'd been selling my stuff behind my back. And that was bad enough. But then I got home and researched the provenance of the original because something about it was ringing alarm bells. Sure enough, the original was owned by this interior minister. He'd bought it at auction eight years before. But I knew the one he had on display was mine.

"When we got back to Elek's place after the reception, I confronted him about it. That's when he told me that he'd been using my forgeries to cover his thefts of the originals. He eagerly offered to cut me in on the action. I literally threw up. Suddenly, I was in way over my head."

I still held his hand and could detect a faint tremor in it. I wondered if it was from his memories or fear of confessing all of this to me.

I asked a stupid but necessary question. "Why didn't you go to the authorities?"

He swiveled his head toward me, and I wished more than anything there had been enough light for me to see into his eyes. "He told me he had enough evidence to pin it all on me. Hundreds of thousands of dollars' worth of stolen artwork and forgeries would put me away in a French prison for a very long time. Meanwhile I had nothing. No evidence of his participation in any of it. It would be his word against mine, and let's not forget he was friends with people like the interior minister of France."

Anger burned in my gut for that young art student.

"How could you fall in love with a man like that?" I blurted without thinking.

"I wasn't in love with him. Ever. But I'll admit it didn't take much for me to become accustomed to living a big life. As soon as he'd talked me into working on jobs with him, I got addicted to the high. It was like being able to nail a forgery only this time there was an actual adrenaline shot that went along with it. And I've always been competitive. So becoming the best at something? Well, that was seductive."

King let out a soft chuckle. "I'm the middle of ten children, Falcon. I wasn't the best at anything. Ever. Hudson was the nicest, West was the smartest, MJ was the most high achieving, Saint was the toughest, Otto was the most sensitive, Hallie was the funniest, Winnie was the moodiest, Cal was this weird kind of sailing expert from a young age, and Sassy was the cutest, sweetest thing we all doted on. Then there was me. I was just... the plainest. The boring one. I didn't excel at anything except copying graphic novel illustrations I liked."

Now it was my time to laugh. "I think you mean most clueless. You're one of the most beautiful, intriguing men I've ever met. You have a mind for strategy, and you're diligent and thorough."

"Stop. I didn't say that to fish for compliments. I'm just... I've just been trying for years now to figure out why I was such an easy catch for him. And all I can think was that I was so desperate to be great at something, to be recognized for my talent and appreciated by others."

"It makes sense." I reached out and ran a hand through his hair again because I could, and for some reason my fingers felt like that's where they belonged. "Why did he leave you on the Van Gogh job?"

"That's a story for another time. I'm sick and tired of talking about Elek Kemény. I'd much rather talk about how to get your clothes off and more of your skin against mine."

I rolled on top of King and brushed my lips across his cheek. "I thought you hated me," I whispered as I continued to kiss him. He made a delicious little sighing sound and reached around to grab my ass.

"Is liking someone a requirement for having sex with them? Asking for a friend."

I could feel his smile under my lips. "Certainly not. It just takes consent and a hard cock." Both my hands went into his hair so I could tilt his head and devour his mouth. When he pulled back gasping for air, his chest heaved.

"Both are yours for the taking." His erection pressed up into my stomach in invitation. I reached down and began shoving at his sleep pants. By the time I got them off, I was far enough down the bed that his cock was in my face.

I nuzzled his sac and kissed his inner thigh, taking my time to enjoy every minute of it. I wasn't stupid enough to think I'd ever get to do it again. Sure, maybe while we were still here in Greece, suspended in this unusual set of circumstances, but I wanted to gather up as many sensory experiences with him to take home, to replay in the quiet darkness of my house.

King's hands landed softly on my head, and his soft sounds of pleasure drifted into the room. There was always something other-worldly about this time of night, but when you were halfway across the globe with a beautiful naked man underneath you, it was something else altogether.

My hands mapped his legs, his hips, his belly, and upwards to his chest while my mouth explored the tender skin around the top of his thighs. His cock was warm and hard, begging for attention, but I loved teasing him, making him wait for it.

I looked up at him. "Do I need to use a condom?"

"Huh?"

"I'm negative and on PrEP, but if you—"

"Negative and PrEP too. No condom. Just... please."

I returned to teasing him relentlessly. Finally, when he made a plaintive whimpering sound, I licked along his length and suckled the tip before taking his cock into my mouth and running my tongue all around it.

"Oh god, yes. *Fuck*," he said, hands tightening on my scalp. "Please don't stop."

I sucked him while I continued to explore his body with my fingers. Muscles twitched under his warm skin as I skated my hands across his shoulders and arms.

"Falcon..." His voice was rough and deep. "You... oh god. I can't... gonna...."

He arched up and shot down my throat, sucking in a sharp breath before muttering curse words and bending his legs up so he could use them to push deeper into my throat for a moment before collapsing underneath me.

One taste of the man and I was addicted.

I moved up, trailing soft kisses along his stomach to his chest and along the column of his throat until I got to his stubbled jaw.

King's eyes were half-lidded as he gazed at me. His hand came up to run fingers through my hair. "That's a much better use of your mouth than grumbling, old man."

I snorted. "You think?"

"Mm-hmm."

My cock was still hard, and he was even sexier postorgasm than before. But there was no way I wanted to disturb his blissed-out state. He looked on the verge of drifting off, but I could tell he didn't want to leave me in the lurch.

"Sleep," I murmured, kissing him on the lips before settling down to snuggle him close. I prayed he wouldn't want to move over to his own bed now that he'd had his orgasm. For some reason, I wanted more from our encounter. Or maybe I just didn't want it to end.

I knew once we were no longer in bed together, the magic would evaporate, leaving us back where we started and where we'd always be.

FBI agent and art thief.

Two people who could never have any kind of future together.

"Falcon?" King's sleepy voice was soft and sweet.

"Hm?"

"Sometimes after an op, I wish someone would hold me down face-first and fuck me into the mattress."

I was too stunned to speak. My dick throbbed back to life against King's hip as my brain went completely offline.

King continued, only this time I could hear the easy flirtation in his sleepy tone. "And, well, we had an op today..."

Before he got the last word out, I'd shoved him over onto his stomach and fumbled the bottle of lube out of my bag. Within moments, I was prepping him as quickly as I could and shoving myself into the tight grip of his body.

CHAPTER FOURTEEN

KING

Thank fuck.

My feelings had been too real, too mushy, too terrifying. The FBI agent had *snuggled* me for god's sake. First he'd reassured me about my family because he'd recognized how upset I was, and then the man had shown me genuine affection by pulling me close and encouraging me to drift off rather than reciprocate.

It was too much. It was giving me ideas. And desires.

Which I knew from experience not to trust. I'd been used before, and I knew I was being used now. Not the sex. I didn't think Falcon was quite that awful. But he was using me to succeed in this mission which would mean he'd succeeded in his job. If all went well, he'd get his promotion and whatever accolades the completion of this op would earn him with the people he respected.

It was a temporary fling at most. There were no real feelings, and if I let myself believe there were, that would lead to me making stupid decisions. I needed to look out for me, for my own goals. And if I developed feelings for one of the agents on the team, that would most definitely muddy the waters.

But Jesus Christ the man could fuck.

As soon as his slicked-up meaty fingers had penetrated me, I'd arched up and pushed back, begging for more. Falcon's larger body lay over top of me, and his big dick speared into me, filling me up until all I could feel was the stretch of the cock I'd been daydreaming about for days.

"Fuck, fuck," I choked out.

"Good?" Falcon grunted.

"*Oh god.*" Was I drooling onto the pillow? Pretty sure I was. "Good. So good." I couldn't think of more words while his fat cock was stroking hard along all the right spots inside of me.

He picked up the pace, hips slamming into my ass as his fingers dug into the skin of my chest and stomach where his arms held me tightly to his front.

"Take it," he growled. After a beat, he pulled back and grabbed the back of my neck with his large grip and pressed the side of my face farther into the pillow. I groaned in pleasure.

He was giving me exactly what I'd wanted.

"That's it," he murmured. "Look at you. So tight. So good at taking my cock."

I was going to come untouched. His words went straight to my dick and made me whimper and beg into the pillow.

"Dirk," I breathed. His pace picked up even more until he was absolutely abusing my ass and squeezing the back of my neck as he shoved me down. He suddenly leaned back in so he could reach around with his other hand and stroke me off.

"Just like that, *fuck.*" He didn't seem to even realize he was speaking, but his words tightened my balls. As soon as his hand grasped my dick, there was no more holding back.

My orgasm screamed through me, and I turned my face into the pillow to muffle my own cries.

His rhythm stuttered and he bit out a muffled curse, pushing harder into me and staying there while he came.

When he was done, we lay together like that with his arms like tight steel bands around my front and his face lying between my shoulder blades. We were both slick with sweat and breathing heavy.

As our breathing slowed, the realization of what we'd done sank in. I'd slept with the FBI agent who'd been hounding me for years, whose career high would be convicting me and putting me in prison for decades.

After Elek had left, I'd promised myself I'd never get involved with someone who had any kind of power over me again.

So why had I done it?

I felt Falcon shift and pull out of me. For some reason, having sex bare like that left me feeling even more vulnerable than usual. I clenched my jaw against the feeling and tried to get up the nerve to get up and return to my own bed so I could act like this hadn't meant anything to me.

But then Falcon's lips brushed along the edge of one of my shoulder blades. His fingers ran lightly down my spine to the top of my ass.

"You're stunning," he said quietly, shocking the hell out of me.

"Thanks." Could I be more awkward? What was I supposed to say to that?

He moved down, following his fingers with openmouthed kisses. My stomach flipped around like a wonky blender.

I turned my face on the pillow to see if I could catch his eyes to find out how he was truly feeling. When he looked up at me, my breath caught.

Falcon's eyes had always been intense. That was the kind of person he was. But the way he looked at me right then... god, it was like the way I imagined Elek looking at the Hungarian crown as he first approached it in the parliament building.

Single-minded desire bordering on obsession.

What kind of game was the man playing?

"Take a shower with me?" he asked, still speaking quietly in the silent house.

I nodded before the suspicious part of me had a chance to take hold and turn into a royal bitch. When Falcon stood, he reached his hand out to help me up. His expression was no longer semi-feral but concerned and affectionate. He was making me dizzy with all this emotion, and I wondered if maybe I was projecting all of it.

It was way more likely the man was thinking, "Yeah, good fuck. Shower, bed, sleep." And here I was assuming he was thinking flowery things about me as a human being.

I let out a scoff halfway to the bathroom door. Falcon turned back to me with a frown. "You okay? Was I too rough?"

Dammit. More mixed signals. "No. Um… no. Not at all. It was…"

Get it together, Kingston. Jesus.

"Really fucking good," I finished.

Falcon's face widened in a relieved grin. This was such a strange new side of him, I was taken aback.

"Yeah, me too," he said before continuing to lead me into the bathroom. "It's been an embarrassingly long time. I was afraid I'd forgotten how to do it."

I barked out a surprised laugh. "Is that possible?"

He turned on the water in the shower and looked back at me over his shoulder. "You never know. According to you, I might have been too old to have a working dick anymore."

Falcon's body was muscular and fit. Even though there was some premature gray smattered among the darker hair on his chest, he was hot as fuck. The man looked like something out of military porn, the kind of scene where you got drilled by your sergeant.

The thought of him in uniform, screaming at me to give him twenty, made my dick plump a little bit.

Falcon noticed.

"Fuck, how young *are* you?"

"Shut up. You're hot." I moved past him into the shower, reaching out a hand first to make sure the temperature was bearable.

"You've already come twice tonight," he said, stepping in behind me and sliding his palms up my back to squeeze my shoulders. It felt amazing.

"Keep touching me like that and I'll be working up to a third," I moaned, letting my head drop forward into the spray.

After a few minutes of silence, Falcon turned me around and put his arms around my back. Our wet dicks touched in a way that seemed even more intimate than the sex we'd had.

"Thank you for telling me about Paris and Elek. How it all started."

I shrugged. "You didn't have to reassure me about my family. That... meant a lot."

His finger came under my chin and tilted it up. "Something about you makes me break rules more than I should, Kingston." Falcon's eyes studied me, his face serious instead of teasing.

"I'm certainly not going to apologize if that's what you're waiting for."

Falcon smiled. "No. I don't expect you to. I'm a grown man in charge of my own actions."

I felt nervous suddenly, like this was the moment he'd pull the rug out from under me. "Is this the part where you tell me it can never happen again?"

Apparently, I'd lowered my eyes again because I felt him lift my chin once more.

"It should be. But no. This is the part where I beg you to sleep in my bed with me so I can touch your naked body all night."

My stomach plummeted down and swooped back up again. Now it was my turn to smile.

"Should I make you beg?"

His laughter was sexy as fuck, and it made me grin even more stupidly. "King Wilde, will you please—"

I didn't let him finish. I jumped up and crushed my mouth to his, throwing my arms around his neck and enjoying the wet slide of our bodies together.

When we finally dried off and got into bed, I was exhausted but giddy, stupid but happy.

And safe in the arms of someone solid, someone trustworthy and dependable. I knew it wasn't a relationship, but it still felt nice being with someone who hopefully was more indicative of my future than my past. He was honest and lawful, the way I wanted to be, moving forward. Unlike the manipulator who still lived inside my head and taunted me from the past.

Just before slipping into deep sleep, a fleeting memory sifted through my consciousness in Elek's heavy accent.

"That agent of yours is going to have a nice night tonight, Kingston. He will finally get his hands on you."

Even in sleep, I couldn't avoid the man. I only hoped the remembered line didn't have any kind of meaning.

When I awoke, there were no longer warm arms around me, and the cool sheets of the bed beside me indicated Falcon had been up for a while. I wondered if this magic bubble feeling could ever be recaptured, but I knew it wouldn't matter for at least eighteen hours or however long of a workday we had ahead of us.

The gala was tonight, and it was time to focus.

I got up and ran fingers through my hair on the way to the bathroom to get cleaned up for the day. When I joined everyone in the kitchen, the only indicator that anything had happened between Falcon and me the night before was the slight pinkening of his cheeks. He didn't look up at me, but clearly he knew when I entered the room.

"The tailor should be here in a few minutes," Linney said. "Grab some food. There are breakfast sandwiches in the oven."

"Thanks," I mumbled. "What else is on the agenda today?"

Ziv typed noisily at the kitchen table. "We got some translation back from our team at the home office. There was some chatter about a housekeeper who'd been caught stealing things. Didn't sound like something huge though. Still, it could have been enough reason to alarm the tunnel exit."

Mouse stood by the coffee maker. "Did you sleep okay?"

I couldn't help but glance over at Falcon. If it was possible, his concentration was even more focused on whatever was on the laptop in front of him. I cleared my throat. "Yeah, good. You?"

"I was too excited to get back to sleep. I kept wondering what else we missed. Did Elek ever steal something else important and display it in his home?"

I thought for a minute. He had plenty of art on the walls of our apartment, but much of it was forged. I remembered something. "He had a dagger. It wasn't a forgery. The Shah Jahan dagger. Have you heard of it?"

Mouse shook his head. Linney's forehead crinkled in thought. I forged ahead. "It's worth millions. And he was very proud of it in the short time between when we stole it and when he sold it. It was in a display case in the living room. Some of my assumptions about the security on the crown are based on how he had the dagger displayed, but I have to assume that he would go all out on the security of the crown in a way he wouldn't for a lesser piece."

Falcon turned to me. Our eyes met for the first time since last night. Heat rush through my stomach, but I tried to ignore it. "King, did he ever have an item he put round-the-clock guards on? Maybe something like the Van Gogh that he only owned for a little while until he could fence it?"

I opened my mouth to say no before I remembered one instance. "Wait, there was one time… We had stolen…"

I paused, unused to just putting it out there. Confessing to a massive art theft in front of several FBI agents wasn't easy. Falcon waited patiently. He must've understood my hesitation.

"Um, we had stolen the John Singer Sargent from the Imperial War Museum in London."

Before I could say anything else, Linney sucked in a breath. "That was you?"

Mouse put his hand over his mouth. Ziv got a knowing smirk on his face. Falcon's nostrils flared and he looked away from me.

I nodded at Linney and continued. "Obviously, we were terrified of being found out. We would have been killed. So Elek arranged for additional security until we were out of danger. I thought of it as more protection for us than for the painting, but I can't be sure. That's the only time I can remember having more security than just Tibor."

Ziv pulled up something on his computer. "Tibor Varga, Elek's manservant?"

"Yeah," I said before taking a quick sip of coffee. "He's sort of a jack-of-all-trades. Part butler, part personal security, part driver, and I guess whatever else Elek wants from him."

Falcon turned back to his own computer and clicked a few keys. "According to our intel, Tibor is still there. The reports say he's quiet but intimidating. I wonder where he falls in the security team now. Do you think he would be in charge of the newer agents?"

"I'm not sure. There's a security consultant Elek would have brought in on the security implementation for the house. He's Serbian, but he lives in Paris. Now that man made me nervous as hell."

Falcon turned to Ziv, but the hacker spoke before Falcon opened his mouth. "On it."

Falcon nodded and turned back to me. At this point it was an unspoken agreement that we were both all business. It was time to go to work. "Do you have a name?"

I shook my head. "Elek only ever referred to him as the security consultant."

Falcon nodded. "What else can you think of? Did you give the information on the security brackets you mentioned to Mouse?"

I nodded before grabbing a breakfast sandwich and joining him at the table. "All of the manufacturers and parts I've ever seen used in Elek's home are on the list I gave to Mouse. I also made a list of all of the things that I've learned about since then that Elek's security consultant may have implemented in the new house. But, keep in mind, I don't have the kind of resources that an agency like Interpol, CIA, MI5, and the FBI have. So I'm sure there are plenty of things I'm unaware of. My specialty is museum-level security. Residential level is easy by comparison."

While Falcon went over my lists with Mouse, I ate my sandwich and got to work. It seemed like the tailor arrived only a few minutes later.

The rest of the day passed quickly. Before I could even catch my breath, it was time to get ready for the gala. Nerves swirled in my gut at the prospect of seeing Elek.

Linney fussed with microphones and microscopic cameras on my tuxedo, Mouse must've showed me how to use the fingerprint retrieval device a thousand times, and Ziv continued to make his opinion about me going into the gala clear to Falcon.

Meanwhile, Falcon looked like he was in a trance. I couldn't decide if it was nerves, or if this was simply how he got into character before an op like this. Either way, his stoicism made my nerves even worse.

A luxury sedan had been delivered to our rental house so Falcon and I could arrive in style. Everyone else followed us in the van.

As soon as we pulled up in front of the address on the invitation, I realized I'd been here before. One of Elek's friends had hosted a party there one summer. It was when Elek had fallen in love with the island. There had been so many people in designer swimwear with fancy cocktails in their hands, it had looked like something from a lifestyles of the rich and famous photo shoot.

Now it looked like we were walking into the winter version of the same party. The place dripped money. But instead of looking uncomfortable, Falcon looked right at home. It made me realize I had never asked about his childhood. I had no idea whether he came from money, where he grew up, or what his background was like at all. And I wanted to know all of those things.

"I've been here before. I didn't realize it until I recognized the house," I admitted.

Falcon looked over at me in surprise, the new red hair and trendy horn-rim glasses throwing me off. "Anything we need to know? I mean, besides what we learned from the blueprints and social media photos."

I studied the house as Falcon pulled the car up the long driveway. "I didn't spend much time inside the house because it was more of a pool party, but I remember there's a ballroom and several smaller salons. If the party has access to all of them, maybe I can find one of the smaller salons to hide out in while you try to put your eyes on our target."

We only had a few moments left before it was our turn with the valet. "You're really going to let me be the one to find the boyfriend?"

"You're the boss, right?" I teased.

"Why do I feel like I'm being manipulated?" he muttered.

After leaving the car with the valet, we entered the large residence past twin gas lanterns mounted next to the wide wooden double doors. As we moved inside, I noticed hundreds of candles lit, some in wall sconces, some in table candelabras, and some in actual candle chandeliers. It was like stepping back in time.

I could hear violin music coming from farther in the house. Servers mingled through the guests with trays of champagne and small bites. Conversation and laughter surrounded us while attendants offered to take anything we wanted to check in the cloakroom. We declined, having left our coats in the car on purpose in case we needed a quick getaway.

As we stepped through the foyer, Falcon reached out and took my hand. It surprised me. I turned to look at him with a raised eyebrow. His cheeks flushed immediately.

"I'm your date, right? The ambassador to France knows David Kennedy is gay, right? So I get to hold your hand."

I grinned at him, squeezing his hand. "Why do you sound so defensive? I'm never going to complain about you holding my hand in public. You're the hottest guy in the room. It only makes me look better if I'm the one who's hand you're holding."

He blushed a deeper red and looked away, scanning the room like a seasoned pro. While I knew he was trying to identify the players among us, he simply looked like any other socialite hunting for his golf buddies. Who knew the man had training?

I guessed that was a silly question.

"David! So good to see you again," a voice called out. I turned my head to see who it was. The man looking at me was familiar, but it wasn't the ambassador.

CHAPTER FIFTEEN

FALCON

"Hi," King said, looking a little unsure of who the man was. But when King spotted the woman on his arm, recognition dawned. "Serena, how lovely to see you again."

He reached out to kiss the woman's cheek before shaking her husband's hand.

"Jacques and Serena, I'd like you to meet my partner, Ethan Reeves." He turned to me. "Jacques and Serena play tennis at the same club I do in Paris. While Serena is perfectly lovely on the court, Jacques is a holy terror."

King winked at them both, and I dutifully barked out a laugh, reaching out to shake hands with Jacques and kiss Serena's cheek with a murmured compliment about her lovely gown.

"What are you doing in Greece?" Serena asked. "We thought you would be back in Colorado with your family."

Colorado? King's family lived in Texas.

"They hired some extra help on the Christmas tree farm this year so I could come to Greece with my sweetheart. I had a wonderful trip here years ago, and Ethan knew," King said, looking at me with affection that took me by surprise, "it was my dream to come back one day."

Suddenly, I remembered it wasn't King Wilde they knew. It was David Kennedy. While King had given me some basic intel on his David Kennedy alias, like where he lived and what he supposedly did for a living, we hadn't had time for lots of background and honestly hadn't thought we'd need it.

I rested my hand possessively on King's lower back. "I couldn't wait any longer to bring him here. The look in his eyes when he talks about Greece is... Well, let's just say I plan on bringing him back many more times in the future." I gazed lovingly at him and moved my hand around to his hip to pull him tighter to my side.

It felt incredible to claim him in public even if it was all an act. Pretending he was truly mine was like having a taste of what it would be like. And it would be pretty damned good.

King leaned in and pressed a kiss to my cheek, giving me a whiff of his expensive cologne. "You spoil me," he murmured before turning back to the couple with a cheeky grin. "Not that I'm complaining."

They chuckled and began gossiping about fellow tennis players, allowing me to continue searching for our target. After a few minutes with no luck, I began politely excusing myself so I could have a better look around. I leaned in to kiss King's temple before telling him I was going to grab us some drinks from the bar. "Would you like anything?" I asked Serena and Jacques. They declined since they already had cocktails in hand.

After meeting King's eyes one last time, I smiled at him. "Be right back, sweetheart."

His eyes widened almost imperceptibly at the endearment, but he quickly schooled his expression and returned my smile. "Take your time. Nobody likes a rushed old-fashioned."

I left the three of them and made my way deeper into the stately home toward the ballroom. There was a bar just inside the giant vaulted room, so I went there first. After placing my drinks order, I rested my elbow on the bar and scanned the room. A deep, booming laugh caught my attention near one of the large round tables against a nearby wall. There stood Elek Kemény holding court with a table full of sycophants hanging on his every word.

He was surprisingly charismatic. I could tell right away that his easy charm and commanding presence attracted people to pay attention to him. He was also larger than I'd expected. Maybe not taller than I was, but he was very muscular. In person, he looked even more built than his brutish butler bodyguard. He looked more like a Hungarian farmer than Hungarian royalty. How anyone could mistake him as descended from the Károlyi line was beyond me.

One of the men sitting closest to where Elek stood looked up at him with stars in his eyes. Demitri was the man whose prints we needed. Now it was a matter of getting the two men separated so we could get close enough to Demitri without tipping Elek off to our unusual interest in his date.

As soon as the bartender handed me the two drinks, I made my way back to King.

"Here you are, sweetheart," I said, handing him the old-fashioned.

"Thanks, babe. Did you have any trouble finding the bar?" he asked, clearly meaning our target.

"I found it right away." I took a sip of my drink. "The ballroom is awfully stuffy though. Let's wait a bit before we go in there if you don't mind."

"Of course." King turned to his friends. "I think I'm going to show Ethan the music room and maybe the terrace views as well. Would you care to join us?"

Please don't join us.

"Oh no, thank you," Serena said. "I'm going to drag Jacques into the ballroom and force him to dance. It was great seeing you and wonderful meeting you, Ethan. Hopefully David will bring you along for our next round-robin."

I smiled at her and nodded. "I'd love that, as long as you promise to go easy on me."

Once they'd wandered off, King took my hand and began leading me toward the back of the house where three sets of wide double doors stood open letting in cold, fresh air to mitigate the heat coming out of the crowded ballroom. He started to duck into a room off to the side but froze for a split second and turned us around.

"You know what? Bad idea. The ambassador is in there, and I think it would be best if we just avoid another bout of small talk if you don't mind."

I didn't mind at all. The last thing I wanted was to watch some beautiful Frenchman flirt with my date. My... work colleague. Whatever.

We made our way out onto the deep, wide stone terrace overlooking a beautiful pool deck teeming with potted plants and flowers. Beyond the pool lay the Aegean Sea, sparkling serenely in the moonlight.

"Gorgeous," King said softly.

I turned to agree but found him staring at me instead of the water. My face heated. "Don't do that. You're going to make me hard," I said under my breath, forgetting about my team listening to our every word.

"Even better," he teased.

I pointed to my button mic and lifted an eyebrow at him. He had the decency to wince in apology even though I was the one who'd said something inappropriate. I reached for his hand again and squeezed before slipping my arm around his waist and pulling him close so I could nuzzle under his ear.

"Our target and his date are together at a round table to the left of the bar just inside the ballroom," I said as softly as I could. King's entire body shuddered as my breath blew into his ear. "I need to separate them so you can get what we need while I distract the date. So this is how we're going to do it."

I continued murmuring in his ear, dropping kisses along his neck while I spoke so it looked to any observer like I was simply lavishing him with endearments while loving on him. There were a few other people cooling off outside, but they weren't close enough to worry too much about.

When I wrapped up my plan and asked if he had anything he wanted to add, I noticed King's Adam's apple bob with a swallow. "Uh-huh," he croaked.

"What is it, sweetheart?" I teased him in a low voice.

He swallowed again. "What is what?"

"You wanted to add something."

"Mmm."

I leaned in and lightly traced the edge of his ear with my tongue.

King sucked in a breath. "Oh god," he breathed, squeezing his eyes closed.

If only we weren't on a damned mission, I could stand out here all night and tease him like this. He was beautiful and wide open. The man didn't hold back how my touches made him feel.

"The op," I reminded him softly.

"Nothing to add," he managed to say. "All good. Please... please stop. I can't..."

But I couldn't. Now that I'd tasted his clean skin, I wanted to remind myself of what his mouth tasted like too. I turned him to face me, and then I lied. "Your friends are coming, and I don't want them to delay us." And then I cupped his face and leaned in to kiss the hell out of him.

King melted in my arms and kissed me back with abandon as if he'd been dying to get his mouth on mine the same way I'd been with him. It was over all too soon when I spotted our target conveniently saunter out onto the terrace. I braced myself, expecting Elek to follow him. If Elek spotted King, it wouldn't be good. Not only would it increase his security at home, but it would also most likely cause a confrontation we wouldn't be able to control.

If Elek came out here, I'd have to keep him from spotting King. And I was fully prepared to pull King back into a kiss for the sake of the mission if need be.

Ahem.

But he didn't follow. Which meant this was our chance to get what we needed. I pulled back and met King's eyes, still holding his face. "Showtime. I'm going to distract the date. Your man is behind you about twenty feet. I'll wait for Linney to tell me when, and then I'll meet you by the front door."

Without thinking, I leaned in and kissed him again like he was my fucking boyfriend or something.

He blinked at me in surprise and then gave me his patented cheeky grin. "Aye, aye, Captain."

I rolled my eyes and made a beeline for the ballroom.

Thankfully, Elek was still holding court at the table. Maybe his date had simply walked out for a cigarette. Either way, we were lucky.

Since Elek didn't seem eager to follow his boyfriend, all I had to do was stand at the bar and order another drink while keeping an eye on him.

Unfortunately, that only lasted until I took the first sip of my fresh drink. And then, it was like a switch flipped and Elek realized his date was missing.

He strode across the room toward the terrace doors, but I was able to cut him off before he exited the ballroom.

"It's Elek, right?" I asked, hoping like hell King had been right when he'd told me a simple hair wig and eyeglasses disguise would be enough to keep the art thief from recognizing me. King had sworn the man didn't pay much attention to the videos and photos since it was details of the investigations he wanted, not visuals of the investigators.

His eyes narrowed at me. "And you are?"

"Ethan Reeves. I'm finally in a position to acquire some higher-level artwork, and someone gave me your name as a collector who might be able to advise me."

His forehead crinkled. "Who gave you my name?"

"Gene Vogler. He's a member of my golf club in the Hamptons, and we get together on occasion for drinks and cigars in the city. The last time we met, he suggested if I ever had a chance to pick your brain, I should be sure to introduce myself to you. Well, imagine my surprise when I overheard someone say your name."

The Hungarian seemed to relax a little at the mention of the contact's name and the corroborating info about the club in the Hamptons. It was intel King had given me.

"What exactly do you want advice about?" he asked, crossing his arms in front of his chest. I tried not to think about those muscular meat sticks causing harm to sweet King Wilde.

"I bought a Renoir at auction last month and hung it in my home office so I can stare at it when I'm supposed to be working," I admitted with a grin. "But I haven't done anything to bump up my home security, and I'm starting to get nervous about it."

Bingo. The art thief was awake and interested.

"Tell me what kind of security you have so far."

"Oh... uh..." I stammered, trying to act suddenly nervous. I looked around behind us. "I guess..." I laughed. "I guess it's not like anyone in here needs the money enough to steal it. I don't know why talking about it makes me so nervous."

Elek smiled. It was predatory. "You can trust me. Besides, I have one of the top security consultants in Paris on retainer. Maybe I can refer you to him."

"Oh, I... well, I'm not sure that's necessary yet. I only have the one piece. Everything else is lesser known like Cross and Laugé."

"What kind of security do you have for those?"

I began to rattle off the things I thought an idiot like Ethan Reeves would have if he didn't know what the fuck he was doing. As I spoke, Elek's face relaxed into a smile. King had been right when he'd said Elek's greed often overrode his smarts. If that was the case, how the hell did he succeed in stealing the unstealable crown?

A soft lilt spoke in my ear. "Time to go."

I stopped speaking and tilted my head at Elek. "You know... I feel like I'm monopolizing your time at this lovely party, and that wasn't my intention. I really just wanted to introduce myself and maybe offer to take you to dinner, if you'd be open to that. I'm here for three more days. Do you have any free time for dinner or drinks? My boyfriend and I would love to host you."

He seemed to consider it.

"Let me know the time and place, and I will check with my partner to see when he is available. Do you have a card?"

I pulled out one of the cards Ziv and Mouse had made for me. "I apologize again for interrupting your evening, but I really look forward to learning how better to protect my collection. I've heard about a Chagall coming up for auction soon, and I need to be ready if I have any hopes of keeping it safe. Thank you so much."

I reached out to shake his hand, trying not to wince as he pulled the asshole move of trying to prove his manliness with his grip. Thank god Ziv had managed to get a copy of Elek's fingerprints from a government database so I didn't have to get them tonight.

I made my way out of the ballroom to the foyer where I recognized the back of King's familiar build. After letting out a deep exhale and handing my valet ticket over to an attendant, I walked right up to him and slid my arms around his front, simply wanting his nearness to negate the manipulative man I'd just spent time with.

"I can smell his cologne on you," King growled under his breath.

I leaned into his ear so I could speak without the sound being picked up on the microphones. "Maybe someone needs to scrub it off me in the shower."

He turned around and launched himself at me, holding on tightly like we were long-lost lovers reuniting after a long separation. His body trembled against mine.

"Hey, hey," I said, rubbing his back. "Are you okay? What happened?"

"Can we leave please?"

"Of course. I already gave them the ticket for the car." I pulled back and studied his face, but I couldn't tell what he was upset about. "Let's go." I took his hand and led him outside where our car was already waiting.

Once we were finally alone in the car and headed out of the estate, King rubbed his hands over his face. "He had a bruise on his jaw."

"What? Who did?"

"Demitri. The new boy toy."

I pulled the car over and shifted into park before pulling out my earpiece and unhooking the hidden mic. I gestured for King to do the same. After telling Linney we were turning everything off now that we were safely away from the op, I slid the electronics into a zip-top bag and stuffed them into the glove compartment.

"C'mere," I said, pulling him in for another hug. "I'm sorry."

"It's fine," he said gruffly, pulling away and looking out the window. "I don't know why it even bothers me. If the kid doesn't want to be thrown around, maybe he should get the hell out."

Silence descended.

I couldn't help but reach over and brush the floppy locks off his forehead. "You of all people know it's not that easy," I said carefully.

"It should be."

"Yes. It definitely should be."

More silence. This time it was more comfortable. I continued brushing my fingers through King's hair.

"You know you can talk to me about it if you want," I told him. "Obviously you don't have to, but—"

I was half expecting him to snap at me, but he turned to me with a sweet smile. "Thank you, but I'm fine. I made my peace with myself about that part of it a long time ago. I just... it was hard seeing that nothing has fucking changed. He's still stealing art. He's still taking advantage of people less powerful than himself. He still thinks he's the most important fucking person in the room."

His anger didn't surprise me, but I had to admit it was frustrating to see how much of a hold Elek still had over King's emotions. It had been two years since the Van Gogh job. According to King, that had been the end of his relationship with the older man.

But here he was two years later still passionately engaged in his hatred. It was clear now that I hadn't needed to make up the lame story about DNA on the Greek coins to get King to help us out. He wasn't doing it for immunity.

He was doing it for revenge against Elek.

Part of me wished he didn't care enough about the guy to get worked up over him one way or another. Was that selfish of me? Sure. But even if King wasn't interested in me, I still wanted him to be free of the stronghold the Hungarian seemed to still have over him.

"Then let's get back to the house and make sure our strategy is flawless so we can take away the thing he values most." I shifted the car into drive and pulled back onto the road. After a few minutes, King shifted in his seat, his thoughts still back at the gala.

"I don't just want him to lose the crown, Falcon. I want him to lose his freedom."

Unfortunately, that wasn't something I was going to be able to accomplish. Nadine's instructions were to carry out this op silently, meaning Elek Kemény would be left alone as soon as we took the crown back.

But I didn't dare tell King that. There was no telling what he'd do.

CHAPTER SIXTEEN

KING

My entire body still jangled with adrenaline and nerves. I'd spotted Elek for the first time in over two years. Seeing him across the large ballroom had been even more nerve-racking than I'd expected. I was hit with the immediate gut feeling that I wasn't good enough or that I needed to work hard to please him. Being faced with that Pavlovian response was both eye-opening and depressing. It illustrated just how much control he'd had over me that I'd never realized.

Coming into contact with Elek's new lover hadn't been a picnic either. I felt like my emotions had gone ten rounds tonight.

But I'd meant what I'd said. I wanted Elek put away.

"King. You know that's not part of our mission," Falcon said carefully.

"It could be."

"Yes, it could be. But one of the goals of the mission is for it to not attract attention in the media or other intelligence agencies."

"Isn't Interpol already involved?" I asked, wishing my brain didn't feel like jumbled up nonsense.

"No. They're involved in our attempts to capture *you*, not our attempts to retrieve the crown. Linney is working with us in an unofficial capacity because she's an integral part of my team and I trust her not to report back to her supervisors at Interpol. This retrieval op is purely an FBI mission. It's not the global task force."

That rang a bell. But also reminded me how little I knew. My brain spun, trying to reframe the situation to fit this new information. "And the fingerprints you have for Elek? How do you have his and not Demitri's?"

Falcon shook his head. "Demitri is a Greek national. His prints aren't in any file I have access to, and it would have been a big deal if I'd requested them from Greece's national intelligence."

I slumped in the leather seat. "I'm surprised your hacker friend couldn't have gotten them," I muttered.

"He could have. But if he'd been caught, it would have been a disaster. Why are you acting grumpy all of a sudden? I thought that was my job."

He was trying to jolly me. It didn't work.

"I'm annoyed. It's one more reminder that I'm not actually a member of this fucking team. There's shit you're not telling me. At every turn I learn something new that changes things."

Falcon turned into the driveway of our rental. "How does this change anything?"

As soon as he put the car in park, I grabbed his shirtfront. "Because it means I don't have immunity with anyone but the US. Did that even occur to you?"

I could tell by the look in his eyes it had.

"Fuck," I spat, pushing him away and turning to get out of the car. "This was such a fucking mistake. God, I knew it."

Instead of heading to the house, I strode in the direction of the cliffs again. I needed room to think. When I heard Falcon's footsteps behind me, I turned to confront him.

"Not this time," I barked at him. "Don't."

He stood and stared at me. I could tell he was torn between doing what I asked and doing what his heart told him I truly needed.

I let out a breath and walked up to him, taking his face in my hands. "Please just let me think for a little while. That... op wasn't easy for me. And I just..."

Falcon's smile was easy, but his eyes were still intense. "Want to be fucked face-first into the mattress?"

I snorted. "That too. But first I need to take a walk. By myself."

Falcon nodded and then clenched his teeth for a bit before saying something he looked like he wanted to take back immediately. "Please don't leave."

My heart squeezed in my chest. I wanted so badly to think he wanted me to stay because he had feelings for me. But the rational part of my brain knew he needed me to stay for the success of this operation. And his career was riding on that. He may have liked me fine, but his career was everything to him. His reputation in the FBI would always take precedence.

I knew what my role was here.

"I'm not leaving," I assured him. "I promise."

Falcon stepped closer and slid his arms around me. I was in danger of becoming addicted to the feeling of him holding me like that. Part of me wondered if that was the point. He sure had an easy way of making me want to stay.

"I know what you're thinking," he said. "And you're wrong." He leaned in to kiss me. It was sweet and all consuming. There was no hint of subterfuge or insincerity in the way he danced his lips along mine, the way his tongue darted in to taste me. This was the true Dirk Falcon. And while I wasn't sure whether or not I could trust him to keep me out of prison, I knew damned well I could trust that kiss.

The man had feelings for me the way I was quickly developing them for him.

And in some ways, that was more terrifying than the thought of prison. Because feelings or not, I knew there wasn't a future in which FBI agent Dirk Falcon could build a life with the notorious art thief Le Chaton.

He pulled away and turned, briskly walking back to the house and leaving me breathless and panting in the cold night air. After a few beats, I turned in the opposite direction and continued my walk to the cliffs.

My fingers itched with the desire to race back over to the gala and peel that fucking painting off the wall. I felt like an addict. This was one of the moments I'd feared when I'd sworn off stealing art anymore.

It wasn't that easy. Not when there were still wrongs to right.

But there would always be stolen artwork in the world. I needed a distraction.

I pulled out my cell phone and dialed MJ. It should be lunchtime in California. She'd already sent me a million pictures of the wedding and the crazy drunken reception that lasted well into the night. They'd all had so much fun, they'd decided to stay a little longer in Napa.

"Hey, baby brother," she said when the call went through. The familiar sound of her voice made something in me relax.

"Hey, yourself. How's it going in Napa?"

"Well, it's been rainy, but I'm not complaining too much. The Marians put on a massive wine tasting for us yesterday afternoon. Needless to say, we got hammered. I'm only just now waking up. How are things there?"

"Fine. I mean, not fine. But... Well, the op is fine, my heart... not so much."

MJ's tone softened. "How so your heart? Tell me what's going on."

I thought for a minute about what I wanted to admit and what I wanted to keep close to the vest. Honestly, I needed a friend. I needed someone I could trust completely, someone who could give me perspective. "I've done something stupid."

"Stupider than stealing priceless works of art?"

"I'm being serious. I think... I think I'm falling for the FBI agent. And, before you say anything, I know how stupid that is. I know I can't trust him. This is the man who's been after me for years, who's wanted to put me in prison, whose entire career is based on prosecuting art thieves. But... I... I don't know. It's like... It's like I can't help it. And I'm not sure I want to."

"Aww," MJ cooed. "Baby brother's falling in love. Finally. Tell me all about the stud muffin."

She didn't get it. "This is not a good thing, MJ. This is awful. There's no future for me with this guy. And more than that, I just realized that my immunity deal does not cover me from prosecution by other entities outside of the US."

I heard a woman's voice speaking softly in the background. I was sure it was MJ's girlfriend, Neckie. "I'm sorry, sis. I didn't mean to interrupt your time with Neckie. Tell her hello for me."

"It's fine. She just asked me if I wanted some coffee. We have some time before she gets back. Listen, about the immunity deal, you told me there was no evidence against you and that we didn't really need to worry about making sure you were covered."

"I know, and that's still true. I can tell the bullshit he told me about the Berlin job was probably just that. Bullshit. But, remember the exclusion in the contract? It says I'm not protected against prosecution and crimes related to the theft of the Hungarian crown. But this whole mission is to steal the crown from the person who has it."

"Honey, you're protected while on a sanctioned mission. That crown mission is sanctioned, right?"

I looked out across the water, noticing the current had picked up, causing whitecaps to form. It was less welcoming than usual, more menacing and dark. It was like the Aegean was reflecting my own mood.

"Yes, it's sanctioned. But..."

"King, do not tell me you're planning something outside of this mission." MJ's bossy sister voice made it very clear that was unacceptable.

"The man who has the crown... He... he was the one who got me into all of this. I want... I want him to get punished."

There was silence from the other end. I wasn't sure if MJ was thinking through what I had said, or if she was gathering herself up to tear me a new one. It turned out to be the latter.

"King, you promised you were done with this life. You wanted to be done. You very specifically told me you wanted to be on the right side of the law from here on out. If you follow the FBI's instructions on this mission, you will be fulfilling your plan for the future. But if you decide to go rogue, to do something stupid like a criminal would do, then you will be right back where you were before. And you'll be no better than the man who got you into this. I want you to think about that."

She was right. That was never in doubt. But that didn't mean it was an easy pill to swallow.

"I just... I just want to see if there's a way to do both. The FBI can get the crown back, and they can nail a longtime art thief in the process. Wouldn't that be a good thing?"

"No!" MJ's shout came through the phone enough to hurt my ear. "You listen to me right now. The minute they have that man in custody, he starts telling them every single thing Kingston Wilde did wrong while you were working together. He tells them every heist you ever planned, every illegal move you ever made, and every illegal move you ever even considered. He tells them where to find evidence of your work, he tells them where your money came from, and he provides all kinds of proof we have to assume he has for your roles in a million thefts you committed together. You're crazy if you want your special agent to get that man in an interrogation room."

The idea of agent Falcon questioning Elek made my blood run cold. Of course she was right. But...

"I have immunity for all of that. Even if he gives them all the proof in the world of what I did when I was with him, the FBI can't prosecute me for any of it. So why do I care?"

MJ sighed. "Now, we're talking in circles. The reason you care is because Interpol can prosecute you, the French national police can prosecute you—hell, every European country has a law enforcement agency that would love to prosecute you. Yes, you have your little book of stolen artwork, but we don't know for sure how well it will work as a bargaining chip. You cannot let that man get taken into custody."

"Fuck."

MJ chuckled softly. "Yes. Exactly. Plus, it's unnecessary. That man is your past. The FBI agent may not be your future, King, but somebody is. And if you want a chance with future man, you have to let past man go."

She didn't know what she was talking about. But she was right about one thing. We were talking in circles. Nothing I could say would make her understand.

I ran fingers through my hair and walked around in circles. "I'm just so mixed up. We went to a party tonight, and Elek was there. I saw him across the room. And I... I..." I blew out a breath. "It just brought up so many old feelings for me."

MJ's voice was kind when she spoke. "I can tell. And I'm sorry. I'm not sure your special agent would be happy about it, but do you want me to come there? Do you need one of us to be there for you? You know any of us would drop anything and come be there in a heartbeat."

Her generous offer made my eyes sting. I shook my head stupidly as if she could see me. "No. Thanks though. I'll be okay. Just needed to get some things off my chest."

After a few beats of silence, MJ's voice came over the line again. "Tell me about your agent. Is he hot?"

I barked out a laugh. "So hot. *Sooo* hot. Like surface of the sun hot. And he's... a good kisser. And... a good lots of other things."

MJ chuckled. "TMI, little brother. I'm surprised to hear you've gotten that close to him. From what I could tell during the contract negotiations, the man is a bit of a stickler for the rules."

I was grinning like a fool. "Oh he is. Believe me, he is. I think it's killing him that he's losing control over himself. Not that I mind— it's kind of fun to watch."

I thought of Falcon waiting for me in the kitchen with the rest of the team. "I'd better go. Listen, MJ, this really helped a lot. Thank you for being there. Always."

"Always. I'm really glad you called. I love you. We all love you."

I took my time returning to the house, but as soon as I was through the front door, the raised voices in the kitchen made me wish I'd hurried.

"What's going on in here?" I asked, noticing Falcon had taken off that ridiculous wig, revealing his short military cut.

Falcon's eyes stayed on his computer while his fingers flew over the keyboard. It was Ziv who looked up at me with an apologetic face. "We have a problem. Demitri Lazarus's fingerprints are setting off all kinds of red flags."

I tried to process what he was saying. "Why?"

Mouse's forehead creased. "Don't know yet. Could be he's an intelligence asset, could be he has diplomatic immunity, or could be suspected of something."

"How did we not already know this?" I asked.

Ziv's tone was defensive. "This isn't a sanctioned mission. Interpol doesn't even know we're here. How the hell would we know the identification or alias of a foreign national?"

I looked at the senior agent in the room. "Falcon?"

Without looking up he told me to take a seat and be quiet for a minute. I could tell he was stressed, and I knew better than to start asking a lot of questions if he was in the middle of something. I took a seat and looked over at Mouse. His expression was serious.

"What country? Greece?"

Mouse shook his head. Linney was the one who answered. "That's what Falcon's trying to find out. He's messaging with his boss."

Falcon's tuxedo jacket was hanging on a hook by the front door, his tie was nowhere to be found, and his shirtsleeves were rolled up, revealing those muscular forearms that made my stomach clench with attraction. I tried not to look.

I cleared my throat and looked at Ziv. "What else? Do we have any intel on his father? Isn't that why Elek trusted him in the first place? He's friends with the kid's father. Right?"

"Well, that's what we thought. Now..." Ziv shrugged. "Who knows?"

Falcon sighed and looked up, raking his hand through his short hair.

"Excellent," Falcon muttered. "A covert FBI mission on foreign soil intersecting with an unknown Greek intelligence asset and/or crime boss. No big deal. I'm sure it's going to be fine."

CHAPTER SEVENTEEN

FALCON

Well, this complicated things. Now we had to wonder why in the world Elek was mixed up with yet another asset of some kind. Was it because of the crown? Another art theft? Or could, by some chance, another intelligence agency have an agent in place for the same reason we did?

To bring Le Chaton to justice.

I looked over at King, who was noticeably agitated by this news. His hair looked like he'd stuck his hand in a light socket. I tried to reassure him. "It's okay. We'll figure this out."

"You can't know it's okay. You and I are both aware of how bad this could be for me." There was tension around King's mouth I hadn't seen since that first night on the plane. I hated to see it now.

"Then we'll take you off the op." I kept my eyes on King's even as Ziv began to bluster.

"Boss, you can't really mean that. King is the only one of us who can get into that room and get his hands on the crown."

"He's right," Linney said softly. "You know he's right. King is our only chance at this. And you need this mission to succeed."

King rubbed his face with his hands. "It's fine. It's fine, I'll do it."

"No." My voice came out low and strong, surprising the entire team. I cleared my throat. "Not until we make sure it's safe, at least. We simply need to regroup and come up with a plan that takes Demitri Lazarus out of the picture. Ziv, find out if there are any airplane tickets or private plane reservations under any name associated with Elek, Demitri, his father, or any other name we can think of associated with this op."

Ziv nodded and went to work on his computer. I could tell Mouse was thinking hard. "Mouse, what do you have?"

His forehead crinkled. "Well, it's kind of crazy, but what if…" He paused, unsure.

"Spit it out, baby boy," Linney said with a kind smile.

Mouse sat forward, clasping his hands together on the table in front of him. "If Greece has an agent with Elek because of suspected art crime… what if… what if we gave Greece's art crime team something else to worry about?"

King's face lit up with a feral grin. "Mouse, my dear friend, I am in love with you. Anything you want, sky's the limit, it's yours. I'm in."

I didn't like what he was implying. "Whatever you're thinking, King, the answer is no."

King clasped his hands together in a prayer. "But Dad… I've been so good. And I know where I can get my hands on some lovely Greek coins and ingots. Pretty please?"

Linney snorted, and Mouse covered a chuckle with his hand.

I rolled my eyes and shook my head at all of them. "Are you fucking crazy? You are proposing that an FBI team plan a heist on foreign soil?"

King shook his head. "No, the FBI doesn't need to be involved at all. I know someone—"

I felt my jaw tighten. "You're not going to Berlin. I can see right through you, Kingston Wilde. No amount of sweet-talking is going to get me to agree."

My computer pinged with a message from Nadine. I let out a breath. "Crisis averted. Demitri is flagged for participating in anti-government riots when he was younger."

"He still *is* younger," Linney said with a snort.

"Dating his daddy's BFF," King said with a melodramatic shudder. "He obviously likes older men. I caught Demitri eyeing up Falcon at the gala."

I shot him a look. "I'm *thirty-eight*. Stop comparing me to your smarmy sixty-year-old ex..."

King's eyes twinkled. "Men get grumpy when they get older, don't they, Mouse?"

Mouse hid his grin behind his hand. "Please don't get me fired."

Ziv cut in. "Found something. It looks like Daddy has a private plane that has made arrangements to leave the island tomorrow with five passengers. According to the preliminary flight plan, the passengers include both Elek and the boy toy."

"That can't be right," I said. "Elek was seriously considering my dinner invitation."

Linney shrugged. "Maybe that just means he'll cancel his trip to have dinner with you. It's not like it's a big inconvenience when you're traveling on a private plane."

I wondered if my impromptu dinner invitation had been the one thing that had screwed up our ability to get both Elek and Demitri out of the way for the crown retrieval op. That would have been just my luck.

"Where are they flying to?" King asked.

Ziv typed a few more keys to confirm. "Paris."

King blew out a breath. "Shit. Now what?"

"What if I cancel the dinner invitation? Or delay it for a couple of weeks? It doesn't really matter since we weren't actually going through with it." But as the words left my mouth, I realized we had the exact opportunity we needed to distract both Elek and Demitri. I looked up and met King's eyes.

He grinned again. "Nope. You and I are having friends for dinner, and it's going to be glorious."

"But it won't be you," I corrected. "It will have to be Mouse since Ziv will be with you and Linney will be on comms." I looked over at the young agent. "Think you can be my boyfriend for the night?"

Mouse's face ignited, his cheeks flaming deep red as he sputtered out what sounded a little bit like an argument. "No. I mean... I can't. That is to say, of course... *not*. Of course not." He tightened his teeth together and winced. "I mean, of course. Yes, sir. I serve at the pleasure of the... you, I guess. Or, whatever. That's fine. It's fine. This is all..."

"Fine?" Linney teased.

"Shut up," Mouse muttered before getting up to fetch a cold bottle of water from the fridge. "I'm dating my boss now. Mother would be so proud."

I bit back a laugh. "You'll do great. It's just going to be a challenge to run the op while two of us are indisposed."

Ziv snorted. "Indisposed, heh."

"Oh dear," Mouse squeaked. "I... will I have to hold your hand? And stuff? Sure, well, that's fine. Of course, it's fine. All part of the... job. Right? Yeah."

I felt King's hand squeeze my knee under the table, and I reached down to grab it and squeeze back. It was the only thing that kept both of us from cracking up.

"I would tell you it's going to be fine," I told Mouse. "But it sounds like you've already got that covered."

As soon as Mouse replied, "Yeah, it's totally fine," the rest of us finally broke. The kitchen filled with laughter, and Mouse's face, if it was possible, got even redder.

When things died down, I spoke up. "Okay, off to bed with us. Tomorrow's going to be another long day, and everybody here needs to catch up on some sleep."

Everyone, including King, looked at me like I had just ripped off my face, revealing an alien in my place.

"Where is our boss, what have you done to him?" Linney asked.

Mouse giggled, and Ziv winked at Linney. King gave me a look that made me blush. I cleared my throat. "Okay, whatever. You all stay awake. I, however, I'm going to bed. And no old-man jokes behind my back after I leave."

I wandered out of the kitchen praying to any god who would

listen that King wouldn't stay up too much longer. I wanted my hands on him again, my mouth, my entire body. Everyone had been right. Normally, I would have stayed up another hour or two, debriefing about the gala op. But my brain couldn't focus. It was too distracted with the cologne-scented nearness of him, the floppy-haired goofiness of him, and the way he had of stringing up all my nerves when my body was close to him.

For the first time ever, I wanted something more than work. I wanted King Wilde.

When I got into the bedroom, I began undressing slowly, taking my time in hopes King would enter the room in time to take over. But he didn't. By the time he came in and closed the door behind himself, I was all the way down to my briefs.

King's eyes jumped right to the bulge at the front of the briefs. "Now that's a way to welcome a man to his bedroom."

I felt my neck heat. "Get your clothes off," I growled.

King's eyes darkened, and his fingers went straight to his shirt buttons. "Yes, sir," he murmured. The sound of his bedroom voice made my briefs even tighter.

So I took them off and made a show of crawling onto King's bed. I turned around and lay back, folding my hands behind my head so I could watch the show. King didn't disappoint.

He kept his eyes pinned on me as he slowly removed each article of clothing. With each piece, he removed a little more of the oxygen in the room as well, until I was panting.

"Should I find some appropriate music on my phone to accompany you?" I asked.

King smiled. "Is the visual stimulation not enough for you? You need auditory stimulation as well?"

He turned and stepped into the bathroom, coming out with a bottle of lube. After squirting some into his hand, he chucked the bottle on a nearby dresser and slathered the lube on his already hard cock. Soon, the squelching noise was all the auditory stimulation I needed.

"Get over here," I said roughly. "Before my palm makes some

auditory stimulation on your ass."

King did as I said, crawling up my body until we were face-to-face. I reached up to take his jaw in my hands to pull him down for a kiss.

We both groaned, relishing the feel of lips and tongue and the long night stretching out lazily ahead of us. I silently thanked the homebuilder for setting this bedroom apart from the others, because I knew when I got inside of King, I wouldn't be able to stay quiet.

After several long minutes of kissing, King pulled back and met my eyes. "Hi," he said with a shy grin. "I wasn't sure..."

He was never insecure outside of the bedroom, so when he expressed it in here, it surprised me. I had to remind myself that Elek had probably done a number on his trust.

"I am. Very sure. Even though I'm well aware of how stupid this probably is." I reached up and ran my fingers through the golden hanks of hair hanging down. "Not that your ego needs any stroking, but I can't seem to resist you. I hope it's not a huge mistake."

King's face was solemn. "I'm not going to betray you. I'm not going to do anything ever again to fuck up your career. I'm... I'm sorry, about... the Van Gogh job. I can't say I would have handled things differently, because I definitely didn't want to go to prison, but I'm sorry about the effect it had on your job."

His words surprised me. Never in a million years would I have expected King Wilde to feel remorse for his actions toward me in the past. He seemed to be sincere, but there was definitely still a part of me that had to remind myself he was a master manipulator, that knew he would do anything to stay free. I only hoped "anything" didn't include faking his interest in me.

"Thank you," I said. I brought his face closer with my hand on the back of his head and took his mouth with mine again. It didn't take long until both of us were writhing against each other, ready for more.

"Want you inside of me," King breathed. "Please."

As I reached for the table between the beds, King rolled off me onto his side. "The lube is on the dresser."

"Mine's right here. I was feeling optimistic earlier." I grabbed the bottle from the drawer and returned to see King's eyes closed in pleasure. He was stroking himself, waiting for me.

"Jesus fuck," I muttered, flipping the cap open as fast as my fingers would allow. "Look at you. *Jesus.*"

I reached between his legs and pushed them farther apart with the back of my hand. My fingers sought his entrance and went to work prepping him. King gasped the minute the cool lube hit his hot skin. I wanted to take in every micro reaction in his entire body: the soft little sounds, the quick breaths, the clenched fists, and the way his throat bared to me as he threw his head back.

King Wilde was living art. He was beautiful, mesmerizing, and thought provoking. I could have stared at him all day long.

"Oh god," King said in a rough voice. "I'm ready. Promise. *Please.*"

I pressed a second finger inside of him, relishing in the heat and squeeze that I was going to feel around my dick.

"You're so fucking gorgeous. I can't keep my eyes off you. I can't keep my hands off you." I clenched my teeth in frustration, knowing I shouldn't say the rest, but I couldn't help it. "I can't keep my thoughts off you."

King's eyes opened wide in surprise, but I looked away, concentrating on moving over him so that I could lose myself in his body and focus on the physical only.

Fucking. This was *fucking.*

King groaned as soon as I began to enter him.

And I forced myself to shut away any trace of true feelings for the enticing man beneath me and focus on the way his body made my body feel. We needed stress relief from the intensity of the gala op.

That's all this was.

Stress relief.

Yeah, keep telling yourself that...

And what the fuck are you going to do when King realizes you've been lying to him about the crown this entire time?

CHAPTER EIGHTEEN

KING

Falcon stretched me wide open, reminding me who had control here, who was in charge. His dominance was powerful and masculine. It checked off all my boxes and would have been more than enough to send me flying.

But then he'd said he hadn't been able to stop thinking of me.

That had made me feel a million times more defenseless, even more at his mercy than ever before.

Even when the agent had threatened my physical freedom, I hadn't felt as vulnerable as I did wondering if he had true feelings for me.

"Look at me. Where did you go?" Falcon asked in a deep grumble. "Stay with me."

I looked up into hooded eyes that seemed to see every part of me. "I'm here."

He stroked in hard and fast, taking my breath away and nudging my entire body up the bed. I threw back my head and bit into my lip to keep from screaming. A desperate whimper came out instead. I wanted more, whatever he was willing to give.

Falcon's eyes stayed on mine as one of his hands moved to the front of my throat. "Do not take your eyes off me."

There was no way in hell I could even if I wanted to.

And I didn't want to.

He held on to my throat while he fucked into me. My heart rammed harder in my chest than his cock did into my body. I reached up and grabbed for his head, pulling him down to kiss me so I could feel his soft lips during the hard fuck.

But as soon as his kisses started, everything changed.

The pace slowed. The tight grip on my throat turned into a sweet caress. The short, hard strokes into my body turned long and seductive.

I held on to the back of his head like it was a life preserver, like if I couldn't keep on kissing him, I'd sink below the surface and be lost forever.

I hated feeling this way. The last time I'd let someone have this kind of control over me was Elek. And hadn't I learned my lesson about that? Hadn't I decided not to let myself get pulled under so easily again?

But this was different. Falcon was different. He was honest and true. Those eyes couldn't hide anything from me even if he wanted to.

"Dirk." I tested the word against his mouth. He groaned and moved to press his cheek against mine.

"Sweetheart, you're killing me."

There was a lump in my throat. "I'm trying so hard not to..." I couldn't finish it.

Fall for you.

His lips mouthed kisses against my jaw until they got to my ear. "Me too, but I can't stop." The words were whispered softly before his hips began pounding again, taking the rest of my breath away.

Had he known what I'd meant? Or had he thought I meant something simpler? *I'm trying so hard not to...*

Come.

Scream.

Laugh.

He pulled out and shoved me onto my front before pulling my

ass back into his pelvis and slamming home again. This time I did scream. Thank fuck I had just enough time to shove a pillow into my mouth first.

In this position, every stroke lit me up inside. I babbled my desperation into the pillow until Falcon's hand found my dick and stroked me off to the rhythm of his thrusts. It only took a few pulls before I was screaming again, this time for my release.

I felt my body tighten around him, and his fingers dug into my hips as his rhythm faltered.

"Kingston," he hissed as he slammed into me one last time and stayed there. "Fuck, fuck, sweetheart. God... oh god, you feel so good. *Fuck.*"

I collapsed flat onto my own wet spot, unable to do much else besides lie there and try to recover some oxygen.

The warm flat of his palm smoothed a line up my spine until his fingers found their way into my hair. He turned my head to the side and leaned up to kiss me softly.

"I don't want to leave your body," he confessed in a whisper. "It's too good."

I reached a hand up to draw my index finger down his stubbled cheek. *"You're* too good."

We watched each other in the silence until our bodies forced us to move. We got up and wandered into the small bathroom to clean up. I turned the shower on while Falcon brushed his teeth. We didn't say anything. Words were too weird. There wasn't really anything to say anyway.

If there were feelings between us, it was too soon to put them into words. And if there weren't... well, then I was grateful for the silence.

I stepped into the hot water and closed my eyes, tilting my chin to my chest and letting the hot spray rain down on my skull. Falcon's arms wrapped around me from behind, and the crinkly hair on his chest lightly abraded my back. I leaned into him, letting the water pound onto my front.

We stood like that for a while. Eventually Falcon's hands began to wander, and he reached for the soap to make the movements slicker. It was more of a skin-worshipping than a washing, and within minutes, I was hard and aching again. I turned in his embrace and tried to return the favor.

"Give me the soap."

"Don't want to. I'm having too much fun with it," Falcon said, sneaking a soap-slick finger down the crease of my ass. I arched into his hand, begging for his attention because apparently I had zero shame and was already desperate for his dick again.

He continued teasing me while I paid him back with my tongue on one of his nipples.

"He's attractive," Falcon said. "I can see why you fell for him."

It took a minute before I realized what he was talking about. I pulled back. "Elek?"

"Yeah," he said, clearing his throat and taking my place under the water. He used the soap that was still in his hand to give himself a quick wash before switching places with me. "He's better-looking in person than I expected."

Talk about a boner killer. Hearing dream guy talking about nightmare man was disorienting.

"Mpfh," I scoffed. "Then maybe you should have asked him out."

Oh god, I was acting like a five-year-old.

But I couldn't help it; after one last rinse, I pushed past him to exit the shower. I grabbed a towel and began to dry off while trying my hardest to ignore Falcon's silence. It was nerve-racking.

When I was dry enough, I hung up the towel and walked my naked, twenty-eight-year-old ass into the bedroom. If there was one area where I could damned well beat out Elek Kemény, it was the youth department. My body was pretty damned acceptable compared to Elek's overindulged one.

I closed my eyes and shook my head. As if Agent Falcon would ever be attracted to someone as slimy as Elek. But then again, not much besides age and opulence separated me from Elek. After all, we were both notorious art thieves. We were both enemies of the FBI's art crimes team. We both danced across the line of right and wrong.

I slipped into my bed and faced the wall. Maybe it was a good thing there would be no more touching or conversation tonight. We had a big day ahead of us and needed the sleep.

Yeah, right.

Against my wishes, every single sound from the bathroom entered my ears, got sorted by my brain, and was finally run through a complicated evaluation process to determine if tooth-brushing was a sign Falcon hated me now for being a brat. Or if an odd fabricky swish sound meant he was covering himself with a towel rather than allowing me to ever see his naked body again.

I was pathetic.

When his bare footsteps finally came closer to the beds, his voice was surprisingly light and teasing.

"I did."

Ignore him.

"Huh?" I asked because I couldn't help it.

Dammit.

"I did ask him out," Falcon clarified.

Jackass.

"Mpfh."

It didn't matter. If it wasn't Elek attracting him away from me tonight, it would be someone else, someone steady, honest, and predictable doing it at some point in the future.

The bed dipped behind me and the covers opened, letting in a chilly draft. I thanked god for Falcon's maturity.

He slid up to me and pulled me back against his chest. I felt the rumble of low laughter. "It's true what they say about dating younger people."

Great, now he was going to make fun of my immaturity. Perhaps I should prove him wrong with the silent treatment.

"They're stupidly jealous for no good reason?" I asked instead.

"No. They keep you on your toes."

"Wait," I said, flipping over to face him. His square jaw was covered in sexy late stubble and a smirk. It made my heart thunder even faster. "Are we… *dating?*"

CHAPTER NINETEEN

FALCON

"No... I don't know, maybe?" I stammered.

I was not a stammerer. In fact, I couldn't remember another situation in which I had felt so wrong-footed. I hadn't even meant to imply we were dating, it just came out. Maybe it was wishful thinking, but now that it was out there between us, I wanted to know what he thought.

King's face widened into a lovely grin which made my heart flip over like a dying fish.

"Is this a joke?" King asked.

"Um, no? Unless... unless you think it's that funny, in which case, yes, it is a joke. Ha ha."

King's hand came up to brush along the side of my face. "You would actually consider dating Le Chaton?"

"Hell no. Not in a million years. I would, however, like to ask King Wilde out to dinner."

King's smile erased all of my nerves. Unless he was playing me, which he very well could be, he seemed just as into me as I was to him.

His eyebrows rose. "And if King Wilde said yes, where would you take him?"

My heart continued its dying fish routine. "Well, I don't date very often, but I have found that some of the best conversations happen while I'm cooking for the guy. Little bit of wine, some finger foods, and then a sit-down meal over candlelight. My apartment isn't nearly as fancy as yours though. No real art on the walls and whatnot. More like museum prints and wishful thinking." Even though I couldn't afford anything real, I did have similar taste in art to what I'd seen in King's apartment in the few minutes we'd been there. It was part of the reason I'd un-handcuffed him. I'd wanted to be able to wander around and peek in doorways while he was gathering his things.

He had a high-end address not far from the Louvre and the Tuileries, but his actual decor was simple and understated. There was an entire hallway full of framed photos of his extended family in all manner of silly candids and more formal shots. His love for his family was the most prominent personal piece of him displayed in the apartment besides his carefully curated art collection.

The rest had been... depressingly cold. All with the exception of his bedroom. I'd only peeked in it for a split second, but I'd gotten a feeling that was where he nested. There were soft blankets and pillows in a comfortable pile on his bed, and homey lamps sat on two bedside tables. Graphic tees and worn-in jeans had been in a folded stack on a dresser with neatly folded socks on top, and a coffee cup and open paperback were on a small side table next to an overstuffed armchair by the window.

The only piece of art in the room was a stunning Henry Scott Tuke bather painting. It was highlighted with a dim spotlight that made the colors of the sand and sea fade softly behind the bright pale skin of the nude male subjects.

I'd wanted to ask him a million questions about it at the time, but then I would have had to admit to snooping in his private space.

King rolled over on top of me until our naked bodies were pressed together. My arms automatically came around his back so my hands could take advantage of all that skin. Soft lips dropped onto the edge of my mouth and brushed across to my ear.

"I would really like that. No one has ever cooked for me on a date before."

I ran my hands through his wet hair, brushing it back from his face. His eyes were striking, even when they weren't focused on me, but when they were? They were mesmerizing.

"Maybe you'll have to make a trip over the river and through the arrondissements so I can show you how the other half live," I suggested. "I even have an extra bedroom if you, uh, decide to stay over."

King's eyes squinted in laughter. "You'd make me sleep in the guest room? That's harsh, Agent Falcon."

I felt my face heat. "No... I just didn't want to assume..."

His smile faded. "I'm sorry about before. I... Well, let's just say I have trust issues. So... I apologize for being immature and jealous."

He handed me the perfect opening to ask for more detail about what happened between him and Elek. "What happened on the Van Gogh job?"

King rolled off me and lay on his side, propping his head on his hand. "He tripped the alarm."

"By accident?"

King flopped onto his back and closed his eyes with a groan. "No. Definitely not. We were arguing. He... he hit me over the head and tied me to the fucking radiator. And then he left and set off the alarm on the way out."

It was more or less what I had expected, but that didn't make it any less surprising. "Why? What the hell were you arguing about?"

"I don't even know. I mean, it was..." King sighed. "I'd begun second-guessing him more and more. I'd finally started realizing I didn't like stealing art just to have it wind up in the hands of people who didn't fully appreciate it or didn't properly care for it. It weighed on me. Made me sick. So I'd started pushing back a little. I guess he finally figured out he no longer had a compliant tool to wield. But that's just a guess."

I was proud of King for having stood up for himself, but I could tell he still felt a lack of closure. "What happened when you confronted him about it?"

He turned his head to look at me again. "I didn't. When I got back to our apartment, the locks had been changed, Tibor—the butler security guy—acted like he'd never seen me before, and Elek blocked my number."

"You're kidding. And you lived together?"

He shrugged. "Yeah, I thought maybe he'd found someone else. I don't know. When he left that night, he told me over comms he had a wife. So that's what I thought until you and your team told me otherwise. What can I say? I'm a gullible idiot."

I hated hearing him talk about himself that way. "No, you aren't. He's a controlling, entitled, pompous jackass."

"And I was in a relationship with him. So what does that make me?"

I reached for his hand and held it. "Naive, maybe. Young, definitely. And most likely an idealist at the time." I took a minute to get up the nerve to ask what I really wanted to know. "Do you miss him?"

King shook his head emphatically. "Not one single bit. I knew the minute he left me there, we were through. But I really would have liked to have gotten my stuff out of the apartment. After that, I started stashing go bags with ID and money all over Europe just in case. I was convinced it was only a matter of time before I would fall prey to another manipulator. It was like… uncovering a fatal character flaw in myself. I thought maybe I was simply destined to fall for people's bullshit because it was how I was wired or something."

I could hear the insecurity in his voice, and it made my heart go out to him. Now that I had seen Elek Kemény in person, I knew just how powerful someone like him could be with a young artist who had stars in their eyes. Especially a young artist who wanted to be recognized for his talents. It was so easy to see how it had happened. But it wasn't as easy for me to understand why he had continued to live a life of crime after separating from the person who'd gotten him into it in the first place.

"Trusting someone isn't a character flaw," I told him. "It's what you're supposed to do in a relationship. And Elek should have been worthy of your trust, should have respected your trust, and if he had truly loved you, he would have. Honestly, I think Elek is all about Elek. It doesn't seem to me that he's capable of true love if it means putting someone else's needs and desires ahead of his own."

King sighed. "Yeah, I get that from an emotional standpoint, but I'll never forget the feeling of standing in that barricaded room waiting to be arrested, knowing he didn't care enough to even help me troubleshoot how to get out of there before the police came. There was no remorse, no apology, and let's not even talk about dividing the spoils."

I realized my hand was rubbing up to his shoulder and back again. His skin was warm from the shower, and the movement of my hand stirred up the lemony scent of the soap. "What did you do after you left my office in DC?"

If it had been a little lighter in the bedroom, I might have seen a blush on his face. I knew King felt guilty for manipulating me that day, and I still regretted making the mistake of believing him. In terms of my job, it had been a fatal error. But getting to know King these past few days... well, I saw more nuance to the story. Obviously, he still deserved to be punished for his actions. But... I had to admit things had changed a little. Now I cared about him too much to want to see him locked away.

The realization twisted me up inside. It was like suddenly having to choose between my job and my personal life. Except I didn't, because the FBI had agreed to let all of his criminal past go. I still wasn't sure how I felt about that.

"I took a circuitous route back to Paris, then went straight to our apartment, expecting a confrontation. But it was like I'd never existed. I told you that part. So then I was even angrier. I daydreamed about revenge, plotted it out many times, and basically spent too much time thinking about the best way to get even." King pushed himself up in bed until he was leaning against the headboard. He bent his knees up in front of him and rested his elbows on them, forking his fingers into his hair. "He has this list."

When he hesitated, I asked for clarification. "What kind of list?"

"A wish list. Every pie-in-the-sky piece he wishes he could add to his collection. I think the bulk of his career was to stockpile enough money to retire in luxury. But he enjoys the game too much to give it up, so once he didn't need the money anymore, he was going to start stealing for fun. He was going to steal all of his favorite things."

All of the pieces started clicking together as King turned his face to meet my eyes. "So I got there first."

It was like heavy dominoes falling over one after the other. Every job where King had left a note instead of stealing a piece of art, every time he had pointed out a weakness in a security system, every job that left our team scratching our heads… I finally knew why. King didn't want those things.

Elek did.

And King didn't want him to have them.

"Wow." Because… what else could I say?

"Yeah," he agreed. "And then there were the jobs where I couldn't help myself. Pieces I knew were in the wrong hands. I didn't set out to be any kind of Robin Hood, but if I knew where Holocaust treasures were, I couldn't just leave them be. There had been jobs I had done with Elek where we had taken one item out of the home or museum and left something else really important. When I was finally on my own, I could do something about it. So I did."

I thought of one of the jobs that had bothered me the most. "Why did you steal those World War I letters from the German Museum? They were important. They humanized the war. People need to see that."

King's jaw tightened. "The couple never gave their permission for their most intimate expressions of love to be shared with the world. I met a woman on a train in Warsaw who told me a story about her grandmother who had written diligently to her husband while he was in the trenches. Their entire love story lived in those letters, but her grandfather got bombed out of the building he was taking shelter in. His knapsack was left behind, so he assumed the letters were gone forever, burned up in a fire. It wasn't until a vacation for their retirement that they saw them there in the museum. They asked for them back and were refused."

He looked down at me with a small smile. "You see, they couldn't prove the letters were theirs, so it was a nonstarter."

This was an area where King and I would most likely never agree. "So you just believed her story. No need for corroboration, no verification of identification, nothing?"

King's eyes sparkled with mischief. "Oh ye of little faith. I surveilled the old couple and witnessed on several occasions them calling each other very specific terms of endearment. The same terms found in the letters in the museum. If I took you there today, to the nursing home where only the wife still lives, you would know in an instant that she is the one he wrote so lovingly about in his journal. If only you could have seen the looks on their faces when their daughter presented them with the mysterious box that had arrived in the mail. One of the best moments of my life."

I blew out a breath. "A romantic criminal. Just my luck."

King chuckled and leaned over to kiss my forehead. "A stereotypical police officer. Just my luck."

I pulled him down on top of me until I could get my hands all over his naked body again. While I envisioned squeezing out another round of orgasms before sliding happily into a coma, King apparently had other ideas.

"Now it's your turn."

I blinked up at him. "What do you mean?"

"Tell me about your last serious relationship."

CHAPTER TWENTY

KING

I wasn't sure there was anything more fun than catching Agent Stoic off guard.

"Uhhh," he hedged.

"Mm-hm. Getting a little taste of your own medicine now, aren't you?" I teased.

"I can't think with your dick wiggling all over me."

There was absolutely zero things sexier than the word dick said in Falcon's deep voice. And the dick agreed.

"Want me to get off?" I asked.

"Yes, but not in the way you mean," he growled.

"Are you kidding? I'm beat. This is all just bullshit posturing. There's no train left in my station, buddy. Find another way of getting there."

Falcon's eyes crinkled as his intense expression softened. "I don't like traveling solo. Much prefer my favorite copilot."

"Now you're simply changing the subject in order to get us off on a tangent. Focus. Love life history. Go."

I slid off him but stayed close, burrowing into his side and resting my head on his chest so I could keep one arm around his middle. He was warm and solid, not to mention he smelled good, and I loved feeling the rumble of his voice against my cheek.

His hands toyed with my hair while he spoke.

"I dated a man named Luca for six years."

"Holy shit," I blurted. "What happened?"

"We didn't want the same things."

I tilted my head up so he could see me roll my eyes. "Elaborate."

"I guess I pressured him to settle down and he didn't like that," Falcon said.

"Pressured, how?"

Falcon sighed. A few of his fingers drew lazy designs on my back. "I bought a house. It was something I'd been wanting us to do together for several years, but he was never ready. I've always been the kind of guy who wants to settle down. It's part of the reason I picked a job at the bureau where I wouldn't have to move around or be gone for long stretches of time."

"And Luca didn't want the picket fence?"

"Guess not. He said he did. Kept saying it was just a matter of timing. There was always something to wait for. A big project at work to complete or a sibling's wedding to get through. And then he'd be ready to look at houses and settle down. I finally decided that he simply didn't want the hassle of making decisions. So I picked a house I knew he'd love, and I surprised him."

"Wow," I said.

"Yeah. Stupid. Never do that to somebody."

I shifted to look at him again. "I disagree. Falcon, that's an amazing gesture, and there are plenty of people out there who would have loved you taking the decision out of their hands."

"Name one," Falcon said.

"My sister MJ. If her girlfriend surprised her with a house picked out to her tastes, she'd be like, 'Thank god. The last thing I wanted to do was spend hours looking at other people's shit.'"

Falcon huffed out a laugh. "Well, maybe I should have been dating MJ, then."

"She's a lesbian. Woulda kicked your ass for even making a move on her," I teased. "She's a tough bitch."

"She's your favorite."

It warmed my chest to hear him say it because even though it was probably more of a guess, it still showed he knew something about me, and more than that... he cared.

"She is. Mostly because she calls me on my bullshit more than anyone else. But I love them all." I paused. "I... I miss them a lot."

Falcon's arms came around me and squeezed. "Then why stay in Paris? Why pursue this revenge game when you have so many people who love you back in Texas?"

"I told you I'd already finished. The only item left on the list was the crown. And there was no way I was going to get to it with live guards standing there 24/7."

"So you meant it when you said you'd retired?" Falcon asked.

I nodded. "Until a certain someone begged me to steal something for him. And I'm a sucker for a pretty face." I batted my eyelashes at him.

Falcon groaned. "That's me. The art heist kingpin."

"Hey, you're planning a heist right now. If you think I'm ever going to let you forget it, you're mistaken. It's the highlight of my career."

"Shut up," Falcon grumbled, leaning in and nuzzling my neck. "I'm on the side of right."

"Pfft. You're on the side of the country too scared to admit to its people it lost a beloved piece of its history."

Falcon's teeth nipped the skin where my neck met my shoulder, giving me an instant hard-on. "I mean against your asshole ex-boyfriend," he said into my skin.

I shivered. "So, you're claiming to be better than a Hungarian crime boss. Hm, I'm impressed. You set a high bar."

I was losing focus to the feel of him, the need for him.

"King?" he asked, reaching down to squeeze my ass cheeks before sliding a finger between them.

"Hmm?"

"Stop talking."

So I did.

Morning came way too soon after a night spent pressed up against Falcon's naked body like a second skin. I'd curled around him and fallen asleep instantly, feeling like I was exactly where I was meant to be.

Regardless of whether that was true or not, my crush on him was deepening, and I knew it was going to be ten times harder to hide what was going on between the two of us from the rest of the team. I simply wasn't that good of an actor.

And I was having feelings. Stupid, vulnerable-making feelings.

So I did the mature thing and acted like I barely knew the guy. I took a seat at the table and got straight to work, not even realizing I hadn't even poured a cup of coffee yet.

We went over everything we had learned at the gala, and I was surprised to hear the details of Falcon's conversation with Elek. I couldn't even picture the two men together. Something about that made my stomach twist. Like... clash of the titans or something.

When Falcon questioned whether or not I thought Elek's interest in his artwork was genuine, I nodded. "Yeah, he wouldn't be able to resist. He doesn't give people enough credit, and he wouldn't assume they'd double-cross him. I'm sure he can't help but think about how easy it will be to get his hands on your artwork. But I guess we'll know more when and if he calls about dinner."

I stood up to finally pour a cup of coffee, letting the familiar smell calm me down. Linney was talking to herself under her breath as she searched through a stack of papers on the table.

"Basically, we'll need to make it look like two rich blokes from the States are on holiday here. Which means..." she muttered, finding the paper she was looking for. "Aha! Found it. Here is the name of a caterer we can use on short notice. I'll go ahead and get everything ready."

I could tell Mouse was still nervous, but he was a diligent worker, so he remained focused on the task ahead. "I'll flesh out the backstory of our fake relationship and my own alias."

Ziv nodded. "I've got your back on that one, Mouse. I can help get everything put online for social media accounts and whatnot. Just give me a name when you have it."

I was impressed with Falcon's team. They worked together flawlessly, and each seemed to know their role. Falcon clearly wasn't a micromanager, since he didn't even raise his head from his own computer when all of them began marking things off the list.

Once everyone was working, I realized that I was the one completely in charge of the heist itself. Not that it came as a surprise to me, but it was still strange to think of this FBI team leaving me purposefully in charge of a solo art heist. How did they know I could be trusted? How in the world could they be sure I wouldn't take off with the crown?

At one point, Falcon looked up at me and winked. It took me by surprise, happening in front of his team the way it did. I wasn't sure anyone but me noticed it, but it still sent a shiver through me. Was he really willing to let his team see him flirting with me?

And what would they say if they knew their strict, gruff senior agent was hooking up with the notorious art thief their whole team had spent years pursuing? Suddenly, I felt guilty. Like I was responsible for putting him in this position. I didn't want his team members to lose respect for him. Did that mean I needed to stay away from him?

I couldn't do that. I wasn't that selfless.

Falcon leaned over and spoke softly. "Are you okay? Is any of this bothering you?"

Those were questions Agent Falcon never would have asked me a week ago. I smiled at him. "I'm good. You know… you know you can trust me, right? I promise."

Falcon's smile dropped. Before he could answer me, I began to babble. "Wow, that sounded guilty? I only meant that with you and Mouse back at the house—now I'm rhyming for god's sake—there won't be as many eyes on me. And I didn't want that to make you more nervous about the op." His forehead had wrinkled even more in confusion, so I forged ahead. "Not that you were nervous about it, but... I'm in this. You know I want the crown out of his hands. And so..."

His face broke into a grin again as he figured out what I was doing. "You're nervous. Why?"

"Me? No," I lied. "I just thought you needed some reassurance. You looked a little... unsure. That's all."

"I trust you, King." His eyes had their typical gray-green intensity, and as much as I wanted to believe him, I still wasn't sure if he was telling the truth. And if he wasn't, I couldn't really blame him. He had absolutely no reason to trust me after all these years. Yes, I had signed a contract. Yes, I had to fulfill this operation in order to get my immunity. But I was also really good at making promises to him I didn't keep. Like the time I told him I didn't have anything to do with the Van Gogh job. And the time I told him I was just running to pack my things at the vineyard.

So, no. He had no reason to trust me. But I would try to show him that I could change, that I could follow through on my promises to him. Even if there was no future between an agent and a thief, I could still show him that a thief could change. And, hell, maybe that would help him give his targets the benefit of the doubt, at least long enough to look at the situation from all sides.

Ziv interrupted him to ask him some questions about surveillance equipment in the other room. When they came back into the kitchen a little while later, Falcon had news.

"Elek called. We're on for tonight."

I blinked up from where I'd been staring at the coffee maker, waiting for it to stop brewing so I could pour a refill. Falcon met my eyes as he resumed his spot at the kitchen table.

"Already? It's not even eight o'clock."

He shrugged. "Maybe he's a morning person. He wanted to make sure I was free tonight since he was leaving town tomorrow."

"Why don't we wait till tomorrow, then? Won't it be easier if he's gone?"

"We can't be sure he's not going to take the crown with him. If he's planning on staying at his place in Paris for a while, he might want to have it there," Falcon explained. And he was right.

"Yeah. Okay. Tonight, then," I agreed, glancing at the others working around the table. Mouse was busy working on the prosthetic fingerprints, Ziv was banging away at his keyboard programming the equipment he'd brought into the room, and Linney was sitting back eating toast with jam while watching Falcon and me.

I turned back to the coffee, mentally popping the little bubble hearts that were probably floating around my head whenever I looked at Falcon now.

The man wanted the white picket fence.

Why did that surprise me? And... it wasn't like that was something I'd ever envisioned for myself. But when he described it... god. It made me feel a strange new mix of emotions. First and foremost, I wanted him to have his dream. More than anything, I wanted him to find someone who wanted what he wanted, someone who wanted more than anything to give him what he needed.

But more than that... I wanted it to be me.

And that was some ridiculous bullshit. Because I wasn't picket fence material. I was solid metal bars material.

"King," Linney said. "Are you waiting for it to cream and sugar itself?"

I realized I'd been staring at a full pot of coffee for an absurdly long time.

"Yes? I don't think that's unreasonable this early in the morning," I explained. "Do you?"

I reached for a mug and did my thing, tossing some bread in the toaster while I was at it. When I finally took my usual seat next to Falcon, I ignored the lemony scent of him.

Kind of.

"After I finish this, I'm going to put together the things I need," I said unnecessarily. "Make sure I have everything I need." Why was I still talking? "And then I need to go over the entry plan again with Ziv." I swallowed. They already knew all of this. What the hell was my problem? "We need to test comms too." How many times would I use the word "need" before I shut up?

Jesus.

Falcon looked up from his laptop and met my eyes. "You okay?"

No. I'm falling for the wrong person. That wasn't part of the plan.

"Of course."

He studied me for a minute, those eyes boring into me as usual. I was getting used to being the bug under his microscope, and it wasn't nearly as intimidating as it had been originally.

"Hmpf," he grunted, turning back to his computer. "Drink your coffee. You're acting weird."

Mouse looked up from his work. "Maybe he's nervous, boss. Give him a break."

Falcon didn't look up but said, "He's not nervous."

"How do you know that?" I asked, feeling more relaxed all of a sudden. "I could be."

He looked up at me and raised a brow. "Yes, you could be. But you're not. And I know that, because—"

For a split second, I pictured him saying "because I fucked all the tension out of you last night."

"—you've done this a million times."

"Maybe not a million," I said. "But you're right. Plus, nerves are inversely proportional to the success of the op."

"Well, shit," Mouse muttered. "We're doomed."

"You're going to be fine," Falcon assured him. "Your part of the op is simply eating dinner at your own place. Nothing to be nervous about."

He was strong and steady, the fearless team leader whose quiet confidence anchored the entire group around him. It was sexy as fuck to watch, especially when he was dressed in a business button-down with the sleeves rolled up.

I nibbled on my toast and tried to think about the crown instead of Dirk Falcon's muscular forearms.

After a few minutes, Ziv stopped typing. "Okay. I'm in their surveillance system and have cut the video loops we need. I'll be able to deactivate the simple door and window contacts, no problem. Not there yet on the motion sensors."

He stretched and stood up to refill his coffee.

"I told you those shouldn't be a problem. They're set above the height of the dogs, so all I have to do is army crawl."

"Yeah, but if I can deactivate them, it'll save us a shit-ton of time."

I shrugged. "You've never seen my belly crawl trophies. They're pretty impressive."

Ziv rolled his eyes, but I could see the slight smirk too.

When I was done eating, I wandered outside to the small storage building at the back of the house. It wasn't big enough to be a garage, but it held the lawn mower and other gardening supplies as well as the crates of supplies the FBI had sent to support our mission here.

At some point Linney and Mouse had organized everything onto two folding tables. I rifled through everything, gathering up the extra items I needed and shopping for anything else that caught my eye. They had a pair of night vision goggles that looked almost like eyeglasses. I grabbed them to test inside the house. I also found a funky little tracker that I wanted to ask Ziv about.

Just as I finished closing the door to the outbuilding, Mouse came racing out of the house. "Come inside, there's something new."

I followed him back to the kitchen where Linney and Ziv seemed to be in a heated argument. As soon as Mouse and I sat down, Falcon told them to be quiet.

"What's going on?" I asked.

"Transcripts from the security guards just came in from conversations late last night. They picked up reference to *crown* and *boat* in the same conversation. They think it was in reference to moving something. Could he be moving the crown onto the boat?"

"I already told you I thought that's where it would have been in the first place."

Falcon sighed. "Shit."

"It probably means he's planning on leaving for a while. I don't think he'd move it to the yacht if he wasn't going to be on the boat with it, but I could be wrong." I tapped a finger on the table while I thought about it. "If it's true that he gave up a ride on Daddy's jet to stay for this dinner... well, he can't exactly fly commercial with a gold coronation crown in his carry-on. And he's certainly not going to trust a shipping company. So, the yacht is the best way to transport it. Maybe he's flying commercial and he's sending Tibor on the boat with the crown. That's a possibility."

Ziv brought up a good point. "It doesn't really matter. Either way, we need to get that crown off the boat before he motors out of the marina late tonight or tomorrow. This changes everything."

I shook my head. This was excellent news for several reasons. "This is so, so much better. I can get in and out of that yacht much more easily than getting in and out of a guarded compound. There's not nearly as much security in place."

Falcon nodded. "All right. What do we need?"

"Scuba equipment for one," I said. "And I'll need Ziv to get eyes on the boat so he can tell me when it's safe to board."

Falcon looked at me, a crease of worry on his forehead. "Have you done this kind of thing before?"

"Many times. Did you ever hear about the string of yacht thefts when the World Cup went through Cape Town?"

"No..." he said, frowning.

"That's how good I am," I said with a wink.

Falcon sighed. "This isn't the way I envisioned my life going."

Linney, Mouse, and Ziv cracked up. I pushed my shoulder into Falcon's. "Relax. My point is, you can count on me to make this happen. I know what I'm doing."

"I don't doubt your ability as an art thief, King," Falcon clarified in a serious tone.

"Then what's your worry here?"

"Missions can be very different when there are emotions involved." His eyes flicked to Mouse, who was paying close attention.

"He's right, King," Mouse added. "I had to help on a mission that involved someone close to me, and it was hell."

"I'm not close to Elek Kemény," I said, trying not to let my annoyance show. I wasn't used to having to deal with other people on an op, and I sure as hell wasn't used to them warning me about my damned emotions.

"We'll talk about it later," Falcon said. "In the meantime, let's go see if the scuba equipment arrived. After you mentioned it on the first day, I put in a request." He stood up and stretched before taking his coffee mug to the sink.

I followed him outside to the shed. We were chatting normally about details of the retrieval mission when we entered the shed. The minute we were inside, he closed the door and grabbed me, shoving me up against it and crushing his mouth against mine. I didn't even have a chance to take a breath before his hands were all over me and his tongue was in my mouth.

This aggressive, handsy motherfucker was such a contrast to the calm, cool, and collected senior agent he'd been in the kitchen, the change filled my dick up in a nanosecond.

"What the hell?" I gasped, pulling away enough to try and assess his mood.

"I woke up this morning so hard for you. I wanted to fuck you while you were sleeping."

"God, why didn't you?"

"I can't even concentrate on my job right now, and some part of me worries that... that maybe that's your intent."

I didn't understand. "What do you mean?"

"You've gotten in my head. I've never been so distracted on a mission before, and it's fucked-up. Please tell me this isn't part of your plan."

I could see the true worry in his eyes, and part of me wanted to soothe and reassure him, but the rest of me was way too angry. He thought I was deliberately targeting him with... some kind of seduction campaign for my own nefarious gains? I shoved off him and backed up. "Fuck you."

"King, I—"

"No. I get questioning it. Believe me, I do. But don't you realize that you're just as likely to be playing me as I am you?"

Falcon's brows furrowed. "Why would I be playing you?"

"I don't know. Revenge? Control? You have a long history of gunning for me, Agent Falcon. You're the last person in the world I should trust right now."

His nostrils flared. "Says the thief."

My heart was hammering in fear. I hadn't been expecting our personal connection to sever itself quite this soon, and the thought it was happening made me feel panicky.

"I'm not a thief anymore."

Falcon's eyes drifted to the tables full of the tools of my trade. I didn't need to point out that those were his supplies, not mine.

I tried to calm down so I could pretend his words hadn't hurt me as much as they had. "Well, good news, Agent Falcon. You'll be rid of me tomorrow. No more having to question my motives." I turned around to look for the scuba equipment.

He didn't make a sound, but suddenly his arms were around me and one hand came up to hold the front of my throat. His lips brushed my ear, and my eyes slid closed. I swallowed a groan of relief at the familiar feel of him behind me.

"I can't be there to keep you safe."

Ahhh. Fear *for* me, not *of* me.

"I can't be here to keep *you* safe," I countered. "And you're going to be at the mercy of an evil man. I'm only going to be at the mercy of some electronics and brainless thugs."

"This wasn't supposed to happen," he said quietly.

"I know."

"What are we going to do after this is over?" he asked.

"I don't know," I said, but I was lying.

I was going to go home to Hobie with my tail between my legs and beg MJ to wrap me in blankets and feed me pints of heartbreak ice cream while Falcon was going to go back to Paris and get recognition for a job well done. He was going to live his best life and find the perfect little househusband to keep his home fires burning while he rid the world of pesky art thieves.

Because that was really the only option.

The door to the house slammed closed which meant someone was coming. The two of us broke apart and quickly went to work looking for the new package of equipment. By the time Linney joined us, everything was fine.

It was *fine*.

And it was time to focus on the job ahead.

CHAPTER TWENTY-ONE

FALCON

Linney arranged the catering, Mouse prepared the house by moving most of our things into the van. We had to assume someone like Elek would take a peek around when he went to the restroom, so we couldn't risk evidence of more than two men staying there. We also wanted to be ready to get the hell out of there as soon as the op was over.

Ziv worked with me to make sure my cover story was solid enough for me to make it through dinner without running out of things to talk about. We'd already told Mouse he could be the submissive, silent type or act like an airhead if he didn't want to participate in the discussions. I secretly hoped he'd feel confident enough to speak since he was our art and antiquities expert. It'd be much easier for him to keep Elek occupied with art chatter than it would me.

Plus, my bad attitude toward the man would be tough to hide. I'd wanted so badly to ask King if Elek had ever hurt him physically, but I knew if I had any specifics, I wouldn't be able to keep from wanting to beat the man when he came to dinner.

Before lunch, King and I took the scuba equipment down to the water. There was a narrow stairway cut into the side of the cliff and a narrow strip of rocky beach below. I'd checked the tidal chart so we made sure not to attempt our testing at high tide.

It was cold as hell with the wind coming off the water and the wall of rock behind us, shading us from any sun this time of day.

King struggled to get the wet suit on over his boxer briefs, and I couldn't do much more than stand there and gawp at him while he did it.

"Thanks," he muttered. "Super helpful."

"God you're good-looking," I said stupidly.

"I'm cold as balls."

"Yeah, and it's making your nipples hard. I'm bearing witness."

King snorted. "Pervert. At least get the regulator ready. Make yourself useful, Grandpa."

"I'm not even forty. I can't help it if premature gray runs in my family," I griped. "And I don't know how to get the regulator ready with a pony bottle."

"It's the same as on a regular bottle, and you're scuba certified which means you know how to do it. You're just stalling."

I waved my hand at his mostly naked body. "Can you blame me? People would pay big money for this kind of show at a club. If I don't watch… it's like… it's like throwing money in the trash. Or something."

He finally struggled the rest of the suit up and pulled the long zip lead over his back to close it. His body in a wet suit was ridiculous. Slim and sleek. Perfect.

"You're drooling," King said with a grin. "It's kinda cute."

"Shut up and get in the water. I still say you're going to regret getting that suit wet before tonight."

King's face turned serious. "I agree, but not testing new equipment is a rookie mistake. And we only have one shot at this if he's leaving tomorrow. No room for mistakes."

I loved this side of him. Watching his competency on a mission was seductive. I shouldn't be impressed with his ability to break into people's houses and steal their prized possessions, but it was hard to deny how much skill it took to succeed as much as he had. And never get caught.

King leaned over and screwed the regulator onto the small air bottle before sliding it into the BCD vest and hooking up the hose to the vest. When he was ready, I lifted it up so he could slip it on.

"Do you worry about running out of air with the smaller bottle?" I asked as he was clipping everything in.

"Nah. If I'm getting into the water at the edge of the marina, it won't take much air to get to and from the yacht in its slip. And I'll be just under the surface too which means I won't use as much with each breath. Worst-case scenario, I have to snorkel. At night, no one will notice."

Everything he had on was black. Even though he was right, it would be hard to see him at night in the water, I still wished it wasn't such a full moon. That was something we couldn't control.

I handed King the face mask and held his fins as we walked toward the water's edge.

"You remember the signals, right?" he asked with a cheeky grin.

I shot him the bird. "This one?"

"Fine. But safety protocol requires me to—"

I leaned in and kissed him to shut him up. His hand came up and held the back of my head firmly to keep me from pulling away. When we finally did end it, I pulled back and met King's eyes.

"I'm not going to let anything happen to you. I promise."

By six that night, Mouse was making a puke nest on the floor in front of the toilet in his bathroom, Linney had set up with her comms equipment in the van, Ziv was bringing up the video feeds from the cameras he'd managed to place around the marina with a drone earlier that afternoon, and King was nowhere to be found.

After searching the house for the millionth time, I let out a frustrated sound.

"He took the car to do some more recon at the marina," Linney said from the dining room. She'd laid out a nice table and was setting out flowers that had been delivered earlier. The food was scheduled to arrive any minute.

"I know," I said, feeling like he'd been gone forever. "Just making sure I knew where everyone was."

She finished arranging things and came to stand in front of me by the open front door. "Don't worry. Ziv put a tracker on him when he wasn't looking, just in case." She crossed her arms in front of her chest. "You know we all like him, right?"

"Who, Ziv? Yeah, he's a good guy."

She lifted her brows. "Really? We're going to play it that way? King."

"Mpfh."

She put her hands on my cheeks. They were cool and dry. "Falcon, honey, it's okay to like the man."

"I know that."

"No," she said, tilting my head down until I was forced to meet her eyes. "I mean it's okay to *like* the man."

We stared at each other.

"No, it isn't," I finally said. "Not really. Not seriously."

"When are you going to tell him?"

My stomach flipped over. "Tell him what?"

She lifted an eyebrow. "That he's going after a forgery."

"I'm hoping he doesn't notice," I said softly.

Her expression bordered on pity. "You should tell him."

"He doesn't have security clearance. I could lose my job."

She pulled her hands away and crossed her arms in front of her chest. "There is more to life than the job. And as much as you like to see things in black and white... life isn't usually like that. It's a whole rainbow. And that man," she said, pointing a thumb toward the direction of the cliffs, "is colorful as shit. You need someone like that."

"He's an art thief."

"He said he's done with that."

I gave her a look. "And we should believe him. Even if he means it now, what if he can't stay away from it?"

She threw up her hands. "What if a meteor lands on all of us tonight? You can play the what-if game all day long, if your goal is to go to sleep in an empty bed at night."

"Lin, how can I spend over four years hunting Le Chaton, convincing the FBI and Interpol he's our biggest target, and then say 'oh by the way, I'm dating him...'?" I asked, leaning back on the open doorjamb and crossing my arms. "I'd lose the respect of all of my peers."

It was unconscionable.

Linney's face was soft, and she projected empathy the way she always did when she was slipping into mothering mode. "You tell them to fuck off. And if that doesn't work, you put him in a situation where he quickly goes from being our biggest target to our biggest asset, a situation in which he saves our asses by keeping the United States government from making a fool out of itself on a global stage."

"No one can know about it," I pointed out. "Remember?"

"They can't know about the US government's role in retrieving the crown, but... they *could* find out about Le Chaton's role in delivering it to the Hungarian Parliament Building." She seemed to be thinking it up on the fly. "What if we make it look like the Greek coins?"

"How do you mean?"

"He puts the crown somewhere in the parliament building with a note about how he got in," she explained. "Make it look like the crown was there the entire time."

Fuck, she was brilliant.

I grabbed her face and kissed her on the forehead. "God, this is why you're on my team. Brilliant. I'm going to go call Nadine. If we get this crown tonight, we start planning the return mission. Thank you."

But when I got Nadine on the phone, everything came to a screeching halt.

"I'm getting pressure to speed up this op," she explained before I had a chance to tell her Linney's idea. "Now that we know where the crown is, what's taking so long to retrieve it?"

Was she kidding? "Nadine, we've only been here four days. How long do you think it takes to plan this kind of operation? There are multiple on-site armed guards, a security patrol, and fingerprint scanners. This isn't a smash and grab in a dark alley."

"I realize that. I simply need to be kept in the loop. When are you going in? Did you hear back from the target about dinner? Give me something I can give James."

I hadn't updated her yet since changing the op target to the yacht, but something in her tone was really bothering me. "We're going to make an attempt at retrieval tonight. If we succeed, we could be in Budapest as early as tomorrow."

"The team at Fort Knox with the original crown is waiting for word from us. They can get to Paris in less than twelve hours when we set things in motion. The sooner we can get this situation cleaned up and behind us, the better."

I closed the door to my bedroom so no one could overhear me question her. "Nadine, what's the plan to place the original in the Hungarian Parliament Building? You asked me to assess whether or not King can sneak it in. I think he can, especially since they aren't guarding an empty display case around the clock right now."

"We will return it, but first we need you to get back here with the stolen forgery. We can't take the chance of having them both out there in the world at the same time. We'll make the exchange in the safety of our office and then determine what's next."

"Can you send the original straight to Budapest? We can fly there with this forgery and save a little time. The sooner we get this back to the Hungarian people, the better."

"I don't feel comfortable having both crowns in Budapest at the same time. We'll do the exchange at your office in Paris."

"But—"

"Agent Falcon," she said, clearly losing her patience. "I understand your desire to close this case as quickly as possible, but I'm not about to take the chance of having two crowns and one of the world's greatest art thieves in a country where I don't have any diplomatic control if things go wrong. Do you understand that?"

I didn't argue with her. "Yes, ma'am. Hopefully we'll have it home tonight or tomorrow."

"Good. Oh, and Agent Falcon?" Nadine asked.

"Yes?"

"Bring King Wilde back with you. I like the idea of using him to sneak it back in. Once you have it in your possession, you can start planning the next mission. And if anything goes wrong and the Hungarians discover him there... they'll assume he was the thief all along. Even if they catch him with the original, they'll have it back and they'll have a thief to put away for the crime. Win-win. We get the heat off the US, and your team finally gets to watch Le Chaton go to prison."

I felt my lips go numb.

"What do you mean?"

"I only mean if something were to go wrong and the Hungarians catch him. Hopefully nothing will happen."

My chest felt too tight. "No, I mean... he can't go to prison. He'd be working for the FBI. He has immunity."

I heard her faint chuckle over the line. "Not from stealing the crown from the Hungarian Parliament Building. That was specifically excluded, remember?"

"But he wouldn't be stealing it," I corrected. "He'd be *returning* it."

"Agent Falcon, if a notorious art thief with a history of stealing any manner of precious works from around the world is found in possession of a recently stolen antiquity, he's going to be arrested and thrown in Hungarian prison. And before you continue to argue with me about this, I would throw his own words back at you. According to King Wilde, he's too good to get caught. So this is all a moot point anyway."

I opened my mouth to argue some more. We'd made a deal with him. All he had to do was help us get the crown back. Then he owed us nothing. But I couldn't risk second-guessing my boss again in the same conversation when I could already tell I was on thin ice.

"Understood," I said before finishing the call and tossing my phone onto one of the beds.

How the hell was I going to warn King about the danger he'd be in without betraying my own chain of command and risking my career?

CHAPTER TWENTY-TWO

KING

When I entered the bedroom, I could tell Falcon had reached an unhealthy level of nerves. His shoulders were around his ears.

"Are you always this bad before ops?" I asked, pulling off my shirt. "Because I have a surefire way of getting rid of pre-heist jitters."

Falcon shook his head. "No... I just had a call with my boss..." He shook his head. "Never mind, I think you're right. I haven't been on a mission this important in a while. If ever. I'm sure it's just nerves. Is that why you were doing more recon?"

I shook my head. "No, that was an important part of the job. But also... I wanted some time to myself. I have this... pre-job ritual thing that I do."

Falcon looked up at me, curiosity sparkling in his eyes. "Tell me."

"Argh," I groaned. "It's so stupid. It's embarrassing."

"Tell Papa Bear what it is."

I laughed. "I changed my mind about calling you Papa Bear. It's too creepy." I blew out a breath. "Okay, here goes. Before my very first heist, I called my sister just to hear her voice. I was nervous and homesick, and I needed something from home to ground me. But I misdialed and got the Hobie librarian by accident."

Falcon was already trying not to laugh. I ignored him and continued.

"Her name is Doreen. And she's known me since I was like three or something. Somehow, she recognized my voice, and we started chatting. It was so... *normal*. It was such a visceral taste of home. But there was no family guilt associated with her, no feeling of having to explain why I hadn't been home for a while. She just... I guess she just gave me a reminder that there are good people in this world. That op went well, and I realized Doreen's calming presence on the phone had worked its magic. So now I call Doreen before every job."

Falcon stared at me. "Are you kidding? Your hometown librarian knows about—"

"No, god no." I rolled my eyes at him. "Of course she doesn't know. I simply call to tell her hello and to ask how her little poodle is and how many tomatoes have grown on her tomato plants or what Netflix show she's been binge-watching with her husband, Ned. And she asks me if I've had any fancy French pastries lately or whether I've discovered a new artist in a museum she should read up on. It's just... grounding, I guess."

Falcon looked at me with suspicion. "So you just took a walk in order to call Doreen the librarian?"

I groaned. "Stop. Now you have to tell me something embarrassing about you. Do you have any pre-mission rituals?"

Falcon gave me a look. "Yeah, I checked my comms unit, my weapon—"

I punched him in the shoulder. "Shut up. I get it. You're calm, cool, and collected Agent Falcon of the FBI. Not all of us are quite as cool as you are."

I continued undressing until I was completely naked and Falcon was staring. Then I sauntered into the bathroom with a little extra swing in my step in hopes he would take it as an invitation. There wasn't enough time for much, but I could at least follow through on the offer of pre-mission relaxation techniques.

But when we were finally together under the hot spray, I felt the tension he still carried in his shoulders and tried to work it out with my fingers. "This isn't normal. You really are worried. What's going on?"

When Falcon clenched his jaw, it looked even broader, more masculine. It was the look that I had originally thought was intimidating when I first saw him in a video press conference.

He spoke in a low voice. "They said they want to use you to sneak the crown back into the parliament building."

That was interesting. "Me? Really?"

Falcon shrugged. "I'd originally floated the idea early on, not really thinking they'd do it. But Linney had a good suggestion." He explained her idea of mimicking what I'd done with the coins in the museum in Berlin.

"You don't really have my DNA, do you?" I asked.

Falcon's lashes were flecked with water droplets, making his stormy eyes even more striking. "I can neither confirm nor deny my use of subterfuge to ensure the desired outcome of a—"

I groaned and slapped my hand over his mouth. "Stop. I don't want to hear you lie to me again, jackass. I would have done it anyway."

He shook my hand off. "Not with us. You would have gone rogue."

Falcon knew me better now than he had at first.

"You didn't know that at the time."

"No," he admitted. "But I do now."

"I just want him to pay, Falcon," I said.

"I know. And I do too. My entire unit does. But there are factors at play in this mission that preclude us from bringing him in."

It was a reminder that Falcon was still holding details back from me which should have made me feel a little relief since I was definitely holding things back from him. Like the fact I now knew the crown wasn't on the yacht.

But I couldn't tell him that without telling him how I found out, and that would definitely result in him taking me off the op.

Falcon got to work shampooing both of us while I grabbed the bar of soap. He continued where I left off. "King, you have to understand how much it bothers me that we can't nail Elek for the crown theft in the process. I mean, why not take out one of the most prolific art thieves in modern history while we have the chance? I'm sure he has other stolen works in his yacht and home. We could always nail him for one of those. But I'm forbidden from doing it."

It wasn't easy listening to him talk about nailing an art thief, but I understood his point.

"It's fine. If he got turned over, he'd take me with him," I reminded him softly. But it really wasn't fine.

Falcon leaned in and kissed me hard instead of saying anything. I wasn't sure if that was a good thing or bad, but as long as his mouth was on mine, I didn't much care either way.

But time was running out, and it was time to get this job done.

After racing through the rest of our shower and dressing in our very different outfits for the night, we stole one last kiss before it was time to leave the sanctuary of our shared bedroom.

I wouldn't be coming back here. And we would no longer be sharing one of these beds.

Falcon's eyes broadcast a million messages, but his mouth only offered one.

"Be safe."

"You too. Don't underestimate him, Falcon. Please."

His thumb came up to smooth a line along my cheek. "My job is easy. You're the one in danger. Promise me if you come up against something… don't… don't take the risk. We can try again another time."

"You know that's not true," I said gently. "But I know what I'm doing. This is what I'm good at. Trust me."

He didn't say the words I wanted to hear. *I do trust you.* But then again, I didn't say them either.

By the time we met the team in the kitchen, I was ready to get a move on. All I wanted was to ruin Elek Kemény's night and present Falcon with the proof I could deliver the goods. He already knew that, obviously, but I wanted to come through for him. I wanted to help him impress his team and his boss in hopes it would go a small way toward making up for all the ways my previous jobs had screwed him over.

Ziv, Linney, and I took the loaded van and headed toward the marina, leaving Falcon and Mouse to entertain their guests. When we left, the caterers were setting out food and Falcon was doing his best to distract Mouse with funny stories about his early days in the FBI. Since the caterers were there and could overhear them, Falcon kept couching the stories as "this movie I saw" which, for some reason, cracked me up. The stories were cracking Mouse up too, so it was a job well done.

Meanwhile, ours was not.

After dropping into the water, making my way to the right slip, getting an expected message over comms that there was no security personnel on the yacht for me to worry about, I climbed aboard and let myself in easily.

Just as I had discovered earlier, there was no crown.

When I got back to the van after a thorough search, I changed out of the gear and into dry clothes.

"What now?" Linney asked.

Ziv and I locked eyes. I could tell he knew what I was going to say before I said it.

"We go to his house."

CHAPTER TWENTY-THREE

FALCON

When Elek still hadn't arrived twenty minutes after the time we'd agreed on, I began to worry. We had a small camera placed near his driveway to record comings and goings, but our receivers and monitors were in the van with Linney. Hopefully she was way too preoccupied with watching King's back to worry about how late Elek was to dinner.

Finally, when half an hour had passed, the Hungarian and his date arrived. I tried not to think of how crazy it was that a pair of undercover American agents were hosting someone temporarily suspected as an undercover Greek intelligence agent for dinner in his own country. It had occurred to me the night before that there could be more unknown factors at play here. But it was way less probable, so I didn't spend too much time worrying about it.

"Come in, come in," I offered with a smile at the door. "So glad you could make it."

Elek was dressed in dark gray suit pants with a lighter gray sport coat. His black button-down had several buttons undone to show a mat of thick chest hair with zero gray in it. Did the man dye the hair on his chest? He had to.

"Thank you for having us," Elek said with a friendly smile. "This is Demitri."

I took in the young man's flashy appearance. According to the information Ziv had been able to scrounge up, he truly was the son of an old friend of Elek's, which made me wonder what his father thought of the union.

"Nice to meet you," I said, shaking his delicate hand. "This is my Joshua." I put my arm around Mouse's shoulder and pulled him into my side. He blushed prettily and gave a shy wave.

"Hi. Nice to meet you. Ethan has told me so much about you. It kind of made me jealous," he said with a little laugh. "I'm not sure if I should be jealous of you or your art reputation. I think my man is enamored with both."

I wanted to turn and stare at my nervous young agent, who apparently wasn't nervous anymore. He'd slipped into his role effortlessly.

"Come on in," he said. "What can I get you to drink?"

For the first hour, we had cocktails and small talk in the formal living room. Thankfully, the villa we'd rented passed quite well for our cover story couple. It was nice and roomy without being overly flashy, and its secluded location near the water was something a couple of American tourists might find appealing if they were looking for privacy.

The small talk was excruciating because it didn't do a very good job of distracting me from my hatred of Elek Kemény. I had plenty of time to assess him physically as well as observe his temperament. He was flattering and somewhat affectionate with Demitri, but there was an obvious thread of control in his interactions with the younger man that bothered me. Obviously, I couldn't help but substitute King for Demitri and imagine what that would look like.

It was one thing to enjoy being controlled in the bedroom and quite another to be told what to eat and what not to talk about.

When it was finally time to move to the dinner table, Mouse managed to move the conversation to art.

"Ethan said you could maybe help us figure out how to put in some better security at the house? I hope so because it makes me really nervous that he's spent this much money on something and we don't really know how best to protect it."

I acted a little embarrassed. "Babe. I'm not an idiot. We have home security. I've done all the online research and stuff. There are art collector forums that recommend different things. I just thought maybe Elek here would help me *upgrade* what we already have."

Elek smiled and nodded. "Happy to. Why don't you tell me what you have now?"

While answering, I said a prayer for anyone who was actually stupid enough to share details of their home security protocol with a stranger.

I tried to act a little cagey just to make it seem a little less easy.

"Well... I, ah..." and so on. Elek seemed to fall for it.

While we spoke about security systems, Demitri pulled Mouse into a separate conversation about a party in Barcelona at New Year's. Apparently many of their fellow European art collector friends were going, and he wondered if we'd be interested in join-ing. For just a moment, I considered taking him up on the offer in hopes of gathering intel among the art set. There was no telling how many forgers and would-be art thieves would be at a function like that if Elek himself was going to be there.

But I had to remind myself to focus on one mission at a time. And right now I was hosting one of the most prolific art thieves of my lifetime. Just because I couldn't prosecute him for the theft of the crown, didn't mean I couldn't come after him later for any of the myriad other jobs he'd done.

And if by some chance I could ever arrest him in the US, it would mean any evidence he had against King wouldn't matter. King's American immunity deal would protect him.

"... someone like Le Chaton," Elek finished saying. I realized I hadn't been paying attention. Fuck.

"I'm sorry?" I said politely.

His eyes were so intense, I couldn't determine whether he was testing me or not.

"I said the security protocols you put in place will determine if your collection is safe from everyday home invasion or the bigger threat which is someone like Le Chaton," he repeated. "And of course, your budget will factor in."

I shuddered. "I've read up on him. The very idea of someone like that targeting my home... well, that's why I wanted to pick your brain. How can you be sure you have the latest technology? It seems like that kind of art thief can get around anything you put in place. I mean, hell, the man stole the crown right out of the Hungarian Parliament Building, and that thing was guarded by live men around the clock."

Elek's booming laugh almost made me jump in my seat. It did make Mouse flinch beside me. I reached for his hand under the table and squeezed. Maybe I shouldn't have baited the man, but I couldn't help myself.

"Nonsense. He did not do that job. He's not that good."

"But... all of the rumors say—"

"They got it wrong."

Nervous excitement made my hands and feet tingle. "How do you know?"

Intense eyes again. "It does not matter how I know." Tension flooded the room until Elek broke it with another laugh. "Besides, it's not like you have the Holy Crown of Hungary in your living room in Wooster."

I'd never told him where my alias lived, but he'd gotten it right.

"Well, no," I said with a laugh, "but I'd certainly like to have more impressive pieces than I have now. Other than the usual places, I don't even know where to look."

"I have a few smaller pieces I'm selling from my personal collection in Paris if you'd like to have a look," he offered before sitting back in his chair and taking a sip of wine.

"What kind of pieces?"

He shrugged. "I have a few lesser-known Warhol illustrations, Miró sketches, and a Degas ballerina sketch. I am also looking for a buyer for an exquisite Pissarro painting. *Sunrise in Hyde Park.* Simply breathtaking."

"Wow," I said, wondering how many were forgeries. "That's... tempting." I turned to Mouse. "Do you think we could make excuses with your family for Christmas? We could go to Paris to see Elek's collection and then go to Barcelona for the party if that's what you'd like."

He bit his bottom lip. "I don't know... my mom would be very upset. Could we... maybe fly home for Christmas and come back?"

I cupped his cheek and tilted his face down to drop a kiss on his forehead. "Of course we can. I know how much you enjoy spoiling your nieces and nephews."

He was right to make our excuses. We needed time to prepare for the gift we'd just been given. An invitation into his home where there was an apartment full of evidence of stolen and forged artwork. It was too good to be true. We'd have an opportunity to nail his ass if the theft of the crown didn't ruin everything for us, which I was sure it most likely would. Elek would have to associate our dinner with a handy distraction once he realized his crown was no longer aboard his yacht.

Mouse stood to begin clearing the table when an unexpected text buzzed my phone.

"Excuse me," I murmured, pulling it out of my pocket. I'd set it so that only Linney's messages would come through during our dinner. Hopefully this was the text to let me know we had the crown. If so, I could cut our dinner short.

They were out of broccoli at the market. Going to the other store.

I read and reread it.

Fuck.

I texted back. *You do not need broccoli that badly. Do not go to the other store.*

"Sorry," I said absently, slipping the phone back into my pocket. "Joshua's mom is a worrywart. If she can't get a hold of him on his phone, she tries mine."

Mouse had come back into the room to clear some more of the

dishes. "Oh, sorry. Did you tell her I turned my phone off for dinner?"

"Yes, dear. She apologized for interrupting. I told her you'd call her tomorrow."

Mouse stepped up behind me and placed a hand on my shoulder before facing our guests. "Who would like some dessert and coffee?"

I needed to stall for a little bit. If they were going to try hitting the house against my wishes, I at least needed to keep Elek and Demitri here as long as I could.

"Actually, sweetheart. Could we hold off a little while first? I'm still full from dinner."

Mouse blew out a breath and put a hand on his flat stomach. He looked sharp in the crisp white button-down and dark trousers he wore. "Oh phew. I thought I was the only one. I had no idea true Greek food was so amazing. I've been stuffing myself the whole time we've been here. I'm going to have to hit the gym extra hard after this vacation."

Elek gave him a creepy, slow-motion once-over. "You have a lovely figure, Joshua. I can't imagine a little indulgence would do anything to take away from it."

The hand Mouse had on my shoulder tightened almost imperceptibly. I put my arm around his waist and looked up at him. "He's right. But maybe you can encourage *me* to hit the gym instead," I teased, trying to lighten the mood.

Elek's attention moved to me. "You are both beautiful, sexy men. In fact," he said, leaning forward, "I would not be opposed to getting to know the both of you a little more... intimately."

Okay. This... was not what I'd expected to happen. But I had to tread carefully, because I couldn't risk them getting upset and leaving.

"Well..." I said with a grin. "Then what do you say we break out the good whiskey? It might help everyone relax a little bit more."

CHAPTER TWENTY-FOUR

KING

We decided I'd go in via the tunnel. It was easy enough to bypass the alarm connectors on the outside of the hatch, and Ziv would disarm the main system with his computer. He'd hacked into it already to prep the video loops.

This was the operation we'd planned originally, so we knew exactly what to do. I triple-checked I had everything I needed before slipping out of the van and into the drainage entrance.

Linney's sweet voice kept me company as I crouch-walked down the tunnel to the hatch. She'd been keeping an ear on Falcon's date night with Elek and assured me they were still at our house. There would still be guards at Elek's of course, but they wouldn't be in the bedroom itself.

When I was ready for Ziv to initiate the system override, I said, "Go."

Ziv's voice was calm when he replied, "Done."

I drilled out the simple lock and pulled the hatch door open. Thankfully, Ziv had eyes inside the house to confirm that there wasn't anyone in the wine cellar to see me enter the room from the tunnel.

I made my way upstairs, following his whispered instructions about guard movement and my own knowledge about the layout. When he confirmed the motion sensors had been deactivated, I entered the main-level hallway, hanging a right before making my way toward the master bedroom. According to Ziv, all of the guards were in the guard room with the exception of one walking around the perimeter of the house outside.

When I got to the bedroom door, I saw the dual fingerprint scanner and a numerical keypad. I went ahead and attached the number scanner, knowing full well Elek would have a long, convoluted string of numbers that would take the scanner longer than usual to determine. Meanwhile, I pulled out the prosthetic fingerprints.

After several minutes, the scanner finally beeped with the right combination of numbers. I placed the fingerprints on the keypad and entered the number. When the lights flashed green and I heard a muted beep, my heart thundered with excitement. Having Elek and Demitri gone for the night had made this much easier.

Once inside the bedroom, I spotted the display case immediately. The crown was lit from inside the case, and the gold of the crown shone brightly. I couldn't believe I was standing in Elek's bedroom looking at the Holy Crown of Hungary.

After approaching the case, I looked for all the indicators on my list of potential security obstacles. Pressure pads, wiring, motion sensors that were attached to the main system, and anything else that looked out of place. There was a pressure pad around the display stand, but I could easily reach across it.

I knelt on the floor outside of the area holding the pressure pad and used my screwdriver to pry off the panel at the base of the display stand. Inside, I found all of the electrical wires. There was wiring for the system we had already deactivated remotely, the lighting, and one other set of wires I didn't recognize. I followed them from the floor up to the base of the glass box holding the crown.

"What are you here for?" I muttered at the wires. I racked my brain to think of all the things it could be until I finally noticed an additional fingerprint scanner mounted underneath the glass box. It had to be Elek's print.

Sure enough, I used the prosthetic with Elek's print and heard a click. When I unscrewed the base of the glass box, it lowered easily into my hands, bringing the crown within reach.

Now all I had to do was release the special fasteners. They were no longer connected to the security system, but they did keep the crown mounted to the display case. Since I couldn't sneak out of the house with a large heavy display case, I had to get the crown off its mount.

I swore half the purpose of these fancy fasteners was to slow down a thief long enough to get caught. But I'd spent hours practicing on them at home and had it down to a science. When the crown finally came free, I slipped it into the slim pouch on my back, set a single Greek coin in its place, and closed up the display case the way I found it.

When I pushed myself up from where I'd been crouching, I almost stumbled onto the pressure pad. I didn't want to assume the pad was connected to the security system Ziv had deactivated, so I didn't know how close I came to screwing everything up. It didn't matter. I had what I needed, and it was time to go.

When I told Ziv I was ready to exit the bedroom, he told me to hold still. Nerves gripped my stomach as I realized that meant the guards were no longer contained to the guard room. I stayed quiet until Ziv gave me the all clear.

He navigated a clear path to the wine cellar for me, and within moments I was safely in the tunnel. As I made my way out, I couldn't help thinking how smoothly that had gone. Which, if it had been the old Elek, would not have surprised me. He wasn't as up on the latest security tech I was. But then, how in the world had he gotten the crown out of the Hungarian Parliament Building?

It still didn't make any sense.

I waited at the end of the tunnel until I heard Linney's familiar voice tell me to come out. I raced to the van and jumped in, sliding the door closed behind me and turning to give Ziv a high five. The three of us were ecstatic. This was what we had come here for, what we had planned meticulously for, and even when the plans had changed, we had overcome the last of an obstacle and still got my hands on the treasure.

I couldn't wait to see Falcon's face when I handed him the crown.

As Linney drove us back toward the small town where we would wait until it was time to pick up Falcon and Mouse, I heard Ziv pecking away at his phone to send Falcon the all clear.

As soon as we were parked on a side street, the three of us huddled in the back of the van to go over the op. I explained in detail what I had found in terms of security, and I expressed my concern over it having been a little too straightforward.

Linney asked, "What could he have done that would have made this harder for you?"

I shrugged. "I mean, if he used a random guard's fingerprint so that it was harder to know which one to get. But then that's a pain in the ass when you want to go to bed. And then, if money isn't an issue, why not put fingerprint scanners at the hatch? Hell, why not put a complete secondary security system in that's wired to a battery backup? Thieves would be slowed down by having to do double the work. Double hacking, double deactivating, double video loops."

Linney put an index finger to her chin. "The only person who would know to come through the tunnel is you. Well, that's not accurate. Whoever built the tunnel would also be suspect, but they would be stymied by all kinds of security protocol before even getting close to the bedroom. And you have to admit, Elek would not expect you to have access to his fingerprint."

"That's a very good point. He knows I can make a prosthetic fingerprint, but he wouldn't in a million years think I could get his fingerprint without his knowledge," I admitted.

"And everything you described is a bit overkill when it's only going to protect you from the absolute topmost elite art thieves, of which there are currently two: you and him," Linney said.

Before we could spend too much time on it, Ziv got a text back from Falcon.

"Let's go," Ziv said with a grin. "Now, who's Hungary?"

Linney and I groaned at the stupid pun.

When we pulled down the long driveway to our rental house, I saw Falcon's luxury sedan from the night before still sitting in the driveway. I'd forgotten about it, but now I wondered why we hadn't just had Falcon and Mouse meet us at the private airport since we had two vehicles.

"Hey, guys," I said, "just drop me off and head toward the airport so you can get the stuff loaded. We'll meet you there."

"Sounds good," Linney said. "Do you want to leave the crown with us?"

I laughed. "Not on your life."

Ziv shot me a look. "If you take off with that thing, I will find you and I will shove it so far up your ass your liver will demand control over an Eastern European country."

"I'm not going anywhere, except to get Falcon and Mouse and meet you at the airport. I promise."

I hopped out of the van and jogged to the front door, making sure to enter the house before they'd pulled out of the driveway just in case they really needed reassurance.

"Who's your daddy?" I called through the house. "If you're ready, come and get it."

Falcon came from the direction of the kitchen, grinning wildly. "You really got it?"

After putting on the cotton gloves I'd stashed in my pocket, I slipped the pack off my back and opened it, setting the crown on a nearby table under a bright lamp. But as soon as I took a closer look, I saw something strange.

I leaned in closer and reached out to touch it carefully.

"Falcon, this is a forgery." My heart was in my throat. *Could it be?*

How the hell had Elek had time and resources to make a forgery this good? And where the hell was the real crown? My heart sank into my stomach.

I'd failed them all. I'd underestimated Elek, and now we were back to square one.

Falcon stood close to me, our shoulders brushing. He leaned in to take a close look.

My hands shook as I pointed to the corona graeca. "Do you see these enamel plaques? They were created using techniques you can't replicate easily today. The scratches and lustre… I just… I know this is a forgery. See how the pearls all have a similar tone? The original is more varied in size and tone. It's practically impossible to forge something with so many different artistic elements." I looked at him. "This isn't the Holy Crown of Hungary, Dirk."

He looked hesitant, and I wondered if he believed me.

"Falcon…" I began. There were more details I could give him, about the nuanced visual effects of the enamel, the lack of aging in the cracks and crevices. About how I'd seen the replica crown in the Carter Presidential Library in Atlanta and knew the difference between a thousand-year-old original and a modern-day forgery. I could see this one was better than the one in the Carter Library, and it might fool plenty of appraisers, but not someone whose bread and butter had once been the study of perfecting forgeries. But before I could say any of that, Mouse came out of the hallway with a bag over his shoulder.

"We ready to go? Oh shit, is that it?"

He pushed between us, but I kept eye contact with Falcon over Mouse's head. Something was going on. Either Falcon knew the truth and wasn't telling me, or someone at the FBI was lying to him.

But why?

"Let's go," Falcon said. "We can talk in the car."

He was right. We needed to be gone before Elek figured out his precious crown was missing. I bundled it back up in the bag and slung it on my back before following the two of them out to the car. Just as we pulled down the driveway, a sleek Mercedes sedan turned in.

Mouse sucked in a breath. "That's Elek's car. He must have forgotten something."

Falcon muttered under his breath, "He didn't forget anything. He knows."

"Go around him," I said, ducking down. "And then speed like hell so we're out of sight before he has a chance to turn around."

"Got it."

He slowed down and rolled down his window as if he was going to stop and ask Elek what he needed. But as soon as Elek slowed to a stop beside us, Falcon floored it, shooting out into the road with a screech of tires.

But Falcon did exactly as I suggested, hauling ass down the deserted road and swinging a hard right onto the main cross street toward the small airport. It was late enough for the roads to be deserted, so he was able to keep up a high rate of speed through the town, turning here and there as Mouse came up with some quick-thinking navigation to keep from being predictable. When we finally came screaming into the airport lot, we were ready to make a run for the plane.

I grabbed Falcon's arm before he reached the airplane stairs. Mouse jogged up ahead of us into the plane.

"Wait. We need to stay here and look for the original. Maybe he still has it, or... shit, did Hungary replace the original with a forgery? Did Elek steal a forgery thinking it was the original?" I loved that idea. That would make my fucking day.

Falcon searched my eyes, clearly torn between doing his job and doing what was right.

I begged him. "Falcon, you know more than you're saying. What the hell is going on?"

"King, just get on the plane. Elek has to know where we were headed, and I'd prefer to lift off before he comes screeching in here."

"But—"

"Let's talk about it when we get in the air," he said, putting his hand on my lower back, under the backpack. "Come on." He nudged me up the stairs while I thought about how to convince him I was right.

But it didn't matter. Because sitting in the closest seats to the front were two overly large meatheads I didn't recognize. I froze midstep, causing Falcon to bump into the back of me, pressing the hard crown into my back through the thin sack it was in.

One of the men stood up and smiled. "Agent Falcon, I'm Agent Martin. Nadine sent us to escort your team safely back to Paris."

CHAPTER TWENTY-FIVE

FALCON

My hands went immediately to King's hips and squeezed in hopes he'd somehow be able to interpret that as my *holy shit, this was not expected* gesture.

"Nice to meet you," I said politely, reaching an arm over King's shoulder to shake the other agent's hand.

The new agent introduced his fellow agent before leaning toward the cockpit and telling the pilots we were good to go.

King moved awkwardly past the agents, clearly trying to keep his sack from being spotted. It was a little silly since the men had to know we wouldn't be there if we didn't have the crown with us.

When we reached the sitting area farther back in the plane, the rest of the team was waiting for us.

"What's with the extra muscle?" Linney asked softly over the sound of the engines ramping up. I glanced out the window but didn't spot any crazed Hungarians peeling into the lot. "Security for…" She glanced at King and back to me. "The crown?"

"No idea," I admitted just as softly. "But Nadine was acting strange earlier on the phone. I was hoping we'd be able to get out of here before she had a chance to do something like this."

I realized it was the first time I'd admitted to blatantly defying orders from a superior. It wasn't a great example to set for my team, and it made me pause. Had I completely lost my mind?

"Why would we need extra agents?" Ziv asked. "It's not like..."

He caught himself before admitting we'd been retrieving a fake the entire time.

I turned to look at King and found him glaring at me. "Yeah, *Dirk*. It's not like... it's *real* or anything."

"Fuck," I muttered before looking back at my team and stating the obvious. "He knows."

"Damn," Ziv said. "Sorry. But it was bound to happen. The man's a forger for god's sake."

"I wasn't allowed to tell you," I said to King. "I'm sorry. I wanted to. Believe me."

Linney added, "He did. It was driving him crazy."

King's walls were coming up before my very eyes. "Yeah. Just doing your job. I get it. We were here to do a job. And now the job is done. Mission successful."

He moved past me and dropped into a seat by the window on the other side of the aisle from the rest of the team, removing the soft bag from his shoulders and tossing it into the seat next to him like it was holding nothing more than a paperback and candy bar for the flight ahead. I took it and put it in an overhead compartment before slipping into the seat.

"King..."

"We don't need to talk about it," he said without looking at me. "I'm going to get some sleep. Adrenaline crash, you know."

I was reminded of what he normally liked to do after an op.

Sometimes after an op, I wish someone would hold me down face-first and fuck me into the mattress.

Memories of doing just that flashed in my mind before I could stop them. I wanted to reach out to him, touch him and reassure him just how much it had killed me to keep the forgery details secret from him.

But was that true?

Because I'd already broken the rules when reassuring him about the undercover agent in Hobie. Why not this? Was it because I truly didn't trust him?

"What do you know about the history of the crown?" I asked him.

He was silent for a long time, and I wondered if he truly had slipped off to sleep that quickly. But then I remembered the flight from California and MJ telling me he was faking it.

"King. I know you're not asleep. What do you know about the history of the crown?" I repeated.

King huffed out a breath and shrugged. "I mean, I know it was used in coronations. At one point the US had it. And it normally lives in the Hungarian Parliament Building. Which is, like, insane with security. There are armed guards around the clock, and some are in charge of watching the crown."

I nodded. "So the part about the US... We had it for several years between World War II and President Carter's time in office."

King's eyes opened long enough to roll. "Yes, I know that."

"The US was originally pressured to return it to Hungary when the Hungarian government was still unstable. Hell, when the entire region was still unstable. So someone took it upon themselves to requisition a forgery in case we ended up having to return it before we fully trusted the Hungarians to keep it safe. The problem is, when the crown was finally returned in the seventies, we returned the wrong one by accident."

King's eyes widened as the implication of it sank in. "Wow. Can you imagine if Hungary had held on to one of our national treasures for safekeeping and then returned a forgery?"

"No, I can't," I said. "But that's irrelevant at this point. And because President Carter's decision to finally return it to Hungary had been such a diplomatic expression of trust and a kind of benediction of sorts, we couldn't risk telling them about the mix-up at the time. We simply had to let it stand."

King sat forward, clearly interested now. "You're kidding. So that's why this is so hush-hush. We need to swap them out before returning it. Right an old wrong."

"Exactly. So now you know why we can't simply go in and arrest Elek. The US can't be involved in this, and that includes an FBI art crimes team being the ones to find the crown," I explained. "We simply need to get the forgery out of circulation and concoct a way of returning the original to where it belongs."

"Where is the original?" he asked, turning in his seat to face me. "And did Elek know he had a forgery?"

"The original is currently on its way to Paris. And you tell me if Elek knew. I hope not."

King shook his head, hair flopping adorably from one side to the other. "No. He was never good at spotting forgeries—that's partly what drew him to me in the first place. Also, people don't tend to look for them unless they have reason to suspect. And if he took this piece off the display under guard at the parliament building, he would have never in a million years expected it to be a forgery."

"Good. If that information got into the wrong hands, it could be a big problem for the US. Once the forgery is destroyed, there at least won't be any proof of the mistake," I said.

"The deception, you mean," King corrected. "Or, what some might call the *theft* of a valuable piece of *art*."

I bit back a sigh. The man deserved his bitterness.

Ziv stood up and stretched before wandering up front to hunt down some drinks and snacks. Mouse pulled a travel blanket out of a nearby compartment and snuggled into the far corner by a window to sleep. Linney stuck in her earbuds and started a movie on her iPad.

That left King and me in awkward silence.

Why did I feel compelled to apologize again for doing my job and following orders?

I clenched my jaw together to keep from saying something stupid.

"I'm pissed off at you," he mumbled, turning toward me and leaning his head on my shoulder. The public display of affection surprised me. I looked up, but no one was paying attention. Besides, according to Linney they all knew anyway. So much for professionalism.

I reached for his hand and threaded my fingers through his. It felt so good to touch him again.

"I know," I admitted softly. "You have a right to be. I'm sorry."

"I don't accept your apology, but I'm going to put it aside for the duration of this flight because I'm exhausted and you're warm and soft."

"Gee, thanks," I muttered, secretly thrilled I was still allowed to touch him. "Every FBI agent's dream is to be described as soft and warm."

"It's better than grumpy and deceptive."

Touché.

I turned and reached for the adjustment on his seat, reclining it back all the way before doing the same to mine. After finding a couple of blankets and throwing one over him, I settled back into my seat and reached for his hand again, pulling him until his head was back on my shoulder.

"Better," I murmured. "Sleep."

It was a five-hour flight to Paris, and we spent every minute of it trying to get as close to each other as possible, trying to make the most of every one of our final moments together.

If there was one thing the forgery situation had made clear, it was that I still didn't fully trust him, and he sure as hell didn't have reason to trust me.

And there was no future between us without trust.

———

As soon as we landed in Paris, the agents escorted us directly to the office, despite the ungodly early hour. When we arrived, Nadine was waiting to take custody of the forgery.

"Well done," she said with a huge smile after peeking into the bag. She didn't remove the crown since there were a few support personnel in this part of the building, but she took a good look at it to confirm we'd accomplished what she'd sent us to do. "Let's go into the conference room and regroup."

We followed her into the room, but before everyone sat down, King asked where the men's room was.

"Oh, sorry," I said. "I should have shown you on the way in. I'll take you." I turned to excuse us, but Nadine stopped me.

"Back out to the reception and hang a left. Agent Falcon, please stay. I want to ask you something while Mr. Wilde is out of the room."

Well, that was awkward. I shot an apologetic glance at King, who just shrugged. Despite our sleep on the plane, he still looked wiped out.

Once he was gone, Nadine closed the door. "If we plan an op to infiltrate the parliament building to return the original crown, I need to make sure we have a secondary support op in place to keep your asset from wandering off with it."

It was on the tip of my tongue to promise her he wouldn't do that, but I decided there was no point. She wasn't going to take my word for it. I had a proven track record of not being diligent enough or thorough enough when it came to Le Chaton.

So I nodded instead.

"Your team will be in charge of the primary op, and Agent Martin here will lead the support op," Nadine continued, gesturing to the agent who'd escorted us back from Greece.

I nodded again.

"Linney will be in charge of making sure Agent Martin's team is read in on the primary op. He will also have custody of the original until Mr. Wilde is ready to enter the parliament building."

She continued to go over some of the logistics, explaining we would spend today creating the infiltration plan and travel to Budapest the following day. By the time she wrapped up her spiel, she nodded to the agent closest to the door.

"Please invite Mr. Wilde to rejoin us."

The agent stepped out and looked around, but there was no King Wilde to be found.

And when he wandered to the men's room to find him, there was no King Wilde in the men's room.

It turned out, there was no King Wilde in the building at all. Our sneaky thief had pulled a runner.

At least this time I hadn't been the one to let him go. I'd simply been following orders.

If only following orders didn't leave me feeling like I'd done the wrong thing.

CHAPTER TWENTY-SIX

KING

In addition to being royally pissed off at the whole forgery deception, I was also feeling squirrelly about Falcon's boss and whatever plans she seemed to have for me next.

I'd fulfilled my obligation to the FBI. They had no reason to keep me.

So I left.

It wasn't like I was going to flee the country or anything, I simply wanted to have a long hot shower and a nice deep sleep in my own bed. I hadn't slept in my apartment in weeks, since before the Berlin job and the Hobie trip. So I made my way out into the winter air of early morning and found the nearest Metro station. Granted, I didn't have any of my things from the trip, but I had the most important items in the cargo pants I still wore.

When I finally returned to my apartment, I was shocked to find my grandparents drinking coffee at my kitchen table with MJ and Neckie.

"What the hell?" I asked.

"He's here," Doc said, standing up and grinning from ear to ear. He held out his arms for a hug, and I fell right into them.

Thank god.

My eyes stung as I felt the familiar solid body against mine and smelled the Old Spice aftershave he always stole from Grandpa's Dopp kit when they traveled together.

"How'd you guys get in here?" I asked. Not that I minded. But as someone who prided himself on being particularly sensitive to home security, it was worth finding out how they'd breached the perimeter.

"You forget who taught you how to pick a lock," MJ muttered into her coffee mug.

"It was Saint," I said with a laugh.

"Yeah, well, he taught me too."

There had been electronic systems to override as well, but I also knew that the doorman could access all of that if my sister knew how to sweet-talk well enough. Which she didn't, but her girlfriend certainly did.

"Hey, Neckie," I said after hugging Grandpa's neck and dropping a kiss on MJ's cheek. "Welcome to Paris. How long have you guys been here?"

"We got in yesterday," Doc explained, sitting back down in the chair next to Grandpa. "I overheard Felix offering MJ and Neckie a ride to Paris on the royal jet and thought that sounded like fun. Felix and Lio had to get back home for some ceremony or something, so they couldn't stick around. Hope you don't mind the impromptu visit."

"Of course not," I said truthfully. "I have plenty of room, and you can tell me all about the wedding. I'm sorry I missed it."

I poured myself some coffee and took a seat. Someone had gone out for fresh pastries and set them out on a platter in the middle of the table. I helped myself while soaking in the familiar chatter of my family all around me. In the moment, I felt the sudden strong urge to move home. I missed them so much.

After a while, Doc and Grandpa moved to the more comfortable seating in the living room, and Neckie said she wanted to go out and wander around to see some things. Before she and MJ left the apartment, MJ pulled me aside.

"How did everything go?"

"It's complicated," I said.

"Yeah, tell me something I don't know. Falling for a law enforcement officer definitely complicates things."

"No, I mean the mission itself. It... turned out to be... part of a bigger picture. Even though I got the crown... they might want my help sneaking it into place."

"No," she said firmly. "Nope. No. You'd need a new immunity contract, King. One that protects you in Budapest."

"That's why I left before they could rope me into it. I needed time to myself to think."

MJ smiled in understanding. "Well, you know those two are going to fall asleep on the sofa for their morning nap," she said, tilting her head at our grandfathers. "So why don't you do the same in your own bed."

"You read my mind," I said. "Have fun with Neckie. There are extra Metro maps in the kitchen drawer if you need one."

She held up her phone. "Got it all on here from my last visit. Thanks."

Once they were gone, I made my excuses to the dozing men on the sofa, taking a moment to appreciate how sweet they were curled up together. Grandpa lay behind Doc with an arm tucked firmly around his middle. Doc's hand rested on top of Grandpa's with their fingers entwined, and Grandpa kept sneaking little kisses to the back of Doc's ear as he murmured something to him.

I wanted that so fucking badly.

As I made my way back to my room, I thought about how much effort I'd spent shoving those desires down since the Van Gogh job. It was obvious to me my feelings for Elek were more a result of wishful thinking than actual love.

I'd had more intimacy and affection in a few stolen moments with Dirk Falcon than I'd ever had with Elek Kemény.

My shower was sparkling clean and more inviting than usual. I blasted all the jets and stepped inside, rolling my shoulders and blowing out a big breath.

It's over. Relax.

Easier said than done. But I tried my best, and by the time I finished the shower, I'd scrubbed myself raw with my favorite loofa and jacked off to the memory of Agent Falcon pounding my ass in Mykonos. I threw on some lounge pants and fell face-first into my comfortable pile of blankets, seeking oblivion.

And that's what I got, for at least a few hours. But then I was woken up by a decidedly nonpaternal hand stroking down my bare back to the top of my ass.

I jumped up with a gasp, thinking one of my grandfathers had finally descended into dementia when I saw Falcon's familiar square jaw and dark stubble. My heart flipped around in my chest.

"What the fuck," I croaked. "You scared me half to death."

I moved back to lean against the headboard before clutching my chest and trying to calm myself down. Falcon sat on the side of the bed and reached out to run fingers through my hair. It was such an affectionate gesture, it didn't help slow down my heart rate at all.

"Sorry," he said. His eyes were soft, and the edges of his lips curled up. The man liked me. He may have been sent there to retrieve me for the job, but there was no doubt in my mind the stoic FBI agent wouldn't soften his gruff demeanor for just anyone.

And that made me putty in his hands. All I'd ever wanted was to be cared for like that. It was a dangerous temptation. It meant I'd do anything for him.

I cleared my throat. "What... what are you doing here?"

"Did you know there are two old men having sex on your sofa?"

I scrambled off the bed and was halfway out of my room before I realized I didn't want to see that. I turned and slunk back to my spot on the bed.

"Gross, but yeah, that doesn't surprise me. They're horndogs sometimes when they think we're not looking. It's kinda sweet."

Falcon nudged me over so he could sit next to me. He kicked off his shoes and got comfortable, leaning his head on my shoulder the way I did to him on the plane.

"Why'd you leave?"

I reached for his hand and began playing with his fingers in mine. "I needed to think. I needed some sleep."

I needed perspective.

"I understand. Nadine hasn't been in the field for a long time. She's forgotten how hard it is to come straight off an op and be thrown into another one."

"Yeah, that sucks for you guys. But once she made a point of excluding me, I remembered quite happily that I didn't work for her. So I came home."

Falcon lifted our hands to his mouth and began leaving open-mouthed kisses on my knuckles.

"She wants you to return the crown for us," he said. "I'm not sure that's a good idea."

I wasn't either, but I wondered if it was for the same reasons. "Why not?"

"You don't have immunity in Budapest," he reminded me unnecessarily.

"Yeah, I was thinking about that. I decided I'll do it anyway."

Falcon dropped my hand and turned to face me. "Why? No. I don't think you should."

Happiness flooded my chest. He was telling me he cared more about me than the mission. I was probably smiling like a fool.

"I want to. I'm good at it. I won't get caught."

Falcon shook his head. "Nadine said the same thing, but I'm not so sure."

I wasn't sure how to feel about that. "Gee, thanks? I mean, I only have a history of eluding law enforcement at every turn…"

"No, King. I mean this time it's different." His brow furrowed in dismay.

"How?" I asked. "There won't be guards in the rotunda since the case is empty. It's the only time I *can* get in without being caught."

"The FBI will be watching your every move," he countered. "What if one of them somehow… tips off the Hungarian police or their National Bureau of Investigation?"

This was a surprise. "You think someone on your team would betray me like that? Seriously?"

I thought I'd won Ziv over during our shared ops, but maybe not.

"No, not someone from my team. I just mean… everything I hear from Nadine about this situation indicates the US will do anything to avoid being associated with the replacement of the crown. They don't want to take the chance of someone discovering our involvement. So you—a well-known art thief who's been acting on his own for years—would make the perfect scapegoat. I don't want to take that chance."

I thought about my own motivations, the last desire to see Elek pay for what he'd done to me and what he was continuing to do to others.

"I'm willing to take that risk," I told him. "Tell Nadine and everyone else that I'll be back at the office in two hours. I want to have lunch with my grandfathers first, okay?" I also needed to make a call, but I wasn't about to tell him that.

Falcon smiled. The worry was still clear in the lines on his handsome face. "Okay."

"Do you want to come to lunch with us? I'd love to introduce you properly this time. My grandfathers are like a second set of parents to me."

He surprised me by saying yes. And as soon as he stepped out of the room to call Nadine with an update, I scrambled to lock myself in the bathroom and call Elek. He'd already unblocked my number and tried calling me ten times while we were in flight. I hadn't mentioned it to Falcon.

"Where the fuck is it?" Elek barked into the phone. "So help me, *macska*, I will—"

I cut him off, ignoring his use of the endearment while threatening me. That was so like him. "I'll exchange it for the Delacroix forgery."

"No. You will return it to me now in exchange for me letting you live."

"Mm, I don't think so. The forgery or I put it back under round-the-clock guards and tell them to replace the old ones with unbribable ones this time." It was a guess, but I was pretty sure that was the only way he could have gotten the crown out in the first place.

"Pick something else," he growled.

"I don't want anything else. I want my painting. I didn't see it in the house, so I took the crown instead. I will be in the parliament building tomorrow night at two in the morning local time. Meet me there to make the exchange or I put it back in the display and phone it in."

I hung up and powered down my phone with shaking hands.

Dear god, please let this work.

CHAPTER TWENTY-SEVEN

FALCON

I had to trust King to do the job without getting caught, and I reminded myself of the many, many jobs he'd managed to complete without getting caught. The only time we'd caught him had been when Elek had deliberately tied the man to a radiator and set off the alarm.

So I set aside my worries at least long enough to enjoy lunch with his family.

It was strange. I'm sure if I felt that way, King felt it even more acutely. There we were, previous sworn enemies and current quasi lovers having a lovely cafe lunch as if we weren't in the middle of a clandestine operation between two countries.

"Une carafe d'eau, s'il vous plaît," I said to the server before turning my attention on King's grandfathers. We'd been introduced in the apartment before King had hustled us down the street to a nearby restaurant. "I apologize again for taking King away from your wedding celebration."

Doc reached over and squeezed King's shoulder. The look on his face was soft with affection for his grandson, and it was nice to see King receiving such loving attention.

"We missed him, but we know he's well respected in his field which must make him very in demand."

I glanced over at King, whose face had turned a mottled watermelon shade. "He is very good at what he does," I confirmed with a grin.

King shot me a look that was half exasperation and half pleading. I winked at him. Whatever he'd told his family about what he did for a living was his business, not mine.

Doc turned to King. "MJ said you were thinking about moving back home. Is that true?"

King's eyes flitted to me again before dropping to his water glass. The movement caused his hair to flop down over his eyes. "Maybe. I don't know yet."

I reached out to brush my hands through his hair again, if only to let me see his eyes more clearly. But as soon as my fingers reached his hair, I froze, realizing what I was doing in front of his grandfathers. I must have looked as caught out as I felt because all three of them laughed.

"It's okay," King said softly. "I mean, it is with me if it is with you."

I leaned in and kissed his cheek, pausing there a few extra beats to inhale his scent and feel his skin against mine.

"I guess I can't keep my hands off you," I admitted.

King's grandfathers' eyes sparkled, and I could tell poor King was in for some major teasing later.

Doc put his arm around his husband. "It took a while before this one was comfortable with PDA. All those early years of being in the closet did a number on him." He looked fondly at King's grandpa. "But I'm the same as you. Can't keep my hands off the man."

"How long have you been together?" I asked.

"Forty-five years. But we've been best friends for over fifty," the other Mr. Wilde said.

"They met in Vietnam," King supplied. "Grandpa flew helicopters and Doc was a medic."

"Wow. That's amazing."

After a quick break to order our lunch, the two men launched into some stories about raising kids together on the ranch. Those quickly segued into stories of a young King which made me laugh until I thought I was going to make a scene.

"I finally realized when he said 'paint horse' he meant actual paint," King's grandpa explained with tears of laughter sneaking out of his eyes. "I wandered into the barn and found my best filly covered in rainbow stripes for the town parade. And by the way, she wasn't even a paint horse. She was an Appaloosa."

King's face was beet red, but he was laughing along with them. "Hey now, I credit myself with inadvertently starting Hobie's first pride parade."

"You were six years old," Doc said. "I'm not sure you knew what pride was."

"Maybe not," King admitted, "but I had it nonetheless."

"High achiever," I added with a wink, squeezing him closer with the arm I had around the back of his chair.

Two women walked up, and I could tell right away which one was King's sister by the suspicious look she was aiming at me.

"You must be MJ," I said, standing to grab extra chairs for them.

"I am. And this is my partner, Neckie."

King stood and helped me squeeze the six chairs around the small four-person table. "Guys, this is Dirk Falcon."

"Sounds like a porn name," MJ muttered.

"Hush," Neckie warned. "Don't be a bitch." She turned to me. "I think it sounds more like a Tom Clancy hero myself. It's nice to meet you, Dirk."

"You too." I waited for them to take their seats before sitting back down. "Did you see anything fun?"

"We went lingerie shopping," Neckie admitted, blushing prettily. "MJ spoiled me."

King groaned and buried his face in his hands. Their grandfathers just continued laughing. I might have mumbled something along the lines of "That's nice."

After a few minutes of small talk, MJ cut through the bullshit.

"Don't fuck him over. You got me?"

I blinked at her.

King groaned again. "Jesus, Em. Cut it out. I can handle my own business."

She cut her eyes at her brother. "It's not your business I'm worried about."

Neckie and the grandfathers sat back and looked at them with knowing smirks. No one intervened to help poor King.

"I don't want him hurt," I said. "In fact, I tried to convince him to be done. He should stay here and enjoy your visit."

MJ looked at King in surprise. "Is that true?"

King glared at me before looking at his sister. "I can handle it. But we need to get going. Can you get Doc and Grandpa back to my place?"

"Of course I can."

"We have GPS on our phones, and your apartment is like ten steps away," Doc said.

"The last time you tried to use GPS, you ended up in Oklahoma," MJ corrected.

Doc threw up his hands. "I was going to Oklahoma!"

"You were going to the stage production of *Oklahoma!* at a theater in Dallas," MJ muttered. "But we're not talking about you, we're talking about King and his stupid inability to let things—"

"I got it," King interrupted, standing up and kissing his grandfathers on the cheeks. "I promise. I'll only be gone a couple of days. Don't leave."

MJ's face softened into one of maternal concern. "I'm not going anywhere. Memorize my number like I told you."

King leaned in to kiss hers and Neckie's cheeks too. "I love you too, big sis."

I gave everyone a wave and told them it was nice meeting them. I hoped like hell the next time I saw MJ wasn't in a Hungarian courtroom.

As we made our way out of the restaurant into the cold

December air, King wrapped a scarf around his neck before reaching for my hand and threading his fingers between mine.

"I like them," I said. "They're sassy like you."

He chuckled. "My baby sister's name is Sassy, so I always think of her when someone uses that word."

We made our way two blocks over to the nearest Metro entrance and descended into the warmth of the station. Once we were seated on the train, King surprised me.

"Tell me why you don't have a family."

"Oh... ah... well, I was what they used to call a change-of-life baby. My parents were in their fifties when they had me. They'd spent years trying to start a family, but it never happened. Then when my mom thought she was going through menopause, it turned out she was pregnant with me.

"Needless to say I was an only child, and by the time I went to college, my parents were in their seventies. My dad died of a stroke when I was at the academy, and my mom died of pneumonia about five years ago. It was right after Luca and I broke up. That's why I took the job here. I just... wanted to leave it all behind. I was gutted. I went from thinking I was finally going to settle down and give my mom grandkids, and suddenly Luca was gone and then she was gone too."

"I'm sorry," King said. I could hear the sincerity in his voice. "I had like... the opposite experience. I can't even begin to know what it's like not to have tons of family around. You must feel... unanchored."

I shrugged, pulling his hand onto my lap so I could hold it with both of my hands. "Even when both of my parents were around, it was a small, quiet family. It's why I chose to go to school at Michigan State. They have a great criminal justice program, but they also have a huge student body. I wanted to be around people and energy. I craved it."

"How did you get into the art side of it?"

The train reached our stop, so we stood to exit with several other people. "That part was more of a fluke. I took an art history class as an elective freshman year and loved it. I ended up taking so many more art history classes, I had almost enough to double major. So I added the French classes and made it happen. Once I had the double criminal justice and art history, it was a no-brainer."

As we walked through the station, we continued talking about our favorite art history classes, specific pieces that had contributed to our love of art, and the aspects of the subject we didn't like so much. King surprised me when he started talking to me about his independent study of famous forgeries.

"There's actually this underground layer of art history centered around forgeries," he explained.

"I've read several books about it," I admitted. "It's fascinating stuff. Just a tiny bit relevant to what I do for a living," I teased.

"Oh, yeah, of course," he said, blushing. "It's just... that's... I feel silly admitting this, but..." King huffed out a laugh and looked up at the sky for a moment before looking back at me and smiling enough to bring out the dimple next to his lips. "I have a designation... a mark that indicates a forgery is mine."

"Why are you telling me this?"

He shrugged and slipped his hands into his pockets. "I don't know. I think... I think I want you to know so I can't... so I won't be tempted to ever do it again. Now you'll be able to catch me."

The admission was surprising, like watching him deliberately tumble down a wall that had been standing between us.

"What's the mark?"

"I find the most horizontal line closest to the lower left corner of the work and make it bolder."

The information sat like a weight between us. It was important because it represented his trust in me. It also represented his commitment to his own future away from art crime.

I bumped his shoulder. "Not quite the same thing as a big flourishing signature, is it?"

"Unfortunately, forger marks are pretty damned subtle," he said with a bashful smile.

"Thank you for telling me," I said after a minute. "That can't have been easy."

He laughed and bumped my shoulder back. "Definitely not. I'm regretting it already."

"Liar," I said, reaching out to wrap my arm around his shoulders and kiss his temple before telling him about some other interesting books I'd read on art history and the current art market. Even though we'd come at it from opposite ends, it was something we had very much in common.

The walk back to my office was deceptive. It felt like a date. We'd had a lovely lunch, I'd met some of his family, and then we'd walked along learning new things about each other.

So when I recognized my office building, it brought me up short. "Oh. We're here."

King dropped my hand like a hot potato, leaving my warm palm to the mercy of the December chill. We approached the building as lovers, but we entered it as colleagues.

I guessed it was better than officer and detainee, but not by much.

When we joined everyone in the conference room, there was news. Mouse blurted it out first.

"Elek booked a commercial flight from Athens to Budapest an hour ago. He arrives in Budapest tonight."

I turned to King, but he looked just as surprised as I felt. What the hell was going on?

CHAPTER TWENTY-EIGHT

KING

I couldn't believe Elek had actually taken the bait. I could only hope he'd brought the painting with him. Even if he left it back in his hotel room, my plan could still work.

We spent the afternoon planning our entry into the Hungarian Parliament Building. It wasn't an easy building to sneak into by any means, but I'd had a couple of years to research how possible it would be if I was ever stupid enough to try it.

And now that the rotunda with the crown display case was no longer under guard, it was actually possible. I explained that part of any good heist in a publicly accessible place like this was a last-minute recon trip to make sure there were no obvious last-minute security additions since the last assessment.

It was a lesson I'd learned the hard way while in Ukraine. The estate hadn't had dogs until the night I'd attempted to break in. It took me an hour to find an all-night market, and even then, I was half-convinced the dogs would be too well trained to be tempted by raw meat. I'd gotten lucky.

Nadine said she'd already sent an agent ahead to do some recon, but that if I felt the need to do a final walk-through, we would be in town the following day early enough to get tourist entry to the building. Thankfully, they still had the rotunda open for visitors since their cover story for the missing crown was a simple regular maintenance break. According to the official record, the crown was with the preservation specialist getting its annual spa treatment.

I wondered what they would have said if they never found the crown.

Ziv and I worked together to make sure he was comfortable with the security systems he'd need to trick, and Linney went over the equipment we needed. Mouse took charge of replicating how I was to place the crown in the display to both secure it and properly position it for accuracy. Nadine reminded me on several occasions that I could always abort the primary mission to return it to its home in the rotunda and hide it somewhere inside the building along with one of my notes. It would be easy to call in an anonymous tip to alert the curator as to its location.

By the time we broke for the night, I had a raging headache. I dreaded going back home and being a complete downer to my family since I'd already ditched them that morning for a nap. To be honest, I wasn't even sure they were expecting me home tonight.

So when Falcon leaned over to murmur in my ear, I wanted to cry with relief. "You're coming home with me, and we're going straight to bed."

I simply nodded, texted MJ, and gathered my things, making sure I had the important items I'd left there earlier. If all went well, I'd never be coming back here again.

———

Falcon's apartment was on the outskirts of the city, but it was charming. He rented the ground floor of a narrow town house that was white-painted brick with glossy black doors and shutters. When we stepped into the apartment, I felt immediately at home. The comfortable furnishings, rich colors, and varied array of house-plants everywhere were so incongruous to the gruff special agent, the first thing I did was bark out a laugh.

Then a pair of matching black-and-white cats uncurled from the sofa and came meandering over to Falcon's feet, periodically stretching and arching to make sure he knew he wasn't that important.

I laughed again and slapped a hand over my mouth. "I'm so sorry," I muffled through my fingers. "You have cats. That's... unexpected." I noticed something else hanging across the back of an overstuffed reading chair. "Is that a cardigan?"

"We should have kicked the fucking grandpas off the sofa and stayed at your place instead," Falcon grumbled, leaning over to pick up one of the cats.

"If you tell me their names are Salt and Pepper, I'm going to—"

"This is Coolie, and that's Gus."

I stepped forward to pet Coolie's head, murmuring to him before looking up at his handsome owner. "If by *any* chance you named your cats after C.M. Coolidge and Gustav Klimt, I will drop to my knees right this minute and blow you where you stand."

Falcon plunked the cat onto the floor and reached for his zipper, a wide grin appearing on his face. "Open up, buttercup."

How was it possible this special agent who'd been gunning for me almost five years had turned out to be my dream man?

I sank to my knees and batted my lashes at him, licking my lips and smacking my mouth in anticipation. "Gimme."

Falcon's rumbling laugh always went straight to my cock, and tonight, with his surprisingly warm and inviting home surrounding us, it was even more intense. He'd let me into his inner sanctum, something I knew he never would have done if he'd been playing me or trying to manipulate me for the purpose of his job.

This was real, just the two of us. And for one brief night, I was going to enjoy it to the limit.

I clasped my hands behind my back and opened my mouth, sticking my tongue out in invitation and locking my gaze on him. His eyes darkened.

"I didn't really mean it," he said in a rough voice.

"I did."

Falcon fished out his cock and smacked it against my tongue, reaching out with his other hand to clasp my chin. "Fuck, you're sexy," he murmured, continuing to paint my lips with his precum before feeding me the tip. I kept my eyes on his as I went to work, licking and sucking and worshipping him with all the gratitude I felt: gratitude for being with him tonight, for being with him at all, for caring enough about me to warn me against the Budapest mission, and finally for his trust in me to complete the job without getting caught.

Never in a million years had I expected this man who'd had so much bitterness toward me in the beginning to invite me into his life in such a personal way. Falcon's home revealed the human side of him, a side I was sure he didn't show to many people. I'd noticed worn-out slippers kicked off by the door, a little rainbow flag propped in a jelly jar of pens and pencils on a bookshelf, and a small plastic Eiffel Tower statue that proved he'd at some point succumbed to one of the street hawkers in any of the many tourist areas of the city.

This was the representation of the real Dirk Falcon, and I wanted to sneak around memorizing every square inch of it.

But first I wanted to swallow his cock and make him scream.

I reached out and grabbed his hands, putting them on the back of my head. He got the message quickly enough and began testing me with shallow thrusts at first until I lurched forward and took him into my throat, showing him what I'd meant.

After that, it was a frenzy. He groaned and thrust, fucking my mouth with increasing speed and depth until saliva dripped from my chin and the choking sounds from my throat heated up the entire room. I hoped the cats had run away long before this, but I didn't know for sure.

Because throughout the whole thing, I kept my eyes on Falcon and he kept his on me.

It was the hottest blow job I'd ever given, and just as he was about to come, I pulled off him to take his load on my face. I'd never done anything like that before, even with Elek. I'd been attracted to

Elek's dominance, but never felt comfortable fully submitting to him.

With Falcon it was totally different. I had this strange desire to prove my submission to him, as if... as if showing him that while the first five years of our relationship had been under my control, it was his turn now.

He was in charge if he wanted to be. I was his for the taking.

After the last of his orgasm had painted my lips, I continued to stare up at him. His fingers had raked into my hair and continued to hold my head in a tight grip. I could tell by the look on his face he understood exactly what I'd been doing, what I'd been trying to tell him with my actions.

"Take off your clothes and get in my bed."

I stood up and turned toward the hallway on the other side of the room, assuming his bedroom was that way, but he grabbed me and pulled me back, slamming his mouth onto mine in a searing kiss.

I whimpered and melted against him, soaking in every bit of the praise he showed me in that kiss. After pulling off, he kissed every streak of his own spunk off my face before kissing me on the lips again.

"Go," he said, nudging me in the direction of the hallway. "Or we'll never make it to the bed."

I found his bedroom easily because the first one I came to was too plain and tidy. It looked like an unused guest room. The one at the end of the hall, however, was a lot like mine. The bed was made with super-soft sheets and a duvet with extra throw blankets. Squishy down pillows were stacked just how he liked them as if he'd slept there last night.

There was a book on his bedside table I recognized as a recent release about the contemporary art market and the rise of mega dealers in the industry. I'd forced myself not to buy it as part of my commitment to a new life outside of the art world, but now that I saw it on his bedside table, I had to laugh.

He was as obsessed about the art world as I was, and he'd been right when he'd joked about having museum posters because it was all he could afford. The framed prints around his apartment were as varied as the pickings in a thrift shop. He had classics like *The Kiss* from his cat's namesake, and more obscure pieces like a Ben Smith wood block print. It was the kind of hodgepodge that would drive a curator crazy trying to make some kind of sense of the display, but in this cozy apartment, it somehow worked.

One of the cats jumped up onto the bed and curled into a tight ball, clearly anticipating a nice cuddle with his man. I had news for him. There was a new kitten in town.

"Scoot over, Gus," I murmured, peeling my clothes off and tossing them over a chair in the corner of the room. When I slid between the cool sheets, I reached out to pet his silky fur. "I think your dad's feeding you in the other room." He didn't budge, and I didn't blame him. The bed was so comfortable, it felt like heaven.

That was the last thing I remembered until morning.

CHAPTER TWENTY-NINE

FALCON

After feeding the boys and making sure there wasn't a note from the neighbor who cat-sit for me, I finally made my way to the bedroom to find King dead asleep curled around Gus. Coolie followed me into the bedroom and jumped up to join them, completing the domestic little tableau that fed into all of my fantasies.

In Greece, I'd made some snap judgments about King. I'd assumed he wasn't the settling-down kind because he seemed right at home in the glitz and glamor of the jet-set art life. I'd watched him schmooze at the gala with other elites who seemed to travel from one luxury destination to another, and I'd assumed he enjoyed that life.

But then today, I'd seen him with his family and heard about a completely different side of him.

His grandfathers had told me about a teenager who'd begged to mow the lawn because he found it meditative. They described a skinny knock-kneed version of King who could often be found hiding in the hayloft of the barn sketching his favorite scenes from around town and the ranch. When King interrupted one of their stories to describe the small town of Hobie, something had lit up in his eyes. I could tell he missed it. As different as a place like that was from his current Parisian life, Hobie seemed to give King a sense of place, of belonging.

His grandfathers told me about King volunteering at a rec center youth program to help teach art to young children after it had been cut from the school budget. King had pointed out that his grandfathers had been the ones to bankroll the program. He'd been trying to take the focus off his good works to put it on his grandfathers' generosity, but Doc hadn't let him.

He'd said, "Remember Winnie's friend Cherry?"

King had groaned and begged them not to tell the story, but I'd put a hand over his mouth and asked politely.

"Cherry was diagnosed with melanoma on her face when she was twelve, which is super rare," Doc had said.

King's soft voice had interrupted. "Doc's late wife, my grandmother, died of melanoma, so it hit us all pretty hard."

The love in Doc's eyes as he continued was palpable. "King here went over to Cherry's parents' house and offered to paint her portrait before the surgery. And then a year later, after her disfiguring treatment and several surgeries to try and repair it, he painted another one, making her look just as gorgeous as before. You could see the strength in her. He just... he just captured it beautifully."

King's grandpa had taken over when Doc had gotten choked up. "Cherry just had her second daughter, and damned if the first doesn't look just like her."

That was when I'd finally put the pieces together.

King Wilde used art as his way of expressing love.

He'd produced forgeries for Elek in hopes Elek would love him. And when that didn't work, he stole art Elek wanted him to steal.

I watched King's sleeping form as I unbuttoned my shirt. He tried to right his wrongs by stealing pieces from wrongful owners and giving them back to rightful owners. He kept Elek from his wish list items as a symbol of withholding his love.

After taking off my clothes, I slid into bed next to him, curling around his back and feeling the comfort of his warm skin. Even though I knew better, I wondered what a life with King Wilde would look like long-term. His family had mentioned him moving back to the States, to Texas. What would he do there? Would he be happy? How would he keep art alive in his life in a way that satisfied him?

Just before drifting off to sleep, I wondered if King's insistence on returning the crown was indicative of his feelings for me. Maybe that was why he was insisting on doing it despite the risks—as proof of his commitment to me, to his new life.

It wasn't until he was entering the Hungarian Parliament Building with the crown the following night that I realized just how wrong I was.

King hadn't done any of this for me. He'd done it for Elek Kemény.

And the truth of that realization cut me deeper than I expected, confirming just how much I'd let myself fall for him in such a short period of time. So when King looked me in the eyes and begged me to trust him, I was once again faced with an impossible choice:

Believe King Wilde's emotion-filled plea, or do my job.

I was back in the middle of the Van Gogh job all over again.

CHAPTER THIRTY

KING

Keeping things from Falcon made me low-key nauseous all day. I'd woken up the morning of the Budapest job sandwiched between a hot slab of man muscle and two tight balls of black-and-white fur. It had taken about three seconds before the cats shot off the bed and I'd felt the slick intrusion of Falcon's hard cock pressing between my cheeks.

I'd tilted my hips back in invitation and enjoyed every second of his body's attention on mine. It was the kind of wake-up I could get used to very easily.

But that had been eighteen hours and another lifetime ago.

Now I was huddled in the back of a rental van on a side street in Budapest feeling like I was truly going to vomit.

What if Elek didn't show up?

Hell, what if he *did*?

Was it selfish of me to want my own closure on all of this? Yes, of course I knew it was. And I knew the risk I was taking with Falcon's career by fucking with his op, but it wasn't nearly as bad as the risk I was taking with his trust in me.

Ziv shoved my shoulder to get my attention. "What the fuck is up with you tonight? Linney just ran a comms test, and you sit there like dead fish."

"Maybe he's nervous," Mouse suggested. "Give him a break, Ziv."

"He's not fucking nervous," Ziv snapped. "Something's going on he's not telling us."

Falcon watched us silently from the front, not saying a word. His stoic face was impossible to read.

"Look," I said, "there's a reason I've never attempted the crown job. This place is a fortress. Can I be allowed a little bit of stage fright?" It wasn't a lie.

Falcon's eyes narrowed the smallest amount.

Please don't hate me after this, I thought for the millionth time.

"Fine, be scared, but test your goddamned comms for Christ's sake," Ziv said with a little less heat.

I did as he said and confirmed everything with Linney before taking another deep breath and mentally rehearsing the entry again.

"Do you want some chewing gum? It helps," Mouse asked, holding out a pack of mint squares. I smiled at him and took a couple, popping them in my mouth and muttering thanks.

"Why can't we just go now since we're ready?" Ziv asked. "I hate all this waiting bullshit."

"I'm going in a few minutes before two," I said for the tenth time. "If you'd like to do the breaking-and-entering portion of this job, by all means, then you go in now. But if you want me to do it, I'm going at the time I've determined I'm least likely to get caught."

Ziv held up his hands in surrender. "Fine. Whatever. I just don't get why—"

"Zip it," Falcon snapped. "King is on this op for a reason. He's the one of us who knows how to sneak into a building without getting caught, and that means even if he said we were doing this at high noon, we'd do it at high noon. The man knows what the fuck he's doing."

Everyone turned to stare at him for his unusual outburst.

His emotional reaction made me even more nervous. If I hadn't had the gum in my mouth, I might have actually puked.

Ever since the agents assigned to track Elek when he landed in Budapest had come up empty, Falcon had been a ball of stress. I didn't blame him. Elek's presence here was a wild card, something completely unpredictable for the by-the-book senior agent. I was sure it was the reason Falcon was so on edge.

It sure as hell was the reason *I* was.

For the third time tonight, I lifted open the top of the box that contained the real crown. The original Holy Crown of Hungary, also known as the Crown of Saint Stephen, glittered on a bed of black velvet. I couldn't believe I was in its presence, much less holding it.

Agent Martin, the heavily armed agent from the plane now solely responsible for escorting the crown, sat on one of the side seats against the wall of the van eyeing me suspiciously. I didn't blame him. If his job was to keep this thing safe, handing it over to anyone, much less a notorious thief, had to rankle.

The poor agent had done a piss-poor job of trying to sneak a bug and a tracker onto me when he climbed into the van next to me, but I'd recognized the "accidental bump" for what it was. The tracker could stay, but the bug was getting caught under my boot heel as soon as I was out of the van.

I looked at my watch again.

"Listen," I said, "If something happens—"

"Nothing's going to happen," Falcon ground out.

"No, but—"

He glared at me. "Nothing's going to happen."

I sighed and turned to Ziv. "If the Hungarian police get involved, get out of here. I can find my own way back to the hotel. That's all I was going to say."

"We're not leaving you," Falcon said.

"Don't be stupid," I barked, finally losing my cool. "It's not good for any of us—for the fucking FBI and Interpol—to be caught at the scene of this fucking thing, and we all know it. If I get caught, I can fend for myself. There's no need for you fuckers to get caught too. It will turn something manageable into a diplomatic shitshow."

He knew I was right, but I needed *him* to know it was okay to protect his team.

Because the Hungarian police were definitely coming.

"I'm asking you to trust me," I said to Falcon. "Promise me you'll go if something goes wrong."

I could see his jaw clenching in frustration. The man was caught between loyalty to his job and his country and a brand-new, delicate thread of loyalty toward me. While it warmed my heart to see his indecision, I needed him to know that he could have both if he would just trust me.

"We'll go," he finally said.

I nodded. "Okay, let's do this."

After slipping the crown box into the soft sack to sling onto my back, I winked at the agent next to me. "Thanks for this. I can't wait to slide it on and pretend to be a king while I'm taking a bubble bath in my secret lair later tonight. I've always wanted a crown of my very own."

The man's nostrils flared as his eyes flicked up to Falcon as if to assess just how crazy the senior agent was for allowing a notorious thief to take off with a priceless artifact. Falcon rolled his eyes at me, but I could see the tiny quirk of his lip too. I just hoped to god it wasn't the last time I saw him smile at me. With what I had planned, there was no way to know how he'd feel toward me in a matter of a few hours. I could only hope he'd understand.

I climbed out of the van and slid into the night.

CHAPTER THIRTY-ONE

FALCON

Watching King enter the Hungarian Parliament Building was excruciating and not because he was breaking the law. He was walking into danger, a situation in which he truly could get sent away to a Hungarian prison. If they charged him with stealing the crown, the people of Hungary wouldn't be satisfied until they had his head on a platter.

I knew he'd done jobs like this a million times before. I knew he was good at it and had a very low likelihood of being detected, much less caught. But I also knew Elek was in town and would be doing everything he could to get his hands back on the crown. And if he couldn't do that, I'd bet big money he wouldn't hesitate to turn King in to Hungarian authorities.

"He'll be okay," Linney said softly from the seat next to mine. We were squeezed together at the bank of comms equipment against the back wall of the van with Ziv and Mouse directly behind us working the monitors on their side. We'd sent the extra agent to go wait in the other van with the secondary team which meant we could finally speak more freely about King without me worrying about saying something too revealing about my feelings for him.

Ziv had hacked into the building's security system and had the camera feeds up on the monitor for the rotunda as well as the expected path King would take to get there.

Suddenly, Ziv snorted out a laugh.

I stiffened, my anxiety spiking. "What is it?"

"He just pulled something out of his pocket and dropped it on the ground. Look."

I leaned back to peer over his shoulder. King was stomping on something with the heel of his shoe.

"What is that?" I asked, squinting at the image.

"My guess is Agent Martin slipped a tracker or something on him when they got into the van."

"Smart man," I muttered, but if that was the case, part of me wondered why King would want to remove a tracker when we all knew where he was going anyway. Was it just the principle of the thing? Not wanting to be treated like a criminal?

"Okay, he's in," Linney confirmed as Ziv, Mouse, and I watched him disappear into the building through a nondescript maintenance door.

I turned back around to follow along on the monitors on our side, listening to Linney's periodic instruction for King to hold or go. My nerves began to calm as King expertly navigated the long staircases, his movements quick and lithe. This was what he was good at, I reminded myself. This was his element. I just needed to relax and let him do his thing.

Easier said than done given what was on the line for him. For all of us.

Everything progressed smoothly until just before he reached the rotunda. Instead of entering the large domed room, he ducked into a side door.

I straightened, leaning toward the monitor. "What's he doing?" I asked, as if any of them would be able to answer me.

"Maybe he heard something," Linney suggested. Her eyes bounced from screen to screen, a furrow appearing on her forehead. "But I don't see anyone nearby."

"Shit," Ziv said, pointing. "Intruder west-wing-terrace-level window."

"What?" I asked, swiveling back around. My heart thumped thickly in my chest as I watched a shadowed figure slipping through an open window and dropping silently to the floor inside before disappearing out of sight of the cameras.

Elek. It had to be.

Fuck. This was going off the rails just like we knew it would.

Why had we gone through with this mission? Why in the world did we think it would be successful?

"Six hundred ninety-one rooms and twenty-eight staircases," Ziv mumbled under his breath. "And... I found you, you bastard."

"Do we tell King?" Linney asked, looking toward me. "He's back in the main hallway now, entering the rotunda."

"Wait," I said. "Ziv, how far from the rotunda is the intruder?"

Ziv clicked through the floor plan, zooming out until even I could see clearly Elek was only four rooms away. Shit, that was way too close for comfort.

"Yeah, Lin," I said. "Better tell him to hurry up."

Her voice was smooth and clear. "Pick up the pace, kitten."

"Don't call me that," King replied immediately. "Don't ever call me that."

Linney turned and blinked at me in surprise. "He knows what Le Chaton means, right? The man speaks French."

"He knows. Just focus on the op."

"Elek, or whoever this fucker is, is getting closer," Ziv warned. "He's one room away. Ascending the final staircase."

I leaned in to the microphone and pressed the button. "You've got company coming from the staircase directly across from you."

Linney gave me a pissy look and took the microphone back from me. "Stay in your lane, boss."

Fuck.

King's next message was mostly static.

"Repeat that?" Linney said.

"Call the Hungarian police. Now." There was an edge to King's words that I recognized as nerves or fear, the same sound he had after the gala when he'd been upset about the bruise on Demitri's jaw.

I hated hearing the stress in his voice when I couldn't be in there to watch his back. He was vulnerable on this op to begin with, and now he was asking us to sound the alarms?

"Ask him what the fuck," I hissed.

"Hey, Texas," Linney said, "You smoking crack?"

"They should have been here by now. *Call them.*"

Ziv and Linney both looked to me for the order.

No fucking way. The words were on the tip of my tongue. No way was I calling the cops, not on King. I didn't give a damn that it would ruin the mission. What mattered was that it would ruin King. If the police arrived and he got caught... I couldn't even let myself finish that thought.

I refused to let anything happen to King. Not when he was under my care. And I was just about to tell him that when he said, "Boss, please trust me. I'm asking you to trust me."

The words hit like a punch to the gut, sucking the air from my lungs.

Trust.

He wasn't asking me as an agent trusting a thief; he was asking me as Dirk to trust King.

If that's what it took for me to prove to him that I trusted him— cared about him—then so be it.

I turned to Ziv. "Call it in."

He hesitated, watching me for a second to see if I would change my mind. "Do it," I said, the command harsher than I expected.

Ziv nodded and turned back to his keyboard, making the call from his computer. A robotic voice said something in Hungarian after the phone was picked up. I had to assume it was something about an intrusion into the parliament building.

I stared at the video feeds on the monitors, my eyes flicking between the screen showing King in the rotunda and Elek slowly approaching. Elek passed under a security light, and I noticed something in his hands. I frowned, leaning closer. "What's he carrying? Is… is that a painting tube?"

What the hell was he doing?

Mouse said, "Why would he have that?"

"He's not stupid enough to steal from the same place twice, is he?" I asked, squinting to see if I could make out any details.

I took the microphone from Linney again. "Texas, what's going on?" I asked, using the same impromptu call sign Linney had picked after kitten was summarily rejected.

There was no answer.

"Texas," I said again, more urgently.

Nothing. I looked to Linney.

She clicked frantically on her own laptop before shaking her head. "He cut the audio."

Mouse leaned forward. "Maybe once he realized it was Elek in the building, he figured this would be a good chance to nail him."

"Wrong choice of words, Mouse," Ziv muttered, keeping a close eye on the camera feeds. They were all we had now, and Elek was finally in the rotunda, approaching the crown display case. My stomach knotted with both fear and anger.

How dare Elek break into the parliament building a second time. And how the hell was King going to react?

"But they'll get King too," I reminded them. "They'll catch him with the crown."

"Not if he puts it in place first and gets the hell out of there," Mouse said.

Why wasn't he doing that? King stood by the display case, not making any move to open it. Instead, he was looking right at the other intruder.

And it was clear as day that King didn't display any surprise at seeing his ex which made my stomach fill with acid. He'd planned this. *They'd* planned this.

Was King Wilde double-crossing us? Had I just made the biggest mistake of my career *again*?

"Linney, get those comms working," I barked even though we all knew if King didn't want us to hear what was going on, there was nothing we could do about it.

I turned to Ziv. "Contact the other team and put it on speaker."

A few clicks and then Agent Martin's voice came over the speakers. "What's the status of the asset?"

I ignored him. "I was hoping you could tell me. Do you have ears inside?"

"No. Your man destroyed the bug the minute he stepped out of the van. The tracker still works though. It shows him dead center of the rotunda."

I murmured thanks before indicating to Ziv to end the call.

"Why destroy the bug and not the tracker?" Mouse asked.

Ziv groaned. "That's what he was destroying. A bug. He wouldn't have worried as much about the tracker unless he was planning on running away from us."

Was he planning on running away from us? At this point, I didn't know squat about what King Wilde had planned. All I knew was that he'd expected me to trust him, but he hadn't trusted me enough to tell me anything.

What if this had all been planned? What if he and Elek were still together? What if...

"They're talking," Linney said, pointing to the monitor.

Sure enough, the two men were standing face-to-face in front of the empty crown display case. I could tell by their body language the words were heated. King tried to turn and walk away, but Elek grabbed him and pulled him back.

Okay, so they weren't together. Or they were, but they were arguing.

"Should we go in there?" I asked.

"Absolutely not," Mouse said at the same time Linney and Ziv said something similar.

"In fact, we need to go," Ziv added.

"No," I said evenly.

"He told us to go if something went wrong," Mouse noted. "Elek showing up and the police on their way is definitely something wrong."

"No," I ground out.

I wasn't leaving King.

Linney put a hand on my shoulder. "He asked you to trust him. And even if you didn't trust him, you can't think having an FBI agent caught in the Hungarian Parliament Building is acceptable. No matter what happens, we can't be caught here. He was right before. We need to leave. The cops are coming."

She was right, but I couldn't bring myself to leave when he was clearly in trouble. What was I supposed to do?

King took the bag with the crown off his back and handed it to Elek just as the sirens finally began to scream.

My entire career came crashing down in front of my eyes as King Wilde handed over the Hungarian Crown to Elek Kemény while I just sat there and watched.

CHAPTER THIRTY-TWO

KING

What the hell was taking the police so long? Maybe Elek's original bribe hadn't been with a guard but with the whole damned police force. I'd hoped they'd get to him before he made it to the rotunda, but now here we were.

Face-to-face for the first time since the Van Gogh job, since he'd bashed me over the head and left me tied to a radiator.

My entire body shook with nerves, but I tried my hardest to fake bravery.

"Let me see my painting," I demanded before he could speak.

"Let me see the crown first."

I turned to leave, but he grabbed me by the bag on my back and yanked me toward him. "Fine," he said, popping open the tube. "Here."

When I saw the raw edges of the canvas inside, I let out a breath of relief. He'd brought it. He'd really brought it. Now if only he'd do what I hoped.

I handed him the bag from my back and reached for the tube in exchange. Elek yanked the tube out of my grasp and held it away from me.

"Crown first, *macska.*"

I stepped back and held up my hands. "Go ahead, then."

Elek tucked the painting tube under his arm and opened the bag before pulling out the crown box. Sirens screamed through the air, finally, and Elek's face snapped up in angry response.

"What the fuck did you do?"

"I didn't do anything. Give me my painting. We need to get out of here," I said, reaching again for the tube. He smacked my hand away and stepped back out of my reach, shoving the box back into the bag and turning to leave with both the tube and the bag.

"Give me my painting," I hissed. "You promised."

"And you believed me? Ah, poor little *macska*, always wanting to trust when you shouldn't trust."

"Elek!" I snapped. "You have the crown. Let me have this last piece. *Please.*"

I waited until he was halfway across the huge space before I rushed him, jumping onto his broad back and trying to wrestle the tube out of his grip. Elek was so much bigger than I was, he shook me off easily. I grabbed at his ankle, holding on for dear life and trying to become dead weight. I just needed him... a little... closer... to the large metal grate on the floor.

Finally we were there. I whipped out a zip tie and looped it through the grate before connecting it to a second one and zipping it loosely around his ankle, all the while complaining loudly and yanking on his leg in hopes he was too engaged in denying me the painting to realize what I was doing.

"What the hell? Let me go," he warned, trying to hold on to the knapsack and painting tube at the same time. "If we want any chance at escaping, we have to go now. Are you crazy? What are you..."

Elek finally realized something was wrong. It wasn't my dead weight holding him in place.

When I heard the shouts of the officers entering the large domed hall, I yanked the ankle tie as tightly as I could and reached for my comms unit.

"Please get out of here," I said. "I hope you're gone. If not, go. Trust me and go," I repeated before finally letting go of his leg.

"I *am* trying to go, you idiot," Elek barked, clearly thinking I'd been talking to him. "My leg—what did you do? Kingston! You fucking fuck!" He wrestled with the tube and the bag with the crown box inside. While he was busy trying to hold on to his spoils, I patted his cargo pockets until I found the multi-tool I knew he most likely had on him.

"Thanks for this," I said, holding it up out of his reach. "I could have used this two years ago, but someone convinced me I didn't need one for the Van Gogh job. At the time, I remember thinking I never wanted to see you again. I was wrong. Seeing you like this right now is so fucking satisfying, I can't even begin to describe it. Good luck, Elek. Or… should I call you *macska?*"

He raged at me as I turned and took off at top speed for an interior door I'd identified from the schematics I'd studied for years in hopes of one day sneaking in to leave a note in protection of the crown.

I followed lit green signs for the exit I needed and finally came to a door with danger warnings and authorized-personnel markings. I pushed through with gloved hands and held my breath.

There it was. A small padlocked grate by the floor with a flood caution sign on it that should lead to tunnels that dumped into the Danube river. I got to work as quickly as I could, pulling out a set of picks. The memory of learning how to pick locks with my brother Saint came unbidden into my mind as my fingers worked from muscle memory.

But this wasn't a childhood prank, and now I was trapped in the basement of the parliament building in Budapest with every law enforcement officer in the entire city converging on my location. As soon as they discovered that someone had breached their precious parliament building for the second time in a matter of weeks and they still didn't have the crown back, all hell was going to break even more loose.

And Falcon is going to hate me.

The padlock finally popped open, and I ignored my stupid internal dialogue in favor of getting myself the hell out of there. Once through the hatch, I crawled forward about ten meters before hanging a right and continuing crawling for twenty meters more. Finally I came to a metal grate that was also padlocked closed as well as wired up with all kinds of alarm sensors. I pulled out the picks again and got to work. I could smell the water of the Danube even though it was too dark to see much of it through the openings in the grate.

Once the lock was popped, I went to work splicing the wires to trick the alarm into thinking everything was fine. As long as I could change over the connection faster than the disconnect blip could register, my exit location would hopefully remain a mystery, at least for a while. I wouldn't know either way since it was a silent alarm, so I moved as fast as I could, opening the hatch when ready and falling from the opening to the water ten meters below.

It was a long drop, and it felt even longer as I twisted through empty air. The night was dark, so I couldn't tell how close I was to the river's surface until I hit it. Frigid water crashed over me, threatening to steal the air from my lungs. I kicked out my arms and legs to keep from sinking too deep. The river was probably only two meters deep, and I didn't want to risk ramming my body into the bottom at top speed.

Once I made it back to the surface, I silently tread water for a moment, catching my breath and listening for any evidence I'd been followed. I could still hear the police sirens and the cops shouting orders, but it all felt far away. Here, down in the river, everything was calmer.

I was safe. For now. I pulled off the thin black face mask I'd been wearing to conceal my identity and reached into a cargo pocket to retrieve the little foldable snorkel I'd stashed there.

I shoved the thick rubber mouthpiece between my teeth and stuck the end just outside the surface, blowing hard to empty it of water before I could begin breathing through it. I didn't have anything as elaborate as a mask, but this would be enough to help me stay under the dark, murky water until I could get some distance between myself and the parliament building.

Since I couldn't see, I stuck my left hand out to feel for the stone wall in hopes it would keep me oriented southward and help push my cold, waterlogged self through the water. I tried not to think about what was in the water. None of the world's big-city rivers were exactly pristine, but the Danube was at least better than it had been in the past.

Since it was December, the water was fucking freezing. I'd estimated it to be around forty degrees Fahrenheit which meant I could stay in it about ten to fifteen minutes before hypothermia would cause some serious problems. I kept my eyes closed and arms out while I thought about the thick duvet and pile of my favorite blankets waiting for me back at my apartment. As soon as I thought about my apartment, I realized I had a long way to go before getting back there.

First I had to get my hands on one of my stashed go bags so I could move on to the next phase of the plan. While I made my way to the nearest bridge so I could climb out of the water without people seeing me, I thought of Falcon and what he must be thinking right now.

Did he hate me? Was he in big trouble with his boss? Or was there any chance he was worried about me? That was too much to wish for.

Would he understand why I did what I did?

I pulled my cold, heavy body from the frigid water and thought of the man who'd shown me time and time again just how much he was willing to trust me. At the scene of the Van Gogh theft when I'd played the victim. At the vineyard when I'd said I just needed to collect my things. In Greece when I'd insisted on attending the gala with him. And when he'd allowed himself to show some vulnerability to me in the bedroom.

At every turn, Dirk Falcon had shown me his giant heart. And even after me fucking him over multiple times, he'd continued to remain rock steady and give me the benefit of the doubt. I wanted to run to him and tell him I was finally done with all of the stupid things I'd asked him to put up with. I wanted to feel his strong arms around me and his deep, rumbling voice reassuring me I hadn't used up the last of his forgiveness.

I didn't know what the hell I would do if I had.

As I moved through the streets toward the public locker that held my stuff, I knew it was time to prove to Dirk Falcon that the trust between us went both ways.

It was the only move I had left.

CHAPTER THIRTY-THREE

FALCON

After catching up with the van several blocks over and regrouping, Nadine finally felt free to speak freely.

"Are you out of your fucking mind? No, I'm the crazy one giving you another chance after showing such piss-poor judgment on the Van Gogh job. You clearly misread this situation, misjudged your own asset. How could your entire team be so far off on this one, Agent Falcon?"

I'd been expecting this, but it still hurt like hell to hear the words out of her mouth. By trusting King, I'd betrayed my job and screwed over my team.

"The end result is exactly what you wanted," I said calmly, trying to do damage control. "A Hungarian national is caught at the scene of the crown heist. There's no connection to us. Win-win all around."

"And your asset? Where the hell is King Wilde?"

I cleared my throat, wondering whether I'd ever get the chance to spank the fuck out of King for putting me in this position.

"He seems to have taken a different way out of the building than originally agreed upon."

On the one hand, I was glad he hadn't gotten trapped inside with

Elek. On the other, the FBI would now consider him a fugitive asset who'd bailed in the middle of a mission after handing over a valuable antiquity to a known criminal.

To put it mildly, I'd never be able to bring him to the company picnic.

"I've already spoken to local police," Nadine said.

My head spun. "Already?"

"They called in help from the task force. I explained we already had a team in Budapest investigating the theft of the crown. According to the police, the suspect they caught inside the rotunda was found in possession of a painting he claims is a forgery sold to him by Le Chaton. Needless to say, the man has offered all kinds of information about the notorious thief in exchange for his own freedom."

Fuck.

"Okay, we need to get over there before Elek says anything else," I said quickly.

"You mean Elek, King's *partner*?" she asked. "Because there's no other way they would have been there in that room at the exact same time unless they'd coordinated it."

I'd thought the same thing, so it was driving me crazy that my heart still wanted to trust King when all evidence pointed to just how much I shouldn't.

I was being an idiot. He'd already proven more interest in either revenge or partnership with Elek than in following my own damned orders or, hell, even being honest with me about his plans. I couldn't have it both ways.

Either he was still working with Elek for some reason—in which case he'd played me yet again and I'd definitely be out of a job—or he wasn't in cahoots with Elek but had, instead, arranged some kind of revenge rendezvous he didn't trust me enough to tell me about.

Neither option was the behavior of someone who gave a shit about me.

To make matters worse? I was so worried about him, I felt like I was losing my mind. I slipped my phone out of my pocket and glanced at it in hopes of some crazy miracle scenario in which King had a phone on him and could reassure me with a call or text.

Assuming he cared enough to do even that.

Nothing. And the more time that passed without contact, the more I had to acknowledge King had his own agenda the whole time.

"So, you're now in charge of this," Nadine continued. "Get over there and prosecute an art thief. Thank god the man they have in custody is the Hungarian and not the American."

What could I do but laugh?

Nadine's mouth quirked up at the edges when I did. "This isn't funny."

"No, I know. It's just... you have to admit, this is kind of exactly the scenario we wanted... Elek Kemény alone in the rotunda with the crown."

"According to the inspector, there's no sign of the crown yet," Nadine warned. "If there is no crown and no King Wilde, this is going to turn into a real shitshow, Agent Falcon," she said, packing up a small laptop into her shoulder bag before slinging it over her shoulder and checking her watch. "I'm giving you the benefit of the doubt right now because I refuse to believe we just handed a thousand-year-old priceless antiquity over to a known art thief. I hope they got that detail wrong. Need I remind you that the last time these two worked together, they stole a two-hundred-million-dollar original Van Gogh off the interior minister's own wall? It's probably in some drug lord's sex den right about now, never to be seen again."

She was right.

I swallowed. "Yes, ma'am. We'll find it." I'd wanted to say King wouldn't do that to me, but what did I know about what King would and wouldn't do? Clearly the man didn't see fit to confide in me.

Once Nadine and her team were gone, Linney, Ziv, Mouse, and I stared at each other.

"Now what?" Ziv asked me.

I ignored the growing fear I had for King's safety. Regardless of all these mixed-up feelings and my concern over my career, I didn't want him hurt. Images of Hungarian police finding him hiding somewhere in the building and doing something rash flashed through my head. I tried to shove them out and concentrate on the task ahead.

"Now we go find that damned crown and put the Hungarian away once and for all."

When we entered the parliament building, the police directed us where to park before escorting us into the rotunda. Elek was hand-cuffed and propped against a column in the center of the room with guards standing close enough to make sure he couldn't escape.

My heart stuttered in my chest when I saw the bag with the crown on the floor. The box lay beside it completely empty. Since the display was also empty, it looked like Nadine had been right. The crown wasn't there.

"Who's in charge?" I called in English and French. It had become a habit after working with Interpol.

"I am," the officer replied in accented English. "Inspector Horváth. You are Agent Dirk Falcon with the art crimes task force, yes?"

I nodded. "What do we have here?"

The man indicated the painting tube an officer held with gloved hands. "Elek Károlyi, a Hungarian national residing in Greece and Paris, was in possession of what he claims is a forged painting sold to him under false pretenses by the thief known as Le Chaton, an American he identified as Kingston Wilde. He also claims Le Chaton was here in the building and had the Holy Crown with him."

"Where did he go?"

The inspector pointed in the direction of a doorway. "There is evidence of someone tampering with a small access door to the river wall."

The river. As in, the Danube. In December. As far as I knew, the man didn't have anything on his person besides an earpiece, a multi-tool, and whatever he may or may not have snuck in his cargo pants pockets when I wasn't looking. He certainly didn't have a wet suit or scuba tank.

And he was presumably all alone with no support. Was his frozen body floating in the damned river right now? What if something had gone wrong? Was he hurt? Was he running through the streets of Budapest with the stolen crown unprotected? What if someone mugged him for it?

I pulled my phone out and checked it again. Nothing.

The inspector was still talking. "We've deployed officers to search the water around the premises, but we don't know how much time he had before we noticed his method of escape. He'd shoved a wedge under one of the doors, presumably to slow us down."

Please let him have gotten away clean.

I knew it wasn't very ethical of me, but regardless of how King felt about me, I wanted him safe.

"Go ahead and take Mr. Károlyi to the station. You can hold him on unlawful entry while we sort all of this out," I told the inspector.

Elek sputtered, overhearing me and looking up. "Who? Me? You must be joking. I'm not the thief here. You forget the forgery and the history of Le Chaton."

Once he took a good look at me, I saw recognition dawn in his face. He looked from me to Mouse and back again. "What the fuck? This is..." He stared at me and squinted. "You're not..."

Elek's brain finally put two and two together and realized the man he'd met as an amateur art collector was actually the lead agent fighting art crimes in the world.

Oops.

I winked at him and enjoyed every minute of his face turning ashen.

"The forgery," Elek demanded. "I have a painting King Wilde forged, and I can tell you where all of his other forgeries are. They are in museums all over the world. This is only one of them."

The implication of his words hit me like a punch to the chest. If he gave us a list of major works that were discovered to be forgeries created by King... god, I didn't even want to think about it. King would go to prison. Since he'd never mentioned forgeries to us in the beginning when we were drafting his immunity agreement, he wasn't protected against them, only against theft. And if what Elek was saying was true... I couldn't even imagine how much trouble King would be in.

And there'd be nothing I could do to save him.

There was no point in stalling. We had a million witnesses to Elek's claim against King about the forgery. "Inspector Horváth, arrest him and get him out of here. Agent Mickey, go ahead and take a look at the painting if you would please."

Several officers escorted Elek out while he screamed in English, French, and Hungarian to anyone who would listen. I had to admit it was satisfying to see him in cuffs. I only hoped they ended up with more to charge him with than unlawful entry.

With the help of a few officers, Mouse found a nearby table and laid out a protective sheet before gently removing the canvas from the tube and unrolling it.

I stepped up next to him and looked to see if I could identify King's mark, but without the original to compare it to, it was impossible.

"I recognize this piece," Mouse murmured. "It's a Delacroix self-portrait. The original hangs in the Louvre."

Fuck.

"So you're sure it's a forgery?" I asked softly.

"No, not at all. I only meant I knew what painting it was. If it's a forgery, it's amazing, Falcon. Truly mind-boggling," he said, the awe clear in his voice. "But I'd need more time with it, and I need to pull up comparison photos of the original from archives from before King's active period. You know how this goes. I need my equipment which is back in the office."

"If it's that good, we need to work under the assumption this is the original," I said.

He stepped back and blew out a breath. "Oh thank god. I mean, I always assume it's the original, but usually it isn't. In this case though... I mean... wow. I've never seen anything like it. I thought I was looking at the best art forgery in history."

"Wait," I said. "You... you think this really could be the original?"

Mouse stared at the painting for a few more beats. "Let me put it this way, there's no way I'll be shoving it back into that cardboard tube just in case."

I thought of the implications of this new development. King hiding the crown before meeting up with Elek... Elek bringing what he thought was one of King's forgeries into the parliament building while King brought... an empty crown box...

Elek got caught in the parliament building holding an original painting that should have been hanging in the Louvre right now while King got away scot-free with the crown.

No. If there was one thing I knew, it was King's belief that the Hungarian people deserved their crown. Which meant... the crown was probably here somewhere or he had plans to bring it back.

And if it was here somewhere, that meant they'd assume Elek had stolen it. Well, not stolen it but... *returned?*

Had there ever been a thief known for sneaking art *in* rather than taking it out?

Why, yes. Yes there had been.

I rubbed my hands over my face to hide my grin.

King had just masterfully set up Elek Kemény to take the fall as Le Chaton.

And I'd just fallen a little bit more in love with him for it.

A clipped few words in Hungarian came from somewhere behind me. I turned to see a uniformed officer escorting a familiar man into the rotunda.

King Wilde strode into the room like he owned the place.

Good god, the man could wear the hell out of a suit.

I blinked to be sure my eyes were working. Yes, that was King Wilde dressed like a damned FBI agent.

"This agent says he's with your team," Horváth translated. "He presented a badge to my men at the door."

"Oh... ah, yes. Yes he is," I stammered, feeling my face heat. Should I have demanded they arrest the man? Maybe, but there he was. King, *my* King. Safe and sound and looking at me with eyes that pleaded understanding. I wanted to touch him. I *needed* to touch him.

I swallowed. "So good of you to join us," I said as drily as I could. "Little late, don't you think? We were *worried*."

He stepped closer and met my eyes. "I'm sorry. I promise it won't happen again."

If I stood any chance at getting through this without grabbing him and holding him close, I couldn't look at him anymore. It wasn't as easy as I'd hoped.

Ziv grinned like a loon, and it was Linney who gave King the side-eye. "Where were you?"

"Showering," he said before running a hand through damp hair. "What have we got?"

Mouse looked at King like he was the second coming of Christ. He might have even drooled. "We might have an original Eugène Delacroix here," Mouse said. "Can you give me your opinion on it?"

King stepped over to the table with the painting on it and crossed his arms in front of his chest. "That's the real thing," he said after a few minutes of contemplation. He murmured a few details, pointing here and there.

"That's what I thought," Mouse said excitedly.

Linney's eyes narrowed. "I don't understand. The man enters the Hungarian Parliament Building with an original painting stolen from the Louvre?"

I lifted a brow at King. "Good question. You're good with art mysteries. Any thoughts? Scratch that. Any thoughts on where the crown might be? Do you think *Le Chaton* might have hidden it somewhere?"

His eyes widened almost imperceptibly. "Yes. Yes, I do. Maybe..."

King wandered around in a circle as if orienting himself in a room he knew almost as well as his apartment.

Finally he wandered in the direction of his original entry point from earlier in the night.

The room he'd ducked into. I was an idiot. How hadn't we put this together yet?

When he came back into the room, he was carrying the crown in his gloved hands. "Did anyone bother to look in the stairwell?"

Suddenly, everyone was in motion. Horvát scrambled to shout instructions to the officers to call in the crown guards, another one of the officers spoke rapidly into his comms unit requesting the curator's team, and Ziv instinctively moved to Mouse's side to help protect the painting and our junior agent from the chaos.

From what I could pick up from the shouted Hungarian and everyone's body language, it was clear they were convinced they'd finally caught the elusive Le Chaton at the scene of the crime.

And his true identity was Elek Kemény.

CHAPTER THIRTY-FOUR

KING

I was so far past exhaustion when we got back to the hotel, I was shaking uncontrollably. Falcon and I hadn't had a single moment alone yet, and wondering how he felt about me now was wearing me thin.

I was terrified I'd ruined everything. The minute I'd seen Elek standing there in the rotunda, I'd regretted everything. He wasn't worth it, had never been worth it.

Why had I risked what was happening with Falcon in order to get this final revenge on a man who'd already taken so much from me?

Dirk and I were finally alone in the elevator, but neither of us said a word or even looked at each other. The tension between us snapped like tight bands, and I thought it was going to suffocate me. As soon as the doors opened, I lurched out and raced to my room, fumbling my key and nearly dropping it on the floor.

I needed inside. I needed time to myself where no one could see how fucking broken I felt. Falcon had barely looked at me all night.

When I finally got the door open, I stepped inside and let out a shaky breath before turning to lock the door and nearly banging my nose on Falcon's chin.

"Sorry!" I croaked before realizing it was the word I needed emblazoned on my forehead. "Sorry. I'm so sorry. I'm so—"

Falcon cut me off with a hard kiss, turning us around and pinning me to the door. His hand came up to clasp the front of my throat and hold me there while he ravaged my mouth and shoved his entire body against my front. His hard cock ground against my flaccid one, perking it right up.

"Don't fucking apologize to me again," he growled, nipping sharply at my jaw and then down my neck. "And don't fucking put yourself in danger like that again. Never again, Kingston. Never again."

I hiccupped and nodded; it was the best I could do under the onslaught.

One of his hands came down to grab the front of my suit pants and squeeze my dick. I squeaked and then groaned, shamelessly begging for more.

Falcon's thick thigh forced my legs apart before he ground his hip into my cock and moved his hand up to grab a fistful of my hair. My neck arched back until I was looking at his dark eyes.

"Please take me," I whispered. "I need you. Please, Dirk."

His hands were a blur, shucking off my suit coat, yanking at my tie, and damned near ripping every button off my shirt. But finally I was completely naked before him.

"You are mine," he said in a rough voice. "I don't know when you're going to get that through your fucking skull. You don't work alone anymore, goddammit. You work with *me*. Do you understand me?"

I nodded again like a bobblehead.

"I can't help you if you don't tell me what the fuck is going on. Don't you get it?" he snapped, rubbing his hands through his hair. "You drive me up the fucking wall."

Falcon's eyes narrowed and he spoke again before I had a chance to. "And don't you dare apologize again."

I nodded and kept my mouth shut.

"Get on the bed," he growled. "Hands and knees."

As I scrambled onto the bed, I heard him move to the bathroom, presumably to find my lube. When he came back, he was still fully dressed.

He tossed the bottle on the bed. "If you want prep, you have about ten seconds to make it happen."

I grabbed the bottle while he reached for his own belt and began unbuckling. We both knew he'd never ever hurt me. He was angry, but more than that, he was scared. I'd seen it the minute I'd walked back into the rotunda and seen his eyes.

The relief in them had been palpable.

As I fingered myself, Dirk's eyes got darker and darker until only the pupils were left.

He reached out and smacked my ass. "Enough."

The man was still wearing all his clothes, but his pants were open and his thick cock jutted out under his pristine white shirttails.

God, the man was sexy as fuck. I arched my back, tilting my ass up in invitation. Dirk groaned and reached for my hips, yanking me back until my ass was against his erection. I wiggled around, trying to feel him between my cheeks. When he finally pressed the tip against my hole, I sucked in a breath in anticipation.

"Please," I murmured for the millionth time.

His wide palm pressed against the middle of my back, holding me down firmly against the bed as his thick cock split me in two. Fuck, he felt good. With Dirk inside of me, I felt full, I felt *owned* in the very best way.

His body came down over the top of me when he bottomed out. "Oh god. Fuck, baby. *Fuck*, you feel so good."

Dirk's lips dragged up my spine, and his hands gentled. Suddenly, instead of being pounded by an angry agent, I was being caressed by an affectionate lover. The change in his demeanor made my eyes smart.

"Please don't do that again," he repeated almost under his breath. His cock stroked in and out of my body, and I felt the graze of his heavy balls against mine when he pushed all the way in. "I was scared for you. I didn't know where you were. They said you were in the water, and I couldn't—" He sucked in a breath. "I couldn't focus because—"

I scrambled out from under him and flipped over, grabbing him and pulling his muscular frame on top of me. I yanked my knees back so he could sink inside of me again.

Our eyes met and stayed locked together while Dirk resumed his slow thrusts in and out of me.

I reached up and held his face before pulling him down to kiss me. "It's done," I said softly against his mouth. "I should have never—"

His mouth crushed mine before I could finish, but it didn't matter. We both knew exactly where the other stood.

Dirk's thrusts got faster and harder, and his hand came down to stroke me off. The fabric of his suit pants scratched against my inner thighs, and his silky blue necktie fell against my bare chest. It was sensory overload in the best way. His grunts, my whimpers, the taste of his sweat on my lips... it was everything I wanted.

And I'd do anything to keep it.

The hand shuttling along my dick shattered all my thoughts until my balls drew up.

"*Agh, fuck.*" As soon as my orgasm hit, I heard Dirk grunt and felt him slam into me one final time.

We stayed pressed together, panting and sweating into each other's skin until Dirk finally pulled out and climbed off me, heading to the bathroom without a word.

I turned over and curled into a ball. My emotions were flayed wide open in a way they'd never been before.

Falcon returned and wiped me down with a warm cloth, murmuring words I could barely make out, but his tone was so affectionate, so gentle and kind, I finally broke, covering my face with my hands to hide my stupid fucking feelings.

"Hey, hey, woah," he said, moving onto the bed. He sat back against the headboard and yanked me onto his lap, reaching one arm around my waist and lifting another up to wipe a thumb under my eye. "Slow down. Why are you crying?"

"I'm not," I said, but it sounded like a sob.

He lifted an eyebrow, and I lost it even more.

"I'm sorry," I said again through tears. I tried to hide myself in his chest, noticing belatedly he'd stripped out of his clothes in the bathroom. "I'm just so tired. I'm sorry."

"Sweetheart, stop saying that." Falcon's voice was so kind and understanding, it only made me cry harder. "C'mere."

He pulled me in for a tight hug and ran strong hands up and down my back, murmuring reassurances into my ear.

I sniffed. "Why are you being so nice to me? I don't deserve it."

Falcon stopped what he was doing and pulled back to look up at me. "You are hurting, and when you're hurting, I'm always going to be nice to you no matter how annoyed I am. That's what you do when you care about someone."

"You care about me." I tested the words on my tongue. They tasted *so good*.

"I do."

"I just... I thought you'd hate me. I worried I'd ruined everything," I admitted, sitting up and fully straddling his waist so I could wipe my eyes with the heels of my hands. "And I'm so tired. All I wanted was to see you and have you hold me, and... and here you are."

"I don't hate you," he said with a soft smile, running his hands up my bare thighs to my waist. "Don't get me wrong, I'm pissed as hell you didn't tell me what you were planning, but if you had, it would have put me in a precarious position."

I nodded. "I know. That's why I couldn't tell you."

Dirk reached a hand up to thread fingers through my hair. "You planned all of this. You set him up."

I nodded again.

"But if you'd been caught in there..." His brows furrowed. "You would have been blamed just as much as he was."

I nodded again. "That's why I had to get the hell out of there."

"Why not just hand him the crown?"

I explained that if I'd actually handed Elek the crown and he'd somehow escaped, it would have been a disaster. I hadn't been sure I'd be able to zip-tie him. And if not, the crown still needed to be safely inside the building.

Dirk seemed to follow what I was saying. "But you got away clean and then came back, impersonating an FBI agent! Why the hell would you do that? It's a crime, King."

I met his eyes. It was important for him to understand.

"I know." I took a breath, but before I could explain, he seemed to understand.

"You were giving me something to arrest you for," he said softly.

"Yes."

"Why?"

"It had to be your choice, Dirk. I needed to know if you truly wanted to send me away, and you deserved a chance to make that decision."

His eyes pinned me in place. "How in the world could you think I wanted to send you away?"

My heart wanted to thump out of my chest and into his.

"I didn't think that. I just..."

"Do you trust me?"

I swallowed thickly, leaning my forehead onto his chest. "Yes. But it scares me."

Dirk's lips brushed the top of my head. "I know."

After a few minutes of him murmuring reassurances, he brought the topic back around.

"Tell me about the painting," Dirk said, leaning in and kissing my neck.

I shivered. "I can't think with your mouth on me," I groaned.

His lips moved down to suck on my collarbone.

"Dirk," I breathed.

He pulled off me with a cheeky grin. "I can't help it. You taste good. Now, tell me about the Delacroix. It's been driving me crazy. What did that have to do with all of this?"

Dirk's fingers came up to brush through my hair, and I preened into his touch.

"He had a forgery," I explained. "The last one of mine in existence. All the other ones have been destroyed."

"I'm figuring that out," he said with a laugh. "He said he has a list."

"Yeah, well, they're all originals, I promise. That was the last one. I saw it on the drone surveillance Ziv did the afternoon of the crown op in Greece."

"Your last-minute recon trip…"

I nodded. "That's when I swapped it out. I'd brought the original with me from Paris."

"The delicate tripod," Dirk said with a groan. "Was an original painting stolen from the Louvre."

"Yeah, sorry. But I had to make sure he had some stolen artwork on him when he got caught since I wasn't willing to hand him the crown."

"Wait, you boarded his yacht without backup?" he asked, pulling back and staring up at me. "Are you crazy? Something could have happened. You didn't have anyone telling you when the coast was clear. We could have—"

I stopped him with a kiss.

"I'm used to doing jobs with no backup," I said. "It was fine. But when I was there, I realized the crown wasn't on the boat. Since there was no way to tell you how I knew that, I had to board the fucking boat all over again that night."

Dirk's hands roamed all over the bare skin of my back, making me shiver with excitement. My dick was already hard as steel.

"Never again," he ground out. "I meant what I said, King."

"Never again. Not without backup."

"Not *at all*," he insisted.

"I'm teasing you," I said, suddenly feeling light and free. "Never again. Not at all."

I slid my arms around his back and laid my cheek against his chest, hoping like hell he believed me.

His hands moved into my hair again. I was so tired, and his touch was so comforting, I almost started to doze and drool.

Several minutes of silence passed before Dirk's deep voice rumbled against my cheek. "I'm falling in love with you."

I squeezed my eyes closed and prayed I hadn't just dreamed that.

"Was that too much? Did I manage to scare you off?"

I lifted my head to stare at him, and he chuckled, reaching out to swipe at my cheek again. "Your eyes are very leaky tonight."

"Do you mean it?"

"Yes," he said, wiping off tears and showing me. "See?"

I punched him lightly in the chest. "No, you idiot. The love thing. Because..."

My lips were numb, and my entire body was shaking.

"It's okay, sweetheart. I'll say it again and again if you need me to," he murmured, wiping off more tears. "I want to be with you. Even if that means staying here in Paris where the art lives or moving to Texas where your family lives. Even if it means you can't keep from nicking a few things here and there, although I'll do my best to stop you." His grin made his chin dimple even deeper. I wanted to lick it.

"No more nicking. I promise. I'm done," I said quickly. I wanted to reassure him, and I knew there was no question which I would choose between stealing art and having him in my life.

I'd choose him every time.

"Kingston Wilde. I'm yours if you'll have me. But I have one condition. No more secrets. No more trying to protect me by holding back. You have to trust me from here on out."

Trust me. Did he have any idea he was asking the impossible?

But it wasn't impossible. Not really. Because I could tell by the look on his face, Dirk meant every word.

"I'm falling in love with you too," I admitted. "So much. I was so scared I'd ruined everything, that I'd—"

He stopped my babbling with a hard kiss. His hand held the back of my head so I couldn't escape.

As if I'd ever want to.

EPILOGUE

FALCON - FIVE MONTHS LATER

The door to our room slammed open, waking me out of a dead sleep and sending the cats rocketing off the bed in search of sanctuary somewhere other than here. King still snored in my arms, but I could tell he was faking. MJ had taught me the signs.

"Get up. I found the perfect place for you guys."

I blinked open one eye and recognized King's brother West in the open doorway. "It's the middle of the night."

"It's seven in the morning," West said. "And I just got a call from Old Man Fowler."

"Do people actually call people Old M—"

"Yes," King muttered. "But don't call his wife Old Lady Fowler. Ask Otto how we know."

Another voice entered the conversation. "I was drunk. That's not fair."

I recognized Otto standing behind West.

"How many of you are there out there?" I asked, not letting go of my boyfriend's sexy-as-fuck body. We were both naked under his grandfathers' ancient stack of quilts.

"I tried to tell them to let you sleep in," MJ's familiar voice chimed in, "but they said something about striking while the iron was hot."

"Wait," King said, sitting up and rubbing his eyes. "You mean Old Man Fowler's place next to your medical practice in town? That big Victorian house?"

West looked like the cat that ate the canary. "Yes! We could be work besties. Lunch breaks, free STI checkups—"

"What?" I asked. "What the fuck is he talking about? No, you know what? We talked about this after last time. No barging in without knocking." I turned to King. "I thought your grandfather promised to put a lock on our door."

He shrugged. "We should get up and go down there. You'd love this place. It's perfect. It's not as big as West's place, but it has a huge wooded backyard that's already fenced in, tons of natural light from big windows, a nice sunporch, and it's only a block off the square."

"Babe, it's seven in the morning," I pointed out. "It feels like... something else... to my body."

"Lunchtime? Because you've got the time change wrong way around. Also, we've been here a week already," King said. "That jet lag bullshit is starting to sound lame."

"No shit," Otto coughed.

"Zip it," I snapped. "When we were here at Christmastime, I specifically remember you making a comment about how your family was always cockblocking you from Seth. Look where you're sitting right now."

Otto looked down at where his hip was against my knee on top of the covers. "Oh, uh, sorry," he said before standing up and shuffling back toward the door. MJ didn't budge from where she'd sat down next to King and started browsing through a real estate catalog that had been on the bedside table.

A scurry of paws and claws on the old wood floors of the farmhouse heralded the incoming arrival of the dogs.

"Oh shit," King said, almost jumping up. I clamped a hand on his wrist.

"You're naked."

"The cats," he squeaked.

"Shit," West said, yelling out the door and down the hall. "Nico! Help! Someone get the dogs!"

"Everybody out," King said. "Dirk's right. It's early. We'll go look at the house later. That means you too," he added to MJ.

"Party pooper," she muttered, tossing the catalog onto the foot of the bed and following the rest of the crew out of the room.

I bolted out of the covers long enough to slam the door behind them and wedge the dresser across the door.

When I turned around, King was snuggling back down into the covers, faking sleep again.

I let out a sigh. "Fine. Let's go look at the house."

He was up and dressing before I finished the sentence.

It was spring in small-town Texas which delighted me even more than I expected. As we wandered across the town square, we saw several families congregating on the grass, chatting and enjoying cups of coffee outside of Nico's bakery. Two kids had ice cream cones that seemed a little out of place that early in the morning.

"Since when do you serve ice cream?" King asked his brother-in-law because, yes, they'd all come with us.

Nico muttered something under his breath about Stevie wearing the pants in the family. I leaned over to whisper in King's ear. "Isn't Stevie with the fire chief?"

King flapped his hand in the air. "Yes. He wears the pants with the chief too. Stevie has lots of pants."

I reached for the flapping hand and twined my fingers with his. "Are you sure about this?"

He looked over at me with an expression of confusion. "What part? The move to Hobie? The consulting firm?"

"All of it. Going into business with me. What if we fight?" It was something I'd brought up a million times back in Paris when we were planning everything. King had been patient with me while I hemmed and hawed about quitting my job. After capturing Le Chaton, I'd finally been promoted to SAIC. It hadn't been easy to walk away from that since I'd spent so long thinking that promotion was all I'd needed to be happy.

But I'd been so damned wrong.

"Oh, we're going to fight. There's no question about that," King said with a laugh. He pointed ahead to where Charlie had just shoved Hudson into someone's shrubbery. "He's pissed because Hudson brought home a barn cat without asking, and it's driving the dog crazy."

"Be serious. You know what I mean. We haven't—"

King stepped forward and turned to face me, stopping my progress down the sidewalk with a hand to my chest. "We haven't known each other that long," he mocked in a deeper "Falcon" voice, "and I just think we should be aware of the challenges we face when two such different people—"

MJ joined in with her mock Falcon voice too. "Come together after such a short period of time."

I stared at them. "I hate all of you."

King walked into my arms and wrapped me in his. "You don't. You love me. And you know how I know that? Because you've told me every day for months."

I leaned down and kissed his soft lips, feeling the contrasting prickly scratch of his heavy scruff. "I do. I love you so much it scares me," I told him. His family members had walked on toward the house, leaving us alone on the quiet patch of sidewalk.

"Don't be scared, Dirk," King said. "Because I love you too, and I want what you want. To settle down and build a life together. I want to take MJ up on her offer of carrying our child one day so we can teach them about art and take them around the world to see all of the amazing cultures. I want to share a home with you and encourage you to do what makes you happy. And if that's not the business we talked about—"

I shook my head. "It is. I promise. MJ's idea of starting the security consulting business was brilliant. There's no one better suited to help people protect their art collections than the two of us together. I just don't want you to feel rushed into anything. I know one of your brothers suggested getting the business up and running in time to have a booth at the Hootenanny in July, but I'm not sure I truly understand what a Hootenanny is. We didn't have those in Michigan."

King snorted. "It's like a pride parade with 50 percent less skin and 100 percent more fried food... wait, actually, now that I think about it, there's almost as much skin. But most of it is sunburnt."

I ran my fingers through his floppy hair. Just being in this man's presence made me feel light and happy. "I love you."

He stopped talking and his jaw clicked closed. "I thought we already went over this?"

"Nadine called me earlier today."

"Mpfh."

My boyfriend wasn't my ex-boss's biggest fan, but I ignored his grunt of disapproval.

"She said a courier delivered something unexpected to her at the office."

"We should catch up with everyone," King said, nodding toward the clutch of Wildes spilling into someone's yard ahead of us. "They're waiting for us."

"She said it was a little notebook filled with the location of countless works of stolen art," I continued. "Enough to keep her team busy for a year if it checks out."

"Mm, handy. Linney, Ziv, and Mouse will be busy," King said.

I pulled him close again, nuzzling his neck before pulling back and grinning at him. "Maybe. Or maybe they'll want to move here once our business can support more people."

King's eyes widened. "You think we could lure them away?"

"Ziv and Mouse want to move back to the States, and Linney confessed her desire to meet a real-life cowboy. I didn't have the heart to tell her all the cowboys I've met here so far are gay."

King laughed. "I'm sure we can rustle up a few straight cowboys. This is Texas after all."

"That notebook was your insurance policy, wasn't it?"

He nodded.

"Baby, why didn't you hold on to it just in case? What if—"

King clapped a hand over my mouth. It was one of his favorite ways of shutting me up. I wished it was something a little sexier like kissing or a spontaneous blow job. But I was learning that wasn't the Wilde way.

"No what-ifs. It's over. All of it is behind me now. No insurance policy needed," he said. "Now can we look at the damned house?"

"Fine," I said, leaning in to kiss him again just for good measure. I'd learned over our Christmas visit that Hobie was a strangely accepting town. Few people seemed to notice PDA. Maybe it wasn't so strange since half the population seemed to be the predominantly gay and extremely handsy Wilde family, but it was still unexpected in small-town Texas. It had been one of the things about Hobie that had made me feel instantly accepted and at home.

We caught up with the rest of the crazy crew and turned to take in the large Victorian home set back from the street and partially covered in overgrown vines and scraggly shrubbery. The house needed a new coat of paint and some aggressive landscaping, but it had a solid, sprawling structure with extra-wide porches and huge windows. The main floor was bigger than the second story and would give us plenty of room to expand the business over time.

West was already chatting excitedly about tearing down the row of overgrown cypress trees between the driveway of this house and the one that served the Victorian home next door that housed his medical practice. MJ argued that King and I might want privacy since we were going to be newlyweds. That was news to me and presumably King as well.

I stared at the hidden gem and imagined all the possibilities. Our residence in the top two stories and our gallery on the ground level. Coolie and Gus sunning themselves in the second-story bay window. Kids one day riding bikes down the shady street to the long, wide driveway—our kids and their cousins.

This house was just scruffy and neglected enough to have not drawn my attention when we'd been to West's office over Christmas. But now that I was looking right at it, I could see it for all its possibilities.

"Dirk," King whispered.

I looked over at him and saw his eyes fill with happy tears. My little cat burglar was feisty most of the time, but every once in a while, his emotions got the better of him. I loved that side of him. He'd never once held back from expressing his true emotions to me, even in the very early days when we were in Greece and he wasn't sure whether or not he could trust me.

I pulled him into a hug and murmured in his ear. "It's perfect."

King laughed through his tears and nodded, pulling back and wiping at his face. "Just think, in fifty years someone will be talking about Old Man Falcon's house," he teased.

"Nah," I said, leaning my forehead against his. "Pretty sure it'll be Old Man Wilde by then."

Up next: Cal Wilde accidentally stows away on a rich man's yacht... and Jonathan Worthington recognizes the opportunity of a lifetime. **NautiCal** *is available now!*

LETTER FROM LUCY

Dear Reader,

Thank you so much for reading *King Me*, book seven in the Forever Wilde series. I wanted to challenge myself to write a heist novel, but I didn't want to lose sight of the romance while doing it. I hope I managed to find balance between the two.

Everything about the Holy Crown of Hungary is true with the important exception of its forgery and recent theft by my fictional characters. The crown has a fascinating history including its time in Fort Knox in the US during and after World War II. I encourage you to check out the photos of the Hungarian Parliament Building's rotunda which houses the unique coronation crown today. You can find them on my Pinterest board for *King Me*.

Book eight in the series is already available. *NautiCal* tells the story of a young, fun-loving Cal Wilde who accidentally stows away on a rich man's yacht in the Caribbean. Steam, sass, and scuba await you in this age-gap, forced-proximity romance!

If you're unfamiliar with the Forever Wilde series, check out the first book *Facing West* which is about Nico, a tattoo artist from San Francisco, returning to his small-town Texas roots to take custody of his sister's baby. There he meets the local uptight physician, West

Wilde, who thinks this urban punk is in no way prepared to take on the care of a newborn. And he's right.

There are already seven novels in the series with more to come, so please stay tuned. Up next will be Cal's story which includes sailing in crystal blue waters.

If you're unfamiliar with the Made Marian series, check out the first book *Borrowing Blue* which is about a straight, divorced vineyard owner agreeing to do a guest a solid. Tristan kisses Blue in the bar one night to make Blue's ex jealous. But when Tristan and Blue discover the wedding weekend they're there for is between Blue's sister and Tristan's brother, what began as one hot kiss turns into lots of big trouble.

Be sure to follow me on Amazon to be notified of new releases, and look for me on Facebook for sneak peeks of upcoming stories.

Feel free to sign up for my newsletter, stop by www.LucyLennox.com or visit me on social media to stay in touch. We have a super fun reader group on Facebook that can be found here:

https://www.facebook.com/groups/lucyslair/

To see fun inspiration photos for all of my novels, visit my Pinterest boards.

Happy reading!

Lucy

ABOUT LUCY LENNOX

Lucy Lennox is the creator of the bestselling Made Marian series, the Forever Wilde series, and co-creator of the Twist of Fate Series with Sloane Kennedy and the After Oscar series with Molly Maddox. Born and raised in the southeast, she is finally putting good use to that English Lit degree.

Lucy enjoys naps, pizza, and procrastinating. She is married to someone who is better at math than romance but who makes her laugh every single day and is the best dancer in the history of ever.

She stays up way too late each night reading M/M romance because that stuff is impossible to put down.

For more information and to stay updated about future releases, please sign up for Lucy's author newsletter on her website.

Connect with Lucy on social media:
www.LucyLennox.com
Lucy@LucyLennox.com

WANT MORE?

Join Lucy's Lair
Get Lucy's New Release Alerts
Like Lucy on Facebook
Follow Lucy on BookBub
Follow Lucy on Amazon
Follow Lucy on Instagram
Follow Lucy on Pinterest

Other books by Lucy:
Made Marian Series
Forever Wilde Series
Aster Valley Series
Virgin Flyer
Say You'll Be Nine
Hostile Takeover
Twist of Fate Series with Sloane Kennedy
After Oscar Series with Molly Maddox
Licking Thicket Series with May Archer
Licking Thicket: Horn of Glory series with May Archer
Honeybridge series with May Archer

Visit Lucy's website at www.LucyLennox.com for a comprehensive list of titles, audio samples, freebies, suggested reading order, and more!

Printed in Great Britain
by Amazon

42730190R00169